Cherry

Lindsey Rosin

Simon Pulse

New York   London   Toronto   Sydney   New Delhi

An imprint of Simon & Schuster Children's Publishing Division
1230 Avenue of the Americas, New York, New York 10020
This Simon Pulse hardcover edition August 2016
Text copyright © 2016 by Lindsey Rosin
Jacket photo copyright © 2016 by MIXA Co. Ltd./Collection/Getty Images
All rights reserved, including the right of reproduction in whole or in part in any form.
SIMON PULSE and colophon are registered trademarks of Simon & Schuster, Inc.
For information about special discounts for bulk purchases, please contact
Simon & Schuster Special Sales at 1-866-506-1949 or business@simonandschuster.com.
The Simon & Schuster Speakers Bureau can bring authors to your live event.
For more information or to book an event contact the Simon & Schuster Speakers
Bureau at 1-866-248-3049 or visit our website at www.simonspeakers.com.
Jacket designed by Regina Flath
Interior designed by Tom Daly
The text of this book was set in Stempel Garamond LT.
Manufactured in the United States of America
2 4 6 8 10 9 7 5 3 1
Library of Congress Cataloging-in-Publication Data
Names: Rosin, Lindsey, author.
Title: Cherry / by Lindsey Rosin.
Description: Simon Pulse hardcover edition. | New York : Simon Pulse, 2016. |
Summary: "Four best friends make a pact to lose their virginity before
they graduate high school"—Provided by publisher.
Identifiers: LCCN 2016005846 (print) | LCCN 2016024435 (ebook) | ISBN
9781481459082 (hardback) | ISBN 9781481459136 (eBook)
Subjects: | CYAC: Coming of age—Fiction. | Best friends—Fiction. |
Virginity—Fiction. | Sex—Fiction. | Self-realization—Fiction. | Dating
(Social customs)—Fiction. | BISAC: JUVENILE FICTION / Social Issues / New
Experience. | JUVENILE FICTION / Social Issues / Dating & Sex. | JUVENILE
FICTION / Social Issues / Friendship.
Classification: LCC PZ7.1.R673 Ch 2016 (print) | LCC PZ7.1.R673 (ebook) | DDC
[Fic]—dc23
LC record available at https://lccn.loc.gov/2016005846

For JSP

The beginning . . .

To be honest, the sex pact wasn't always part of the plan.

Layla Baxter started it.

She announced it super casually to the rest of the girls—Alex, Zoe, and Emma—between bites of froyo, as if it were simply another addition to her massive, ever evolving to-do list. "I added a new bullet point today," she said as she mixed a fresh spoonful of Sno-Caps into her frozen yogurt. Every Sunday afternoon at exactly 4:00 p.m. The Crew (as the girls were commonly known) would meet at their favorite froyo spot, The Bigg Chill, and huddle around their regular table for an important hour of sugar and gossip.

"Oh yeah?" Zoe asked, humoring Layla.

"Yeah. Well. Actually . . ." Layla smiled. "I added *three* new bullet points. Three felt like the right number." Layla swept her long blond hair up into her signature bun, which was always equal parts messy and adorable. With Layla, *everything* was an "always." Everything had an order or a pattern or some sort of special meaning. True to form, she always—*always*—ordered the same frozen yogurt combination: a chocolate, peanut butter swirl with Sno-Caps on the side.

Zoe Reed also always ordered the same flavor: classic, plain vanilla. Vanilla really was Zoe's favorite flavor, but beyond that the truth was she also made most of her life choices with the hope of drawing as little attention to herself as possible. She blamed the habit on her bright red, almost orangeish hair. It was frizzy, dry, and nearly unmanageable, but unless Zoe wanted to rock some sort of buzz cut—which was obviously out of the question—there wasn't much she could do to improve the situation. She was stuck with it. With the hair. And the red. And the frizz. Which meant that everything *else* about Zoe had to be toned down accordingly. Even her frozen yogurt flavor: always vanilla.

"Lay, you gonna actually tell us about your new bullet points," Alex prodded, "or are you just gonna be a cocktease about it?"

"Alex. I am not being a tease—" Layla fought back playfully.

"Except you totally are. . . ." Alex smirked.

Unlike Layla or Zoe, Alex Campbell wasn't into the "always." She preferred randomness. Chaos, even. Alex was always looking for something new and exciting. Case in point: She had never (*ever*) ordered the same flavor twice. The Bigg Chill changed its flavors every week, and so every week Alex would make a big deal about trying all of them and then inevitably end up with the most eccentric option of the bunch, something like Chocolate Pistachio or Oreo Cheesecake. Today, it was Caramel Custard.

When you looked as naturally good as Alex, it was easy to pull off the boldest kind of choice. Alex had soul piercing blue eyes, light chocolate skin, and endlessly long legs. The overall combination was, in a word, stunning.

"Okay, okay . . . ," Layla said, getting back on track. "At some point between this very moment, right now, and approximately six months from now, on graduation day—"

"Really? Hi," Emma interrupted. "I thought we weren't talking about that."

"About what—graduation?"

"La, la, la," Emma sang, sticking her fingers in her ears.

"Oh, come on," Layla said. "Our high school graduation"—more *la, la, las* from Emma—"is happening whether we talk about it or not."

"I know it's *happening*, but that doesn't mean we need to dwell—"

"I'm not *dwelling*—I'm just saying it's the due date for my new bullets."

"Okay. But then I'm just asking why it has to be the end of the school year?"

"It seems fitting and thematically appropriate. One door closing, another door opening." Layla had clearly already given the timeline a great deal of thought. Of course, Layla didn't do much of anything without giving it a great deal of thought.

"Don't worry, Em," Alex chimed in, "I'm sure Layla will just add even more bullet points to her list soon. Then there'll be a new due date anyway."

"You know, some people say that success means never getting to the bottom of your to-do list," Layla retorted.

"Because those people never actually finish anything?" Alex laughed.

"No, because they're always busy adding more things to do."

"That makes no sense."

"It actually makes so much sense. And I'd very much appreciate if you could please stop hating on my life system?"

"Only if you stop saying supercool things like 'life system'?"

"Oh, you love it—"

"Layla, I love *you*, but that's not the same thing—"

"Yes, okay," Emma said, interrupting Layla and Alex's familiar back-and-forth. "That's great and all, but can we please just stop talking about it?"

Emma O'Malley plunged her plastic spoon into her Cookies 'n Cream froyo, piling on an oversized bite. Emma's weekly order was typically somewhere right between Alex's peculiar and Zoe's plain. In other words, she liked to keep things interesting, but she didn't feel the need to stray too far from the status quo. Emma's "always" was an extra order of rainbow sprinkles, which she got on the side for everyone to share. Emma was especially thoughtful like that.

However, at this moment, all Emma could think about

was trying *not* to think about graduation . . . and she was failing.

Under normal circumstances, Emma was the most laid-back member of The Crew, the girl most likely to go with the flow, but senior year was throwing her off her game. Emma liked the way things were right now—her friends, her parents, her classes, and her job as senior photo editor of the school yearbook—and she didn't really understand why any of it had to change.

"Ooooo-kay," Layla said, starting her announcement over again. "Before the-day-that-Emma-will-not-let-us-name, I am going to, in no particular order: get an A in Mr. Moore's AP Lit class . . ."

"Yes. Super doable," Zoe interjected.

"Put blond highlights in my hair . . ."

"Ugh, *finally*," Alex approved. Layla had been talking about getting highlights almost literally forever.

"Aaaaand," Layla said, pausing slightly for dramatic effect, "I am going to have sex with Logan."

Layla's sexclamation made Zoe spit rainbow sprinkles across the table.

A saliva-covered red sprinkle landed on Alex's hand. "Ew. Zoe, c'mon."

"Sorry—sorry," Zoe said as she scrambled to pass Alex a napkin. "I was very much not expecting that."

"The highlights?" Layla asked playfully.

"The Logan."

Layla and Logan had been together for more than two years, so it wasn't entirely surprising that Layla was ready to do it . . . but actually hearing the words "I am going to have sex" come out of her mouth was a whole new sensation. All of a sudden, sex was something The Crew actually *did*. Or at least it was something Layla did. Or was *going* to do. Or something.

"I'm ready," Layla added definitively.

"Wow," Zoe said. Or maybe she only thought it. She wasn't sure if the "wow" had actually managed to come out of her lips or if it was still stuck, rattling around inside her head.

"I like this," Alex said. "But why not just go for it?"

"I *am* gonna just 'go for it.' That's exactly what I'm saying."

"No, I know, but then why do you need to do it with a due date?"

"Oh. Have you met me?"

"Yes. You plan everything —"

"*Ev-er-y-thing.*"

"Right, but what if this time you were just, like, *Hey. Logan. I want you inside me.*"

"Ohmigod, Alex." Zoe blushed.

"What? I have a feeling he'd be down."

"Yes, I feel that too" — Layla laughed — "but I can't just say that —"

"You *could*, actually —"

"You know spontaneity makes me nauseous. Besides, a due date is an essential element of any well plotted plan. *Otherwise* it's just, like, what's the point of having a plan in the first place?"

"That's exactly what I'm trying to say," Alex explained. "Maybe you don't *need* a plan."

"Again: Have you met me?!" Layla countered as one of the cell phones vibrated from the phone stack in the middle of the table. "I think that's mine. Probably Logan," she said.

The Crew had decided—well, Layla had decided and everyone else agreed—that froyo Sunday would be a phone free zone. The girls would always stack their phones on the table when they first sat down, and the only way they were allowed to check a text message before they got up was if someone else in The Crew read it first.

"You want me to check?" Emma offered.

"All good," Layla said. "I think his flight just landed. I'm sure he's fine."

"More than fine. He's about to have sex."

"Not, like, *immediately* about to . . ."

"Right, 'cause spontaneity makes us nauseous," Alex teased.

"Exactly." Layla winked, knowing full well that Alex was making fun of her.

"But for real, Lay," Alex said, trying again. "The first time you attempt to have sex you can't just, like . . . force it. I mean . . . there are moving parts involved. Body parts." Alex was the only member of The Crew who wasn't a virgin. She'd done it only one time before, but that was still one more time than anybody else at the table.

"I know it's gonna take time to figure it all out," Layla insisted. "That's why the ultimate due date is six months away—plenty of time to work out the kinks."

"So basically you're saying you want to have a lot of sex." Alex grinned.

"A lot of *good* sex," Layla clarified.

"I think it's supposed to be good even when it's bad," Emma chimed in.

"No-o—it can definitely be bad," Alex maintained.

"Right. But I think it's also like pizza: Like, when it's good, it's really good, and then when it's bad it's still pretty good," Emma said with a laugh, which made Alex and Layla laugh too. Zoe joined in halfheartedly, but the entire conversation was making her anxious.

"I'm gluten free," Zoe managed to add.

"What does that have to do with anything?"

"It makes it harder to find good pizza."

"Zoe, it's a metaphor."

"I know . . ." Zoe stuck some more vanilla froyo in her mouth.

"I'm thinking Logan and I will do it for the first time on Valentine's Day," Layla said proudly, as if she were the first person in the history of premeditated sex dates to select the national holiday of flowers and candy and Hallmark cards. "It's gonna be perfect."

"Were you always this corny?" Alex laughed.

"I am not corny—"

"I bet you want rose petals and candles too."

"Who *doesn't* want rose petals and candles?"

"Me, for starters," Emma said.

"Me, for seconds," Alex agreed.

"Okay, okay," Layla said, turning toward Alex, "We can't all be lucky enough to lose it on make-out rock behind the boathouse at Camp Waziyatah."

"It was make-out *ledge*, thankyouverymuch."

The girls knew that Alex's camp boy was named Cameron, and that he was "tall" and "hot" and "lived in Massachusetts," but that was pretty much it. Alex wasn't really a big talker no matter what the subject was, but she definitely didn't like to kiss and tell. Probably because then she'd have to be talking all the time. More often than not, she was tired of her boy-of-the-moment before the end of their first make-out session.

"Okay, fine. Make-out *ledge*," Layla corrected. "I'm sure it was magical."

"Yeah, well . . ." Alex paused, searching for the right words to explain what had happened. She knew "magical" certainly wasn't going to be one of them. "I think the first time's gonna be awkward no matter what you do."

"So you're saying I should *plan* for awkward," Layla said, translating Alex's advice into a language she could understand.

"If you must . . ." Alex grinned, knowing full well that Layla *obviously* must. "All I'm trying to say is that it's probably smart not to expect . . ."

"An orgasm?" Layla offered.

"Ohmigod," Zoe said, squirming in her chair.

"Oh my God, *yes*, Zoe, we're talking about *orgasms*," Alex teased.

"I realize that, but . . ." Zoe's face turned red, and she

couldn't finish the rest of her thought. She was still wrapping her head around Layla's sex date, and the thought of Alex's orgasms, or *anyone's* orgasms, or really just the entire *concept* of an orgasm was a lot right now.

"Just think of them like . . . *fireworks*," Layla said.

"Fireworks . . . ," Alex repeated, trying the word on for size.

"I actually love fireworks." Emma laughed.

"Okay, *okay*. Thank you, but now I hear you all saying 'fireworks,' and it just sounds like 'orgasm' anyway, so . . ."

"Zoe, if it *really* sounded like an orgasm—"

"Ohmigod, Alex, I swear, if you start moaning right now . . ."

Alex, Layla, and Emma exploded into another fit of giggles, as Zoe shook her head and heaped another spoonful of rainbow sprinkles onto her vanilla frozen yogurt.

"I like that we're talking about this," Layla said once all the laughter had quieted down again.

"Me too," Emma agreed.

"Me three," Alex piled on.

Layla, Emma, and Alex all turned toward Zoe.

She shook her head.

"Is that a no?" Layla asked.

"We've already established that I'm bright red, and I'm pretty positive I have massive pit stains and a rash on my chest . . ."

"*That's* your answer?"

"I don't know . . ."

"Oh, c'mon, Zoe," Layla pushed. "We're having a

bonding moment like we've never had before, and all you're gonna give us is an 'I don't know'?"

"I love-hate this conversation. Is that a possible correct answer?"

"Zo, it's not a test," Emma said through a fresh wave of giggles.

"Okay, well, whatever it is, I'm one hundred percent having a love-hate relationship with it," Zoe managed to say before getting swept up into Emma's laughter. Alex and Layla were already there too, laughing so hard they couldn't breathe, and it was simply impossible to tell whose laughter was whose because it all just mixed together so perfectly.

That's how it worked.

Layla, Zoe, Alex, and Emma had been an inseparable foursome ever since the fateful day they were all randomly assigned to the same desk cluster in Miss Morgan's first-grade class. All these years later they were still just as close as ever.

"Most people aren't this lucky," Layla said, as always.

"Not even close," Alex, Emma, and Zoe answered.

Then Layla swirled another spoonful of Sno-Caps into her frozen yogurt—and a brand-new thought bubbled up into her brain . . .

Zoe was the first to see Layla's face light up. "Oh no," she said knowingly.

"'Oh no' what?" Layla laughed.

"I see you, Layla. I see all the gears in your pretty little head spinning like crazy. Like that time you decided we should toilet paper Xander Murphy's house. Or the night you made us go skinny-dipping at Zuma—"

"Hey, I did not *make* you do anything—"

"Layla," Zoe said, wiping her clammy hands onto her jeans, "I know what this face means . . ."

"That I often have good ideas?" Layla asked, loving everything about this moment.

"Wait, *what* is a good idea?" Emma asked.

"Yeah, what are you talking about?" Alex asked. "Unlike Zoe, I don't have psychic powers."

"Layla thinks we *all* should have sex," Zoe blurted.

"Together?" Alex laughed.

"Ohmigod, no," Zoe squeaked, too nervous and awkward and rashy to even entertain that kind of joke.

"Wait. But what if we really did?" Layla asked, getting all sorts of excited. "I swear I wasn't thinking that when we first sat down this afternoon, but now that I hear Zoe say it out loud—"

"Please don't blame me—"

"Zoe. There's no *blame*. This is brilliant."

"Wait. You're serious?" Emma asked.

"Yes. We should all have sex. Before graduation."

Emma shook her head at Layla's use of the G-word.

"I think we're forgetting that Alex has already *had* sex," Zoe said, as if that somehow made it impossible or unnecessary for the other girls to do it too.

"Yeah, but she still hasn't had *good* sex, no offense—"

"Okay, but *no*," Zoe said, still fighting the idea. "You have a boyfriend. Alex always has a million options.

Emma's adorable. And then there's me over here with my frizzy hair and freckles and permanently red cheeks. I just got my braces off two weeks ago!"

"Luckily, 'braces off' exponentially increases your sex appeal," Alex teased.

"No. No one looks at me and thinks about wanting to have sex."

"That's not true," Alex pushed back. "I could be thinking about it right now . . ."

"Yeah, yeah . . . ," Zoe said, shaking her head again.

"Zoe," Layla insisted, "you could totally have sex if you want to."

"I do want to!"

It took Zoe a moment to realize that those four little words had actually come out of her mouth and into the sugarcoated air of The Bigg Chill. Now the words were echoing off the froyo machines and the wall of glass windows and all the tables and toppings and people in between. "Ohmigod . . ."

"Ohhhh my God *yes*," Layla replied, all singsongy.

"No. Stop. No more smiling . . . ," Zoe said. "My point is that—"

"Your *point* is that you want to have sex," Alex piled on.

"No—"

"Don't you mean *yes*?" Emma joined in. "I'm positive I already heard you say yes."

"No, still *no*. My point is that I don't exactly have a lot of options."

"That is false," Emma said.

"If you want to have sex, you can find a way to have sex," Layla insisted.

"The last thing I wanna do is just 'find a way.' I'm not gonna sleep with a random or lower my standards because Layla had a stupid idea—"

"It's *not* a stupid idea. In fact, I think the sex pact might be the single greatest idea I've ever had."

"*Sex pact?* Since when is there a sex pact?" Zoe was now officially freaking out.

"Well, now that we've established we all *want* to have sex—"

"*Good* sex," Alex interjected.

"Duh, yes. Now that we've established we all want to have good sex, I think we all should."

"I'm down." Emma laughed.

"Totally," Alex agreed.

"Ohmigod . . ." Zoe blushed.

"Is that a yes?" Layla asked.

Zoe couldn't quite believe it, but the truth was "yes" it was.

"It's *hap-pen-ing*," Layla declared triumphantly. "I think step one is to put the positive intention out into the universe." Layla loved step-by-step instructions almost as much as she loved her lists and due dates. "Before high school ends, we are going to do this together."

"But not *together* together," Alex teased.

"Right. We'll do it . . . *concurrently*. With the right person in the right place at the right time . . ." Alex and Emma nodded firmly in agreement. Zoe managed to tip her head forward slightly, which was more than good enough for Layla. "We're having *sex!*" she exclaimed.

And that was it.

One serving of frozen yogurt later, sex was no longer simply a daydream or a wet dream or a piece of juicy gossip that happened to somebody else.

All of a sudden, it was something the girls actually did, something they all wanted to do—and were going to do, *together*—before high school graduation.

169 days until graduation...

LAYLA almost couldn't believe it.

The Crew had a sex pact.

And the sex pact had a due date.

And the whole thing was happening.

In Layla's head, plans and dreams were basically the same thing, but suddenly this one felt like it was actually gonna come true. Obviously, there were still variables to consider and the need for contingencies and everything, but Layla loved that sort of thing: the planning and the overplanning. She realized it might even be thematically appropriate to say she got off on it, which made her grin, equally embarrassed and excited.

ALL THE FEELS, Layla texted Alex, Emma, and Zoe in The Chat, which is what The Crew called their ongoing text message conversation. *I am having all of the feelings at the very same time.*

RELAX, Alex texted back. "Relax" was a pretty

standard Alex response, but Layla could not simply relax. She tried not to get too far ahead of herself, she really, truly did, but her mind was always racing away from her. Like even right now it was racing into the future—past the pact and the due date—all the way into the next year and then into the next decade, until all of a sudden all she could think about was the fire pit where The Crew would spend all of their future nights together. Of course this fire pit would be located in the backyard of the property that the girls would communally purchase, where they would build four separate, but architecturally cohesive, houses, one for each girl, and they'd all live happily ever after with their husbands and their children—and each other, obviously. The compound, as Layla called it in her dreams slash plans, would materialize sometime shortly after the girls wore the same blush-colored bridesmaid dresses to each other's weddings, but not before they all took a coordinated sabbatical from their successful and well established careers to travel through Europe.

Layla took a deep breath and managed to reel her thoughts of the future back into the present where she was lying on her bed, holding her cell phone up in the air, and watching a string of texts pour into The Chat from her best friends, who—thankfully—seemed to be full of just as many feelings as she was. Layla already knew that she was ready to have sex with Logan, but the fact that her best friends had just piled onto the plan with her was the icing on the cake.

Or no, not the icing . . . it was the cherry on top.

IT'S ALL HAPPENING and I couldn't be happier, she texted.

It was Sunday, January 4. High school graduation was Monday, June 22. Therefore, according to Layla's precise calculations, there were exactly 169 days until graduation and the official "doing it" due date. How thematically appropriate, Layla thought. The "sixty-nine" of it all felt like a giant wink from the universe, like a sexy, numerological "all systems go!"

As Layla double-checked her math, recounting the days from January to June, she could feel that same splendid smile, the one Zoe had caught on to at the yogurt place, creeping back across her face. She realized the smile had most likely been stuck there ever since she got home from froyo. It had probably been there all the way through dinner, too. Thankfully, no one else in the Baxter family seemed to notice. Layla's younger sister, Maxine, had spent the whole meal lobbying their mom for permission to go on the upcoming middle school ski trip, while her dad and little brother, Avery, were engaged in a heated discussion about their fantasy basketball league. Luckily, all of this mundane commotion let Layla off the hook. She didn't have to explain why she was unusually quiet. Or why her toe wouldn't stop tapping under the table. Or account for the fact that she had somehow eaten all the lima beans off her plate even though she absolutely *hated* lima beans.

The only real explanation for all of Layla's strange behavior was that she was too busy thinking. She was *always* thinking, but if her parents or siblings had asked her what she was busy thinking about *tonight*, she would've turned as bright and red as Zoe's hair. Behind Layla's calm face and that plastered smile there were approximately a million thoughts running through her head: almost all of them were X-rated, and every single one was moving at a mile a minute.

After dinner Layla *re*-recounted the days a third time just so she could be entirely, 100 percent sure that she was planning accordingly. As expected, she was right the first two times: 169 days until the doing it due date. Then, she glanced at the clock on her phone. It was almost 9:00 p.m. She had one more winter break homework assignment to finish. There was a big basket of laundry to fold. Her nails desperately needed a fresh coat of paint. But all she'd managed to accomplish since she came home from The Bigg Chill almost four hours ago (besides sending about two *hundred* text messages to The Chat, of course) was to count the days on her calendar three times and survive dinner.

Finally, the doorbell rang.

"Lay-la!" her mom called from downstairs. "Guess who's here?!"

Layla didn't have to guess.

She fixed her bun and reached for her lip gloss, semi-stalling. She couldn't just go barreling down the stairs, even though she wanted to. It took every ounce of self-control she had to hold back her response until after her mom yelled for her a second time.

"Coming!" she finally yelled back, trying to make it seem

like she'd been in the middle of something super important. She waited one more moment and then walked slowly to the top of the staircase. The second she saw Logan, a knot in her stomach loosened. She hadn't even realized the knot had been there in the first place. Logan had only been on vacation for a week and a half, but it felt like forever. He grinned at her with his entire face as she made her way down the stairs, his one perfect dimple on full display. The dimple was so small, and seemingly insignificant, and yet it made Layla melt every single time.

"Layla, you never told me that Logan's grandparents live in Miami," her mom scolded, as if that were a very important detail about her boyfriend that she absolutely needed to know. (It wasn't.) Or as if their family had some sort of close connection to Miami. (They didn't.)

"Sorry," Layla said, as much to Logan as to her mom. She must've been grilling him. *What did you do for the holidays? Is Florida nice this time of year? Are you glad to be home?*

"We're gonna go outside," Layla said, grabbing Logan's hand and pulling him gently but quickly toward the back door.

"Nice to see you, Ms. Baxter! And happy New Year!" Logan called back over his shoulder as they made their way outside. He was the kind of teenage boy who knew how to talk to parents: He looked them in the eye. He answered their questions. He remembered to wish them a happy New Year. Layla's mom and dad bragged about Logan as if he were one of their own kids. Layla found it mildly embarrassing, but she couldn't exactly blame them. There was a lot to brag about. Logan was president of the senior class, which meant he was also president of the entire student body. He had gotten in early decision to his first-choice college, the University of Pennsylvania. *And* in his spare time Logan was organizing a school-wide fund-raiser to help fight pediatric cancer.

He was also a phenomenal kisser.

Layla was obviously the only one who bragged about that last part, but it really was the best.

As soon as they made their way outside—and out of her mom's sight line—Logan pulled Layla in close, kissing her hard, like she knew he'd been wanting to since the first moment he saw her at the top of the stairs. Logan's kisses were fast at first, and then slow, and then somehow both at the very same time. He slid his hands up Layla's back, and then to her neck, pulling her in even closer . . . he pressed his lips even harder against her lips—and then pushed his hips up against hers even harder than that.

"Come here," she said when they finally came up for air, grabbing Logan's hand and pulling him across the grass and up onto the trampoline in the corner of her yard so they could continue the make-out session.

Layla's parents had what they called an "open door" policy. Logan was pretty much always invited to come over to the house, but all the doors to any room he and Layla were in had to stay open at all times, which meant that the backyard was actually their most private hangout spot.

After a few more minutes of kissing—all fast and slow

and hard and soft—Layla pulled back to ask, "Do you remember what you asked me the night before you left for Florida?"

"Is that a trick question?"

Of course Layla knew he would remember.

They had been making out on this very trampoline, except he was the one who'd stopped their kisses to ask her a question. He'd asked if she wanted to have sex. His voice had cracked as the words came out of his mouth, which made Layla laugh. She really was laughing at the crack in his voice and not the actual question, but Logan assumed that her laughter simply meant no, so he backed off the question as quickly as he'd brought it up in the first place.

They hadn't talked or texted about it since . . . until now.

"My answer is yes."

"*Yes?*" Logan's voice cracked, even more than it had the time before. "As in *yes*, you want to have sex with me?"

Layla nodded.

"*Now?*"

"Not now." She smiled.

"Okay. But . . . soon?" Logan asked excitedly, flashing that perfect dimple again. As always, it drove Layla absolutely crazy. "I know you've probably got a whole plan worked out already," he added, "but, um . . . you should know that I have a condom in my glove compartment."

"Oh. Okay. For emergencies?" Layla teased.

"For realistic situations," Logan teased right back. "At least I know better than to keep it in my wallet."

"Thanks for that."

"You sure you don't just wanna go upstairs?"

"I'm super sure that my parents aren't going to let us into my bedroom without the open door policy in full effect, so unless you want to do it for the first time with the door wide open . . ."

"How about my car?"

"Your car is at the very top of my list of places where we are not going to have sex."

"You would have a list like that." Logan laughed.

"I don't *actually* have anything written down, but I can tell you right now there is no possible way I am going to lose my virginity in your car."

"Right. Right. Okay. *Your* car would be a much better option—"

"*Logan*," Layla said, loving him even more than she did a moment before.

"What? Your backseat is far more spacious, and you have leather seats, so . . ."

"I can't with you." Layla grinned before rolling up on top of him and pressing her lips back onto his.

"I can't with *you*!" Logan teased through kisses. "You can't just stick your tongue into my mouth and expect this conversation to be over . . ."

Layla knew that their conversation was far from over, in fact, it was just getting started, but as far as tonight was concerned, there wasn't going to be any more talking, only kissing . . . and maybe a few other things. Layla reached for Logan's hand and slipped it up under her shirt. He unhooked the clasp on her bra and then pulled it down, sliding his hands onto her boobs. Her nipples were already hard, mostly because it was cold outside, but also because Logan's lips were warm and his fingertips were everywhere and his hips were pushing against hers along with the rise and fall of the trampoline.

ZOE's chest had grown an entire cup size since the beginning of winter break.

She hadn't measured them exactly or anything, but now, basically without any proper warning, her boobs were popping out of all of her bras. Zoe also considered the alternate possibility that maybe every single one of her bras had simultaneously shrunk in the laundry at the exact same time, but she had to admit that seemed rather unlikely.

Zoe stood in her bathroom, wrapped in a towel, having just gotten out of the shower. Normally, she didn't spend much time staring in the mirror—that was really more of a Layla or Alex thing to do—but she couldn't stop admiring her new braceless teeth. Maybe it was the fact that Alex had said her lack of braces increased her sex appeal exponentially, but even Zoe had to admit that her smile looked good. Honestly, she knew her newly upgraded boobs looked good too, but that felt weird to even think about. *Then* she felt weird for feeling weird about thinking about it, and then all of the weirdness quickly amplified in her head until there was nothing left to do but unwrap her towel and force herself to take a look. . . .

When Zoe saw her topless reflection, the first word that came to mind was "pale." The second word was "red," for her hair. The third word was "freckles," because they were basically everywhere. But *then* the next word was "nipple," followed closely by the word "boob," and then, undeniably, "big." It had become simply impossible to deny the fact that her boobs were decidedly larger than they'd been even just a few weeks before. Still, Zoe could only look at them for so long before achieving a maximum level of weirdness and had to reach for her towel again. As she rewrapped herself, one of the bathroom doors began to swing open, which caused Zoe to shriek and her older brother to slam the door shut again as quickly as possible.

Zoe's brother, Joey—or J, as Zoe called him so as not to acknowledge the embarrassing fact that their first names rhymed—was two years older than Zoe. He was a sophomore at UC Berkeley and still home from school on winter break. Zoe's and Joey's bedrooms were connected by a Jack and Jill–style bathroom. The layout wasn't such a big deal when they were younger, but now it was clearly causing some growing pains.

"I'm sorry!" Joey yelled through the closed door.

"What happened to knocking?" Zoe yelled back.

Joey knocked softly, making a joke out of it.

"Great, thanks . . . ," Zoe scoffed, pulling her towel more firmly around her.

"Zoe Reed," Joey teased with a loud, booming voice. "It's your brother. I am moments away from attempting to open the door to the bathroom again. Brace yourself."

"Yeah, okay. Got it," Zoe said as Joey reopened the

door. "I know you're all used to coed showers at the dorms or whatever, but come on."

"Come on, yourself." Joey laughed. "You could also try locking the door. Or, you know, maybe don't just stand naked in front of the mirror forever."

"J," Zoe said sternly, not even sort of ready to laugh about such a close call. "Tell me right now you didn't see anything. If you did, I think I will die."

"Zo, please don't die. I saw nothing."

"Thank God. But also, I wasn't just, like, standing naked. I took a shower."

"All right, all right," Joey said, backing off. "I am sorry for cramping your style. I'll be back at school soon enough, and then I promise you'll miss me and these awkward encounters." As anxious as Zoe was, Joey was just the opposite: calm and collected, always unfazed. Zoe envied that about him. He turned his attention toward the mirror, running his fingers through his hair, spiking it up on top. Although Joey's reddish highlights clearly identified him as a member of the Reed family, he didn't have the same bright red color that Zoe did. Not even close. Zoe and Joey both had the same deep brown eyes, but beyond that they barely looked related. Zoe joked that Joey had taken all the attractive qualities out of the Reed family gene pool and left her with nothing but frizz and freckles.

"Going somewhere?" Zoe asked.

"Yeah. Shawn is having a party. Track people." Joey had been on the track team in high school. He was a pole-vaulter, and he wasn't half bad, but Zoe knew he had mostly joined the team just to hang out with his friends. "You wanna come?"

"It's a school night."

"Right. *High school* . . ."

"Oh, whatever. Have fun."

"I will, but I actually need your tree first." Zoe's bedroom was in the front of the house, and there was a giant sycamore tree right outside her window. Zoe was too anxious and awkward to try and use it, but it gave her brother the pole-vaulter a perfect escape route into the front yard.

"Really? You're sneaking out? I thought you were a big college man now?"

"Ye-ah. You've met our parents . . ." Joey exhaled, running his fingers through his hair again. "Their house, their rules . . . Mom turned the alarm on, like, an hour ago."

"Lame," Zoe commiserated.

"Totally. But here's the beginning and end of tonight's unsolicited brotherly advice: Pick your battles. Always. But *especially* with Mom and Dad." Zoe nodded, appreciating her brother. She and Joey had fought like crazy when they were younger, but for the past few years, ever since Zoe started high school, their relationship had been shifting toward being friends rather than just siblings. Zoe's cell phone vibrated even louder than usual as it rattled on top of the tiles next to the bathroom sink. And then it buzzed three more times as a new flood of texts poured into The Chat. "Say hi to The Crew for me."

"The Crew doesn't care about you . . ."

"Cool, cool. Appreciate that."

"Love you, bro."

"Love you too, sis. Just leave your window open for me? Please? Thanks." Joey slid out the window without waiting for a response, climbed onto the nearest tree branch, and swung down to the front lawn in one fluid, seemingly effortless movement. He'd perfected the art of sneaking out of the Reed house.

Zoe focused her attention back on her phone, scrolling through all the new texts in The Chat. Layla was providing a detailed recap of her and Logan's latest epic trampoline make-out session. Zoe put on her pajamas, comfy flannel pants and an oversized T-shirt, as Layla's texts continued. Zoe loved reading the texts in The Chat, but she never really had much to contribute to the conversation. Besides, at this moment, her hair required all of her immediate attention. She had a whole hair routine. First, Dream Curls spray. Second, Daily Moisturizer mousse. Then, Frizz-Ease serum, which she referred to as her secret weapon. And then finally Dep gel. She crunched the thick gel into her red locks as hard as she could. Barring any natural sleep-induced hair disasters, Zoe would wake up with dry, moderately acceptable curls.

Then her phone buzzed again.

Another text.

This one was from Dylan: *Ready?*

Zoe noticed that the clock on her phone read 11:11.

She kissed her hand, touched the phone, and then kissed her hand again. Layla wasn't the only one who believed in little signs from the universe. Zoe had no clue what this particular sign meant, but she always seemed to catch the clock at 11:11, and after today's sex pact conversation, she felt like it must be at least marginally important.

Normally, Dylan didn't text her until closer to midnight, but Caroline, Dylan's girlfriend, must've gone to bed early. Caroline was the captain of the varsity cheerleading squad. Zoe would have to sprout two more cup sizes in order to catch up to her. Not that Zoe was trying to catch anyone. She actually liked Caroline. She was a big upgrade from Dylan's last blond, skinny girlfriend. And the one before that, too. Dylan Riley was a serial monogamist. He was tall, almost six-four, and thin. He'd probably describe himself using the word "lanky." He kept his blond hair short, usually in a buzz cut. And he had an eight-pack. *Eight.* As in two more abs than the already impressive six-pack. Not that Zoe went out of her way to notice his abs or anything, but Dylan was cocaptain of the varsity water polo team, and their uniform Speedos didn't exactly leave much of anything to the imagination.

Zoe closed her bedroom door, turned off the lights, and then jumped into bed. She called Dylan's cell phone. He picked up on the first ring.

"Hey, hey," he said, as always.

"Am-I-sexy?" she asked, the question tumbling out of her mouth, all quick and jumbled, as if it were a secret.

"What?" Dylan asked, his voice getting squeaky for a moment.

"Okay, fine," Zoe said with an exhale. "I'm not gonna make you say no."

"Last time I checked, 'what' and 'no' are not even sorta the same thing."

"Then you already heard my question."

"I didn't. Swear."

"You just want to make me say 'sexy' again."

"I *promise* I didn't hear you before, but now that you said 'sexy,' I want to hear it for real. Also, I am positive that your face is matching your hair color right now."

"My face matching my hair is the story of at least fifty percent of my life."

"Nah. Only, like, forty percent," Dylan teased. "And now you've got this giant, brace-free smile on your face . . . you're probably blinding the bedbugs with your ridiculously bright white teeth."

"Yeah, yeah . . . thanks."

"I'm sure it's all matching your pasty skin now too."

"Pasty? You really want to talk about who is more pasty? Last time I checked, we were both painfully pale," Zoe fought back, making Dylan laugh.

Point for Zoe.

Then the conversation got quiet for a moment, but it wasn't an uncomfortable kind of quiet. Zoe and Dylan both knew the importance of a good pause. Zoe felt like knowing when to stop talking was almost as important as knowing what to say in the first place, and she and Dylan had spent enough hours on the phone to perfect both. Almost every night they would talk for an hour or two or sometimes even three if there was something particularly exciting to talk about. The tradition had started back in ninth grade when they were lab partners in freshman Chem class. Their last names ("Reed" and "Riley") were next to each other alphabetically, so they'd been paired up. Most lab partners split up the assignments and then copied each other's work during passing period on the way to class, but Zoe felt like she needed to do the whole assignment in order to understand it, and Dylan wasn't going to let her do all of his work for him, so they got in the habit of doing their homework together on the phone every night.

In the beginning their conversations were quick and entirely academic. They didn't have much in common. Zoe was in the theater crowd. She liked show tunes and jazz hands. Dylan liked contact sports and video games. The truth was they *still* didn't have much in common, but something about their friendship just seemed to work. And it worked best on the phone.

So, every night, Dylan would text Zoe when he was ready to talk. And then Zoe would call him. And he would pick up on the first ring. And he'd say "hey hey" and then they'd spend the next few hours talking to each other and trying not to fall asleep. The funny part about these nightly falling asleep phone calls—"phonefalls" as Dylan and Zoe called them—was that they were entirely platonic. Even though Zoe and Dylan agreed that it was more or less impossible for boys and girls to simply be friends—the "sex thing" really did always seem to get in the way—they also believed they were the exception to the rule.

After the comfortable pause had passed, Dylan returned his attention to Zoe's initial phonefall question.

"But really, what were you trying to ask? Something about something sexy?"

"It was nothing. I didn't say anything."

"Z. You are the worst. Liar. Ever. We've been through this . . ."

"*D*," she said, matching his playful tone, "I am not lying—"

"It's okay. You're a pasty, freckled, red-haired liar . . ."

"Ohmigod . . ." Zoe giggled.

And then Zoe and Dylan went on like that for another hour or two, laughing and teasing and talking and pausing, appreciating their conversation and the quiet spaces inside of it until finally, somehow, they managed to drift off to sleep.

168 days until graduation . . .

ALEX was pressed up against the largest rock on make-out ledge.

Cameron was leaning up against her, his tongue in her mouth, his hands everywhere.

And it was all happening so fast.

Cameron paused just long enough to pull his jeans down to his ankles, and Alex's black Converse high-tops sunk down below her into the soft summer grass. Of all the things Alex had thought about when she imagined having sex for the first time, the location of her shoes was not one of them. If she *had* thought about it, Alex probably would've assumed that her shoes would just simply be off, lying on the floor next to the bed or something. Of course that assumption would also require that there would be a bed in the first place. Alex never thought that her first time might happen outside. On a cluster of rocks. With her Converse sneakers sinking down into the grass . . .

. . . but that's what was happening.

The air was cold against Alex's cheeks, but Cameron's breath was soft and warm as he moved his kisses from her lips to her neck and then up onto her earlobe. Whatever he was doing with his lips and his tongue sent a tingle all the way down to her toes and then back up into her arms, which she then realized were entirely covered in goose bumps. Alex looked at Cameron, locking in on his gaze, his green eyes were bright and wide and alive, and this feeling of incredible closeness washed over her, making Alex feel as if she and Cameron were the only two people in the entire world who could possibly exist in this moment. Alex leaned in for another kiss, but before she could find Cameron's lips . . .

Her cell phone rumbled on the top of her wooden nightstand, jerking her awake.

It took Alex a moment to confirm that she was only *dreaming* about that night with Cameron at sleepaway camp, and not, somehow, reliving it. It was confusing because she'd woken up with real goose bumps on her arms, and the feeling that they'd morphed from her dreamland into the real world, but there wasn't any actual morphing involved. The goose bumps were just as real as the *car horn* coming from her neighbor's driveway.

Shit.

Alex's one and only New Year's resolution had been to not be late for car pool anymore.

She wasn't big on unnecessary commitments, and resolutions certainly fell into that category, but she also wasn't above self-improvement. Even she had to admit that punctuality was her weakest link. But now it was only the first day of the new semester, and she was already mucking it up. She glanced at her phone. It was a quarter to eight. She could've sworn she had set her alarm before falling asleep the night before, but it seemed to have betrayed her. The honking continued, growing louder and longer, as Oliver Miller, the literal boy next door and Alex's car pool driver, waited impatiently in his car.

Alex jumped out of bed, ripped off her pajama pants, and beelined for the bathroom. Toothpaste, hairbrush, clean underwear, fresh socks—it more or less happened all at once. Her dad was out of town on business, per usual, and her mom had left early with her twin brother, Max, who went to a specialty school on the other side of town. She grabbed her cell phone and a banana and her shoes and her backpack and her wallet and tore out the front door— still barefoot.

Alex was a sprinter on the track team, so she certainly knew how to move quickly, but normally when she ran she would have a chance to stretch first, she wouldn't've just woken up, and she wouldn't be trying to balance all her possessions in her arms at the same time. Her super speed commonly led to stupid jokes about how she liked to move fast in other places as well—like between the sheets, for example. One time she even showed up to school and found the word "slut" spray-painted on the front of her locker. That was a particularly shitty day.

The upside was that Alex was fast enough to leave most

of her haters in the dust. She was also fast enough to be recruited by Stanford, which, gratefully, took all of the academic pressure off her upcoming second semester. Her main concern these days—besides pledging to not always be late for car pool—had to do with the hundred-meter dash. The Southern California high school record hadn't been touched in nearly a decade, but Alex had a real chance to break it, and she was determined to make it happen. If she were to make her own Layla-like to-do list, "break the state record" would be the one and only thing on it.

"I'm sorry, I'm sorry—" Alex said as she jumped into the passenger seat of Oliver's black Jeep Grand Cherokee.

"What happened?" Oliver asked as he peeled out of the driveway.

"My alarm clock didn't go off. I swear I set it for 7:05, but I think it must've been p.m. instead of a.m., 'cause I was using it to sleep late over winter break . . ."

"That is far too much information."

"You asked what happened."

"Yeah, but I don't really care," Oliver said, which was the type of statement that contributed to his reputation for being an asshole. "I swear, I'm just going to start leaving without you."

Even when Oliver said ugly things like that, he was still really nice to look at. Today, he wore his red and black varsity basketball jersey over a white T-shirt. He was the starting shooting guard and the top scorer on the team, and yet somehow he managed to be even cockier off the court than he was on it.

"You are not gonna leave me. You've been saying that all year."

"'Cause you've been *late* all year," Oliver said, rolling his eyes.

"We both know this ten minute drive is the best part of your entire day."

"Please, don't flatter yourself," Oliver jabbed back. "Aren't there enough boys at school who will do that for you?"

Now it was Alex's turn to roll her eyes. She was used to getting compliments, but she didn't care too much about them. They were mostly about the way she looked, and the infuriating truth was that she didn't actually *do* anything to look this way. She woke up like this. Literally. Four and a half minutes ago, she had still been in bed. Alex wasn't complaining—she *liked* the way she looked—but she cared way more about what her track performance looked like than what *she* looked like. Sometimes it seemed like she was the only one who felt that way.

Alex put her foot up on the glove compartment so she could pull on her sneaker, a black New Balance running shoe. Then she reached for the second one, realizing it was a bright pink Nike cross-trainer instead of a match black one.

"Oh damn."

"We don't have time to go back," Oliver said, noticing the mismatch.

"Ugh. I know," Alex said as she pulled on the pink shoe. "Whatever. I'll make it work."

"Knowing you," Oliver smirked, "you'll probably start a new schoolwide fashion trend."

"I don't think anyone's paying much attention to my shoes."

"I'm paying attention," Oliver said without missing a beat. "To everything."

It was statements like that one that managed to counterbalance Oliver's reputation for being an asshole—and made him so crushable. If Oliver thought *Alex* got a lot of compliments, he should hear the way girls talked about him in the locker room. But Alex wasn't going to tell him that. Oliver had more than enough of an ego already, which was a shame, because if it weren't for that, Alex might have had an actual crush on him. She would've been lying if she said she wasn't *attracted* to him, but that was more or less unavoidable, considering the way he looked and carried himself, all confidence and charm. All year, their morning car rides had been overflowing with sexual tension.

Alex glanced up at the rearview mirror and caught him staring at her. Most boys would've been flustered and looked away quickly, but not Oliver. He kept staring, owning the moment. He had no fear.

Alex didn't have any fear either, but she wasn't interested in being pulled in any farther. Oliver had already succeeded in providing her with a fresh set of goose bumps.

Like it or not, they were completely out of her control.

EMMA could not stop taking pictures of Nick . . . and his lips.

She'd taken about five *dozen* pictures, but none of them were quite right. To make matters worse, Emma had no clue what would actually make them "right" or what she wanted them to be "right" for, but there was only so much she could worry about all at once.

Nick had been talking to the yearbook staff for the past seven minutes, ever since the first bell rang signaling the start of homeroom. He was the editor in chief, so he had a lot of ground to cover, but Nick barely even paused to breathe as he laid out the schedule for the rest of the year, breaking down the delivery calendar and explaining when they would need to lock in the layout as well as all the text and candid photographs for the yearbook. It was all super nerdy, but Emma thought it was fun, too, and so did Nick, which might be why they got along so well.

When Nick first started talking, he had run his fingers through his hair, leaving himself with an accidental Mohawk. Emma was sitting in her usual spot in the back corner of the room, and even though she was only half awake—and definitely not a morning person—something about Nick's hair had compelled her to look alive and take a picture.

Emma didn't know why she was suddenly so obsessed with taking his picture. To be fair, she didn't know why she wanted to do almost anything, but at least she knew when she just simply had to do something. Right now, she had to take Nick's picture. She had started by framing his whole head, including the accidental Mohawk, but then she zeroed in on his face, and now, finally, she was just focused on his lips.

Emma always noticed people's lips.

It was the first thing she was drawn to whenever she looked at someone—boys, girls, adults, whoever—but especially when it was someone she had never seen before. Mostly, she'd just stare at the lips' size and shape and shade, but then, inevitably, she would wonder what it would be like to kiss them. And it didn't just happen with the kids at school, either. It was teachers, too. Like, Mr. Moore in English. Or even full-fledged adults like Dr. Saperstein, her dentist. Emma knew it was a weird habit, but like so much of the weirdness in her life, it was completely involuntary. At least with Nick she didn't have to wonder what it might be like to kiss him, since it had already happened on at least three or maybe four different occasions. It always seemed to happen at a party, usually while one (or both) of them was slightly (or even very) drunk. But their kisses were mostly just casual and never got in the way of their ability to work on the yearbook together.

After eleven solid minutes Nick finally stopped talking and took his first extended breath of the second semester of their senior year. Emma seized the rare, quiet moment and snapped yet another picture of him. This time his lips were closed. *Finally*, that felt right. As always, Emma was thankful to her camera for giving her purpose. Without it, she knew she probably would've been stuck awkwardly staring at Nick's lips forever.

When Emma was about nine years old, her staring became so prolonged and intense that her teacher, Ms. Benton, recommended she go see a therapist. Even her parents had to admit she was a bona fide creeper, which was not an official diagnosis but still quite accurate. It turned out that Emma was totally fine. She just had an überlong attention span, which was rare. Most of Emma's friends could get bored watching a six second video, but Emma could sit and stare at people for hours. It didn't even matter what they were doing, exactly; she just had this overwhelming urge to look at them. If Emma did the looking all by herself, it was weird and felt invasive. If she did it with a camera in her hands, she could call it art, and it felt important.

She snapped a few more quick pictures of Nick's lips. They were full and pink. A solid, masculine sort of pink. And they always tasted like ChapStick.

Now that she thought about it, her own lips were actually pretty chapped. Maybe she should just walk right up to the front of the classroom and kiss Nick. Of course, the more practical thing to do would've been to just *borrow* his ChapStick and use it herself, but at this moment all she wanted to do was stand up and go plant a wet, slippery kiss on his ChapSticky lips.

Emma was really glad that no one could get inside her head. More than half of her thoughts were incredibly embarrassing, even though she was the only one who knew about them. Emma exhaled, trying to clear her mind. She ran her fingers through her straight black hair, pushing it into place behind her ears. As features went, Emma liked her ears. They were symmetrical and round and not too big. In fact, Emma really liked the way she looked in general. She felt like it all just kind of worked. She had olive skin and deep, dark brown eyes that slanted ever so slightly, commonly prompting people to ask her where she was from. "Born and raised in Southern California" was her first answer, but when people grew more persistent and/or rude, she'd go on to explain that her dad was Irish American and her mom was Japanese American, which made her one-fourth Asian and three-fourths Cauc*asian*, which also has the word "asian" in it and always made Emma crack a smile. Not because she thought it was funny, but because it was a strange quirk of words and spelling.

It was weird, just like Emma.

"Em, can you do me a favor?" Nick asked from across the room. Everyone else had already begun working on their assignments. "Can you show the newbie how to use the page layout software?" Emma nodded, glad to have something productive to do. She walked over to the bank of computers where Savannah, "the newbie" girl, was sitting.

Savannah was petite, rocking a pixie cut and thick glasses. Emma couldn't help but notice that her thin lips were a light, bright, grapefruit shade of pink. Emma had the feeling that their lips might be the exact same color, but she wouldn't be entirely sure until the next time she looked in a mirror.

Emma slid down into the empty chair next to Savannah and immediately got a weird sensation of déjà vu. Her forehead crinkled.

"Everything chill up there?" Savannah asked, gesturing toward her head.

"Oh yeah . . . sorry . . . just having too many thoughts all at once."

"Tell me about it," Savannah said, seemingly unfazed.

Emma knew that was a common expression, but something about Savannah's tone made it sound like she might actually want to hear a real answer, so Emma responded honestly, opening the door to her weirdness ever so slightly.

"I'm having déjà vu all of a sudden," she said.

"*Tell me about it*," Savannah said again, with newly added emphasis.

Emma thought she just had.

"Sorry . . . ," Savannah added quickly. "You said 'déjà vu,' and apparently I thought that meant it was okay for me to act like a total weirdo . . ." Emma was glad she wasn't the only person in the room who was capable of such weirdness. "Okay, *anyway*," Savannah said. "I'm Savannah."

"Hi. Emma."

"Hi."

166 days until graduation . . .

LAYLA couldn't stop smiling.

"Uh-oh," Zoe said warily as Layla joined the rest of The Crew at their usual lunch table in the middle of campus. "The last time your face looked like that, you convinced everyone at this table that we should all have sex together."

"But not *together* together," Emma teased.

"Don't worry. This is still that same face," Layla said, still just excited as she'd been on Sunday. It had been about sixty-five hours since the girls agreed to the sex pact, and Layla was pretty sure she'd been grinning continuously ever since. "Guys. It's happening. All of it. First, I bought a box of blond highlights on the way to school this morning. Then, I asked Mr. Moore for an extra credit assignment in AP English and informed him—and also *the universe*—that I will be getting my grade up to an A by the end of the semester."

"What did the universe have to say about that?" Zoe asked.

"*Ob-vi-ously*, the universe is thrilled. Thanks for asking. And so is Logan. I'm sorry you didn't get to see the look on his face that night."

"Was that before or after you were sucking on it on the trampoline?" Alex asked.

"It was when I told him we're gonna have sex."

"Wait, wait. You told *Logan*?" Zoe squirmed. "I thought we weren't telling anyone about the pact." To be fair, The Crew hadn't officially decided whether or not they were telling anyone, but, as an ongoing rule, whatever happened at the froyo table stayed at the froyo table.

"I didn't tell him about the sex pact. But I *did* tell him that we're gonna have sex. As in, him and me. I figured he should know that much." Layla winked and then instantly regretted it. She was not a winker.

"You told us before you told Logan?" Emma laughed.

"Well, yeah." Layla didn't even think that was strange. *Of course* she'd tell the girls first. "But he wouldn't care. He's just so excited. It's gonna be his first time too, so . . ."

"Sometimes I forget he's a virgin," Emma said.

"I know, right? He's good at sex *stuff*, but he hasn't actually . . ."

"What do you mean by 'stuff' exactly?" Zoe asked before Layla could finish her sentence.

"She means he gives good head," Alex offered.

"Ohmigod . . ."

"Well, no," Layla said, correcting Alex. "I mean he's

a good kisser—*phenomenal*, actually—and he knows—"

"Hell. No," Alex interrupted. "Don't tell me he's never gone down on you."

He hadn't.

He'd never even really tried.

And Layla had never thought to ask him.

"I don't think I'd like it," she said.

"How do you know if he hasn't done it?"

"I don't know . . . I just . . . I mean . . . have you thought about where his head would have to be in order to do that?"

"Um, yes. Yes, I have." Alex grinned.

"I'm pretty sure he'd do it if I asked him to. I think he's done it before, 'cause he mentioned that it tastes like fish . . ."

"Layla. It does not taste like fish," Alex insisted.

"How do you know?" Emma laughed.

"I don't *personally*, but I know that fish crap is some super silly boy bullshit Logan's trying to pull."

"Yep. Total bullshit," Emma added. "And it's not like *dick* tastes all that great or whatever."

"Exactly," Alex agreed. "Boys want head, but then they don't want to give it back. Not only is that lame, but it also sucks because it's, like, probably the best way to orgasm—"

"Ohmigod, ohmigod . . ."

"Or *firework* or whatever we're calling it for Zoe . . ."

"I can think of a few other *best* ways." Emma said with a bit of a laugh.

✻ ✻ ✻

EMMA didn't realize that was such a bold statement . . .

. . . but it made Alex smirk and Zoe squirm and Layla's mouth drop open.

"Emma. O'Malley," Layla said after a moment. "Tell. Me. Everything."

"There's not really a whole lot to tell," Emma said, suddenly feeling shy.

It was hard to believe that after more then ten years of friendship and thousands of school lunches and hundreds of helpings of frozen yogurt that there could still be new topics for The Crew to discuss, but the truth was they'd never really talked about this before. Orgasms were completely uncharted territory. They'd talked about kissing, almost endlessly. About tongues and teeth and saliva. They'd talked about breasts and nipples and the appropriate amount of squeezage. About which boob moves turned them on and which ones made them feel like a cow being milked. They swapped stories about hickeys and dick pics and which boys knew how to unhook a bra with only one hand. They'd talked about what to do with their lips or tongues or teeth or hands whenever they were in close proximity to a boy's lips or tongue or neck or penis. They'd talked about penis size and shape and width and color. About shaving and waxing and even what made them wet . . .

. . . but they'd never really talked about this.

At least not until now.

"But you've . . . you've fireworked?" Layla asked. Emma nodded. "With who?"

"Oh. Mostly it's just . . . well, *me*. I have a vibrator."

"Whoa," Zoe said.

"Well. It's not, like, a *vibrator* vibrator," Emma clarified. "I think it's supposed to be like a back massager or something, but it vibrates, so . . ."

"How often do you use it?" Layla asked.

"Um . . ." Emma thought for a minute. "Not, like, a lot . . . but sometimes."

"Same," Alex added. "I don't have a vibrator, though."

"I've never tried . . . ," Layla admitted.

"Ever?" Alex asked, sounding genuinely surprised.

"Yeah, no . . . ," Layla said, making a mental note to at least consider adding "masturbate" to her to-do list.

"I haven't either," Zoe offered. "But you guys obviously knew that already."

"I made sure to put a couple links about it in the Sex Doc."

"*The Sex Doc*? Is that what we're calling that *textbook* you sent us?" Alex grinned.

"You're welcome." Layla smiled. "Did you read it?"

ZOE shook her head.

"There's, like, a thousand articles . . . ," Zoe said as if that were the only reason she hadn't read Layla's extensive Google Document of sexcentric information yet. Unsurprisingly, the whole thing made Zoe nervous. From what she'd skimmed last night, the doc was basically a data dump of everything and anything anyone could possible want to know about sex alphabetized and color-coded by subject matter: what to do, how to do it, where to do it, when to do it, how to be safe about it. There was a whole section on birth control and condoms and morning-after pills. There were links to first person articles about losing your virginity and an extensive collection of YouTube videos. It was basically the most Layla thing ever, Zoe thought as she unzipped her hoodie. She wasn't sure what the most "her" thing ever would be, but it definitely wouldn't be something like that . . .

"Whoa," Emma said, her eyes on Zoe.

"Whoa, what?" Zoe looked down at her tank top. "Did I spill something?"

"It's . . . *your boobs.*"

"Ohmigod, stop."

"They're hot, Zo," Alex added. "Just use them wisely . . ."

"Ha. Right." Zoe blushed. "I don't know the first *thing* about using them."

"I'm sure you'll figure it out pretty quick."

Zoe was still getting used to having them attached to her body let alone trying to figure out what to actually do with them. Zoe turned to Alex, hoping to change the subject. "Speaking of figuring it out, I have an important question for the sexpert."

ALEX was definitely *not* a sexpert.

"Okay, but in comparison to the rest of the table you are," Zoe insisted.

"Maybe your answer is somewhere in the Sex Doc,"

Alex said, but Zoe was already forging ahead with her question.

"So, last night, when I was talking to Dylan—"

"Wait, you two are *still* doing that?" Layla asked.

"Oh. Yeah. We fall asleep on the phone almost every night."

"Forget the sleeping part," Alex said. "Who *talks* on the phone?"

"Me! My fingers are too fat for texting."

"Zoe."

"What? They are. And autocorrect hates me. I'm completely unkeyboardinated and can't type without making every mistake possible. I also never know what to type in the first place."

"But you somehow know what to say for hours every single night?"

"Yeah. It's really so much better. You should try it sometime."

"I can't imagine having that much to say to the same person, even Logan," Layla said.

"Yeah, I don't know." Zoe smiled. "It's really just the easiest . . ." Then she ran her fingers through her hair again and launched back into her question for Alex, *the sexpert*, which basically boiled down to: Does the G-spot actually exist?

The truth was, Alex had absolutely no clue what a G-spot was, let alone whether it existed.

What she *did* know was that there was only so much longer she could go without setting the record straight

50

about what actually happened with Cameron at sleep-away camp.

Or, more accurately, what *didn't* happen.

There was a good reason why Alex's sex dreams always ended in exactly the same place, right before the actual sex part . . .

It was because she never really made it to the actual sex part.

165 days until graduation . . .

ALEX never meant to lie about it.

Technically, she didn't *actually* lie about what had happened, but she also definitely didn't have sex with Cameron that night at camp.

It was an honest misunderstanding, she thought as she laced up her shoes in the locker room before track practice. Surely the girls would get that too, at least once she had a chance to really explain it to them. Still, the thought wasn't doing much to quell the growing pit in Alex's stomach. Now that the sex pact was in play, she knew she would have to set things straight with The Crew as soon as possible . . . but getting up the nerve to do it was the hard part.

As Alex walked out of the locker room, she heard a chorus of laughter coming from Coach Kolbert's office at the end of the hallway. Coach K, as everybody called him, had been coaching track for almost twenty years, longer than all kids on the team had even been alive. They teased him about being an old man, and he had no problem teasing the "young kids" right back. He was wise, but also playful, which was why everybody loved him so much. Alex watched him for a moment through his office window as he laughed with a few older boys she recognized as former members of the track team. They were all recent graduates. Alex figured they must've still been home from college for winter break.

One of the boys in particular caught her eye.

It was Joey Reed.

Alex always found it rather funny that his name rhymed with Zoe's, but apparently that was a total accident. Mr. and Mrs. Reed were formal people and only called him by his full name, Joseph, for the first six years of his life. It wasn't until he got to elementary school that people started calling him Joey. By that point Zoe was already four years old, and they certainly weren't going to change *her* name, so there was nothing anyone could do to stop the rhyming: Joey and Zoe forever.

Alex had known Joey ever since she and Zoe met back in first grade, but they become friends in their own right more recently through their time on the track team. Joey hung out with the kind of stupid boys who liked to play pranks or make lame jokes, but he wasn't like that. Joey was a sweetheart, and he'd go out of his way to apologize for his friends. Alex watched Joey and the other boys closely for another minute as they kept talking to Coach K. College life seemed to be agreeing with all of them. They were only a year or two older than she was, but they looked so much more mature and comfortable in their own skin. And their bodies, too. Especially Joey. Especially *his* body. Alex didn't want to walk over and interrupt the reunion, but she hoped he would look out in her direction so she could wave hello.

He didn't.

Things didn't always work out the way she wanted them to.

Oh, well.

An hour later, in the midst of track practice, Alex still hadn't been able to stop thinking about Joey. She should've just gotten over herself and said hello. It was stupid she hadn't, but it was too late to do anything about it now. Especially right now, at this moment, as she sprinted around the track, pushing herself as hard as she could. She could feel the blood pulsing from the ends of her fingertips all the way down to the tips of her toes. She could feel her knees buckling beneath her. But mostly she could feel every single second of time as it slid away from her.

She knew too much time had slipped off the clock even before she crossed the finish line.

"Almost," Coach K said, looking at his stopwatch.

Alex let out an exasperated *groan*. She had been stuck at "almost" for months now—and she hated it. "Almost" doing something just meant that you almost *didn't* do it as much as you almost did. "Almost" certainly wasn't going to help her break the state record.

"You're so close," Coach K said, trying to find the bright side.

But Alex didn't want "close" and she didn't want "almost," either.

She wanted *actually*.

It didn't matter that she was *close* to breaking the record, just like it didn't matter that she was *close* to having sex with Cameron. She still wasn't the record holder, and she was still technically a virgin. At this moment, Alex wasn't sure which "still" was worse.

"You're just getting in your own way," Coach K said, sensing Alex needed more of a pep talk. He was talking about breaking the state record, but he might as well have been talking about everything else in her life too. "I can see you're all up in your head right now, overthinking yourself, second-guessing every choice you've ever made, revisiting all your old mistakes . . ." Alex nodded, mildly worried that he might be reading her mind. "But you know as well as I do that's not going to get you where you want to go. That's only going to send you backward. And you don't need to go back. You've already been there, right?" Alex nodded again, but more subtly this time. "Yeah?" Coach K asked, pushing for an actual response.

"Yeah," she grunted back, frustrated.

"Good. Get angry," he pushed, "because as far as I'm concerned, this record is already yours. But just because we think something doesn't mean it's just going to hap-pen," Coach K said, choosing his words in such a way as to make Alex even more certain that he could read her mind. "Victories have to be achieved, but I know—*I believe*—that you can do this. You will do this. But I need your faith to be bigger than your fear, Ms. Campbell."

Alex needed that too.

"Let's do one last lap and then call it a day," he said.

She walked back to the starting line with her hands clasped on top of her ponytail, trying to empty her lungs and her thoughts at the same time. She did her best to push unhelpful words like "failure" and "Cameron" and "lie" and "virgin" to the edge of her mind, but as she worked to clear space in her head, she couldn't help but think about how hard she had to try to do so, which made her think about her twin brother, Max, and about how hard he had to work to do just about anything. Even though she was never entirely sure what was going on inside his head, she always felt like she understood him. She and Max had a special twin bond. They connected over their shared love of *Star Wars*. Really, Max was the one who loved *Star Wars*, but Alex loved how much he loved it, and then that just made her actually love it too. Max could quote every word any character said in any of the movies, but he always liked Yoda's words best— never quite in the right order, but somehow always making sense anyway.

One of Max's favorite Yoda sayings was "Do or do not. There is no try." Alex liked that too, because it didn't pretend that "almost" was acceptable. You either succeeded or you failed—there was no in between. There was no "close." There was no "almost." There were no points for trying or planning or expecting.

Max was only two minutes and thirty-five seconds

younger than Alex, but that time—that "only"—was everything.

Alex, always the fast one, came out first, while Max got stuck backward or upside down or something. The doctors went in and grabbed him, but those first two minutes and thirty-five seconds had already changed everything. Immediately, expectations were recalibrated. Bars were lowered. Dreams were reimagined. Alex knew her parents loved her and Max equally, but they all knew that she was capable of so much more than he was, so they expected more from her too.

To put it simply, Alex had to be both the good daughter *and* the good son. Maybe that's why she was such a tomboy. Maybe that's why she liked to play sports. Maybe that's why she approached making out with more of a "boy mentality"— or whatever that meant. The irony was that if she actually *was* a son, no one would've ever written "slut" on her locker. She probably would've been called a stud or a pimp, like Oliver. He hooked up with everyone all the time, and he was "the man." She made out with guys semifrequently, admittedly more often than most girls but not *all* the time, and she was called a ho. And, ironically, everyone thought she was even *more* of a slut because she'd had sex before, which she actually *hadn't*, so it was all just a jumbled mess. And all of it was still swirling around in Alex's head even as Coach K blew the whistle to start the last lap of the day.

Alex sprinted hard off the starting line, running as fast as she could, but it wasn't enough.

This time was even less "almost" than the lap before.

"It's okay. We'll pick it up again tomorrow," Coach K said.

It actually *wasn't* okay, but arguing just felt like another lost cause.

A few minutes later Alex walked toward the parking lot, carrying her backpack and gym bag and all of her thoughts and fears and expectations. It was more than she knew what to do with. She was sweaty and frustrated and tired, and annoyed that her mom wouldn't be able to pick her up for at least another hour . . . and that's when she saw Oliver, sitting on the front hood of his car, texting. His hair was still wet from a recent shower. "Hey, you," he called as she approached.

"Hey, *me*?"

"Yes, you. Who else would I be waiting for?" Alex smiled. "Maybe don't answer that . . ." Oliver smiled back. "Do you want me to give you a ride?" he asked, his innocent tone not exactly matching the gleam in his eyes.

Alex raised her eyebrows, a new, bold smirk stretching across her face as she considering the wording of Oliver's question.

"A ride in my *car*," he clarified. Alex added Oliver to the list of people she suspected might be able to read her thoughts. "You coming?" he asked one more time. "I'm not gonna beg."

Oliver didn't have to beg. Alex was in. Literally. Figuratively. *Actually.*

She climbed into the front seat of his SUV, flashing him her trademarked Mona Lisa smile.

"You gonna tell me what that smile means?"

Even if Alex had wanted to tell him—which she didn't—she honestly *couldn't*, because she rarely knew what it meant herself. It was the kind of smile that says yes as much as it says no—even though the truth was that smiles didn't actually say anything at all.

It was the kind of smile that had gotten Alex into trouble before, and probably would again.

"Whatever it means," Oliver said after a moment, "it's driving me crazy."

The look on Oliver's face was driving Alex crazy too, but she didn't tell him that.

She didn't have to. She was certain he already knew.

158 days until graduation . . .

LAYLA felt like Vanessa was doing it on purpose.

And by "it" she meant *everything.*

Vanessa Martin was the most popular/unpopular girl in the sophomore class. Opinions were evenly drawn between gender lines. The boys all loved her low cut tank tops and her push-up bras and her super short shorts. They loved her flirty laugh and the way she was always sucking on something, be it a lollipop or a strand of her hair. At the same time, the girls generally hated all the things the boys loved about her.

The part that annoyed Layla the most was that everything about Vanessa felt so calculated. It wasn't *just* that she knew what she was doing; she also seemed to know the kind of reaction it would elicit. Case in point: She had been sucking on the cap of her pen since the student council meeting started almost forty minutes ago.

Not just sucking, but *sucking.*

And it didn't look like she was going to let up anytime soon.

Layla didn't blame Vanessa for *wanting* a reaction; she just wished she would own up to it a little more. If you're in a meeting sucking on a pen cap for forty minutes, you're going to give all the student council boys hard-ons and you're going to piss off all the girls. Don't act all shocked when your guy "friends" want to hook up and your girl "friends" don't actually like you.

"Does anybody have any new business?" Logan asked from the front of the classroom.

"Oh, his *voice*," Vanessa whispered to Layla as if it were part of some inside joke between them. It wasn't. "Don't you, like, *die* every time he talks to you?"

No. She didn't, like, die.

Somehow, Layla managed a fake smile in Vanessa's direction, but her beady, calculated eyes were already locked back on Logan. Layla could practically see her mentally undressing him. There was no new business, so Logan wrapped up the meeting, telling everyone to have a good week and that he'd see them next Thursday.

"Sucks there's so much time between meetings, huh?" Vanessa whispered to Layla again. Layla couldn't help but notice her use of the word "suck." How appropriate . . .

A few minutes later, Layla and Logan walked toward the senior parking lot, hand in hand. Layla couldn't stop stewing about Vanessa. "I just don't like her . . ."

"Yes, it's very Captain Obvious of you—"

"But it's like she has no idea. She thinks we're best

friends. And she is completely, shamelessly in love with you."

"Lay, she flirts with *everyone*—"

"So then you admit she's flirting with you?" Layla teased.

"I think I've always admitted that—"

"Oh no. You usually try to say she's just being nice."

"She *is* being nice—"

"'Nice' is not even sort of a strong enough word. It feels like all she wants in life is just to get inside your pants—"

"Whatever. Everything in my pants is already entirely occupied by you." Logan flashed a smile and that dimple and then pulled Layla in close, pressing his waist up against hers.

"Oh, hi," Layla said, teasing him—and his hard-on. "You sure that's for me, though? Not just left over from Vanessa's extended pen-sucking exhibition?"

"Pen sucking? I hadn't noticed," Logan tried to say with a straight face, but Layla knew he'd noticed. All the boys always did. There was no point in trying to deny it. "Hey, so is it annoying or still sort of cute to remind you that I have a condom in my glove compartment?"

"It was never cute."

"A little bit cute? No?"

"Nope." Layla let the dust settle for a moment before telling Logan that she wanted to have sex for the first time on Valentine's Day.

"All right," he said with a nod. It looked like he was doing the mental math in his head. It was twenty-nine days away, just over four weeks. Layla had obviously already counted. "That'll be cool. Losing the V-cards on V-day."

"A little less cool when you make it sound all corny like that."

"The *day* is corny—there's not much I can do about that."

"Actually, I think there's a lot you can do . . ."

"Oh. Is this your way of telling me that you want a whole production?"

"Not, like, a *production* . . ."

"But a scavenger hunt or something like that?"

Layla smiled. Yes, something *exactly* like that.

Logan pulled her hand up to his lips and kissed her fingers. "For a second I thought you were going to do your best Vanessa impression," she said, laughing.

"Oh, you mean like this?" Logan playfully slipped Layla's pointer finger into his mouth and sucked hard. She yanked her hand back.

"Ew, Logan. Slobber."

"You wanna try me?" Logan held out his hand, wiggling his fingers.

"No thank you . . ."

"Fine. Whatever. I'm sure I could get Vanessa to do it," Logan said as he finally pulled his car out of the parking lot.

He was joking.

And Layla knew he was joking.

But something about the way he said it, or maybe something about the fullness of his smile *as* he said it or maybe just something about the twinkle in his eye as the words came out of his mouth . . . whatever it was, *something* about the moment didn't sit right with Layla.

She simply couldn't shake it.

ZOE couldn't quite reach the tallest leaves.

She was standing on her toes on the highest rung of the ladder, trying to paint the top of the wooden trees, but so far she was failing. She could feel the ladder wobbling beneath her.

"Please don't fall!" Austin shouted from the back of the theater.

Zoe was startled by the sound of his voice, and it made her sway on her heels. She had to crouch down on the top step to steady herself. She didn't realize anyone else was around, but apparently Austin had been watching from the tech booth.

"Sorry for the scare," he said. "I'd just be super sad and embarrassed for you if you fell. But then I'd also have to laugh at you."

"I would also be sad and embarrassed too," Zoe said, already laughing. She realized she probably looked pretty ridiculous up there, covered in green paint. This year's spring musical was *Into the Woods*, and, as the stage manager, a big part of Zoe's job was to make sure that the woods on the stage looked like actual woods. So far this involved a lot of brown and green paint and was only turning out to be a mildly successful endeavor.

"You need a hand?" Austin asked, walking toward the stage.

"Yes. And longer legs and arms," Zoe said, instantly feeling lame about it.

"What?" Austin asked before realizing it was a bad joke, "Oh, ha, right, yes," he added quickly. Austin was a nice guy like that. He held the ladder as Zoe climbed down and even offered Zoe his hand as she jumped off the bottom step. Zoe's hand was sweaty and covered in paint, but she reached for Austin's anyway. She wanted to know what his fingers felt like.

"You greened me," he said, looking at his hand after Zoe had let go.

"Oh no. Here." Zoe held out the bottom of her already paint-covered tank top so he could wipe off his hand on it. Austin looked at Zoe for an extra beat, catching her eyes as if to confirm that she wouldn't mind. Really, she wouldn't. "It's all good. I'm a mess already."

"You're not at all," Austin said sincerely as he wiped his hand.

Then, Austin shifted his weight in his shoes, seemingly nervous. Zoe wasn't exactly sure why he was nervous, but she was nervous too, so it sort of made sense.

Austin ran his hand over his short hair and then looked down at his shifting feet. Zoe followed his gaze, down his body, and it suddenly occurred to her that she'd never really noticed his body before. She'd noticed his dark skin and his deep brown eyes and the shape of his hands and maybe even his neck and the curve of his ears, which were slightly larger than average and maybe even a little bit pointed in an adorable sort of way, but she'd never really noticed his body. Maybe it was because he was usually sitting in the tech booth designing lighting cues. Or maybe it was because he and Zoe hadn't actually spent that much time together. Yes, they'd been in the same place, at rehearsal, for hours and hours, but they weren't really *together*.

Not like this, anyway.

Not this close.

Even though they weren't even touching, Zoe could feel him and his presence and his body and the way it was right there, taking up all the space next to hers.

"You have some, um, some more green," Austin managed to say, getting bashful as he pointed in the general vicinity of Zoe's chest.

Zoe looked down.

Yep.

There was a big glob of green on her chest, right between her boobs.

Not only had Austin *noticed* her boobs, but he'd basically just *told* her that he noticed—and that made Zoe smile. And then blush, too. She hoped her face was only a *little* red and didn't look like a full-on fire engine, which is what it felt like. All the red and green was probably making her look like a giant Christmas elf. She wiped the paint off her chest as slickly as she could, which wasn't very.

After some mildly awkward silence, Austin asked Zoe if she liked The Other Team. "It's this band," he explained. "My buddy's the drummer. They play at house parties sometimes."

"Oh yeah," Zoe said, pretending like maybe she had

heard of them. She didn't go to all that many house parties, but when she did, they certainly weren't cool enough to have live bands.

"Yeah. They're good," Austin continued, "and they have a show coming up at the Roxy this Saturday. A bunch of the tech guys are gonna go, so if you want to come too, that would be . . ."

"Cool," Zoe said, completing Austin's sentence for him.

"Cool," Austin agreed. And then they just stood there on the empty stage, grinning at each other until Austin finally regained his ability to speak. "Um . . . ," he started timidly, "can you do me a favor and stand in my spotlight for a minute?"

"Oh sure, but I bet you say that to all the girls," Zoe said, trying to maybe flirt with him. In her head, it had sounded like something a pretty actress would say in a movie. In reality, Austin just looked pretty confused, and the whole exchange made Zoe feel self-conscious. "Where do you need me?" she asked, getting things back on track.

Austin pointed to a mark in the center of the stage and then scampered back to the light booth. He turned on the spotlight and worked to focus it. Now it was Austin's turn to make Zoe nervous. It was mostly the spotlight's fault. At least all she had to do was stand still. "Got it!" he said after what seemed like an eternity. "Looks perfect!"

"Thanks," Zoe said as a new feeling of excitement washed over her.

It was the kind of feeling that made her want to break into song.

She wasn't *really* going to start singing, mostly because she couldn't carry a tune to save her life, but she felt like a real life version of the characters in the musicals she loved so much. The kind of a character who lived in a magical, musical world where it was normal and acceptable and maybe even *encouraged* to break out into song at any given moment.

At this moment, Zoe could hear a whole orchestra in her head; the instruments were playing the opening notes from the song "I Know Things Now," which was Zoe's favorite song from *Into the Woods* and might also be her favorite Sondheim song of all time, which was a very big deal considering how many incredible Sondheim songs existed in the universe. "I Know Things Now" is the song Little Red Riding Hood sings about her first encounter with the wolf. At first Little Red describes the meeting as being exciting, but then she clarifies that it's actually both exciting *and* scary, which was exactly how Zoe felt at this very moment.

Excited and scared.

She was both at the same time.

Austin and his spotlight and his voice and his smile and the way his body felt next to hers—and the way *her* body felt next to his—was the most thrilling *and* terrifying thing that had happened to Zoe in a very long time.

Quite possibly, ever.

157 days until graduation . . .

EMMA had been tossing and turning for what felt like forever.

She rolled over and glanced at her digital alarm clock.

12:02 a.m.

It was already tomorrow, and she was still awake . . .

Clearly *something* was bothering her.

She'd been in an especially bad mood for the past few weeks or maybe even the past few *months*. Basically since the very beginning of the school year. She was pretty confident that it all had something to do with the calendar and the unwavering finality of G-day, and the way the future simply wouldn't stop approaching the present, but she didn't know what to do about it.

All she *wanted* to do was go to sleep, but she couldn't manage to turn off her brain. She was having too many thoughts and feelings—and overthinking and overfeeling all of them. Sometimes, when Emma really couldn't sleep and just needed to take a break from herself, and her thoughts, and her brain and everything, she would masturbate.

But right now *that* didn't even sound like fun.

Even if Emma somehow managed to get up enough excitement to actually go for it, she didn't feel like she was going to be able to *finish* it . . . and the thought of ending up without any, well, fireworks made her more frustrated than anything else.

Still, she took her vibrator out of the bottom drawer of her nightstand and turned it on, hoping maybe the sound would *un*frustrate her. Or at least just *un*frustrate her enough to get her in the mood. Sometimes that worked.

This time it didn't.

ZOE wanted to go to sleep, but she couldn't stop staring at her phone.

It was almost 12:15 a.m., and Zoe's phone had been buzzing for the last few minutes as Layla sent a string of motivational quotes to The Chat. Layla loved quotes. And she seemed to love them even more when they were displayed on abstract pictures or on top of sunsets or on seascapes or color backgrounds. Zoe liked Layla's quotes, but she was much more partial to song lyrics. Something about the music made the words feel more important, Zoe thought.

She was almost always listening to music, and tonight she'd made it all the way through her Songs of the Moment playlist *twice*. Zoe was constantly updating her SOTM mix, but it always consisted of about two hours of pop songs, classic favorites, and show tunes. She could happily listen to her mix, almost endlessly, but at this point, she was just stalling and waiting for Dylan's nightly *Ready?* text message. It was Dylan's job to text first, but it was already much later than usual, so Zoe figured if there was gonna be a phonefall, she'd have to break tradition.

Ready? she texted him.

Ten minutes passed. No response.

Just as she was about to give up and go to sleep, her phone rang.

She picked up on the first ring. "Sorry," Dylan said — instead of his usual 'hey, hey' — before Zoe even had a chance to say hello. "I just got off the phone with Caroline, I swear . . ."

"Everything okay?"

"She was being dramatic . . ." Dylan was clearly in a mood.

"I'm glad you're all right. I was starting to think you might be lying in a ditch somewhere."

"No ditch, just my bed," he said, softening ever so slightly.

"Oh, okay, so then you basically forgot about me. That's cool too," Zoe teased, still trying to pull Dylan out of his bad mood.

"Z. Puh-lease. I could never forget about you," Dylan replied, sounding a bit more like his goofy self again. "I'm sorry. It was just stupid Caroline bullshit that went on for way too long. It's fine. Whatever. What's up with you?"

"So much," Zoe said excitedly, thrilled to finally have Dylan's attention. "At rehearsal this afternoon, the lighting designer—Austin—do you know him?"

"Do I?"

"I don't know. Austin Jones. He's tall-ish. Cute. Black. He's a theater kid."

"Oh yeah, one of those losers . . ." Dylan chuckled.

Zoe knew Dylan was just teasing, but she'd been waiting so patiently to tell him about the paint and the concert and the spotlight and the way everything with Austin was both exciting *and* scary, so Dylan's jab seemed rather insensitive. "We're going to see The Other Team on Saturday," she replied.

"Which team?"

"The Other Team. It's a band, not an actual team. Some of the other tech people are coming to the concert too, so it's like a group thing, but still . . ."

Zoe waited, hoping for even just a medium amount of excitement from Dylan, but all she got was a little bit of a grunt. It might even have just been a cough.

"Well. It was cute."

"I'm sure."

"And then he asked me to stand in his spotlight," Zoe added, as if that might mean something to Dylan.

It didn't.

And Zoe couldn't figure out how to explain it to him.

155 days until graduation . . .

EMMA still had no idea what was bothering her.

The girls were seated at their usual froyo table, phones stacked in the middle as always, listening to Zoe recount all the adorable details of her first date with Austin. Like the way she'd done her hair—half up and half down—and how he'd nervously rung her doorbell and then had been forced to talk to Zoe's dad, who wasn't *really* intimidating, but his broad shoulders and full beard seemed to make teenage boys rather anxious. But then it turned out that *Austin's* dad was driving them to the concert, so that made Zoe's dad like the situation a whole lot more. Zoe and Austin hadn't kissed, which Alex assessed was mostly due to the fact that Austin's dad was their carpool driver. Zoe explained that they kind-of almost held hands a couple of times during the concert and stood next to each other the entire time. It was all cute sounding, and very "Zoe" and Emma wanted to get excited about the date night like Layla and Alex seemed to be, but she was mostly just distracted and frustrated. It wasn't Zoe's fault.

It wasn't *anyone's* fault.

At this point Emma was even annoying herself.

After Zoe finished her story, Layla turned her attention to Emma and asked her for a "progress report" on the sex pact. Layla meant well enough, but it was exactly the opposite of what Emma needed right now. Layla had asked Zoe the same question, but the difference was that Zoe had some actual progress—an entire date night—to report.

Right now Emma had nothing.

She could barely even figure out how to complete a sentence.

"I don't . . . I just . . ." Okay, forget *finishing* a sentence, apparently Emma couldn't even figure out how to *start* one.

All she knew for sure was that Layla wasn't helping.

"I just . . . I think you're making this whole thing very stressful," Emma finally managed to "report" between bites of caramel frozen yogurt.

"What whole thing?"

"The pact. Obviously," Emma huffed.

"Not *obviously*. Em, lately you think everything is stressful."

"Yes, but . . . ," Emma said, attempting to start another sentence, but trailed off, deciding to focus on her rainbow sprinkles instead.

"Maybe there's a better phrase we could be using instead of 'progress report,'" Zoe chimed in, trying to help.

"The problem isn't what we're *calling* it." Emma could feel a bit of sharpness in her voice, and she didn't like it at all.

"Then what *is* the problem?" Layla pushed back.

"I don't know . . ." Emma exhaled. "It's only been two weeks since you first said the words 'sex pact' and it's like you're already expecting us to have it all figured out. You're the only one who has a boyfriend."

"Aw. No. I don't mean it like that," Layla said sweetly. "I just want to know where your head's at."

Yeah.

That was pretty much the only thing anybody—her parents, her friends, her teachers—wanted to know these days: Where was Emma's head?

Literally: It was sitting on top of her shoulders.

Beyond that . . . she had no clue.

The clock was ticking and time was flying and there was nothing Emma could do to stop it. She wanted to enjoy the second semester of her senior year and have fun with her best friends and laugh about boys and penises and sex pacts, but she just . . . couldn't.

"Everything is just feeling like a lot right now."

"All the feels?" Layla asked with a smile.

"Something like that . . . ," Emma said, forcing a smile in return. Layla's heart was in the right place, but Emma's heart and head, and whatever else was involved in her decision making process, had already reached peak emotional capacity. There simply wasn't room for anything else. Not a Sex Doc. Or weekly progress reports. And *especially* not all the feels, either.

Honestly, Emma didn't have room for *any* of the feels. She would've been perfectly happy to give them all back, but that didn't seem to be an option.

ZOE had already spent too many hours waiting for Dylan's *You ready?* text message.

Again, he was running late.

And, *again*, she felt like an idiot.

All she wanted to do was tell him about her date with Austin, but he wasn't responding to any of her text messages. She sent a text to The Chat—*Dylan's avoiding me*—just to make sure her cell phone worked and it had service and the ability to deliver messages to other cell phones.

He's jealous, Alex texted back immediately.

Then Layla chatted a picture of a typewriter with the quote *"Love means never having to ask 'Did you get my text message?'"* written on it.

Zoe wanted to text back that Dylan clearly didn't love her, non-mystery solved, but that seemed like too much effort. Mostly she wished she could forget about Dylan entirely. He'd been so distracted by Caroline recently that she could barely remember the last time they had a real, satisfying conversation. Now she finally, actually had something worthwhile to tell him and didn't want to miss her chance.

She tried sending Dylan one more text: *Are you okay?*

Still nothing.

She put her phone down on her desk, willing it to buzz.

Just as she was about to give up entirely, it did.

Hey.

That was it. The incoming text was one word, three letters, one period.

Zoe had to recheck the text and then *re-*recheck it, three times altogether, before realizing that the incoming message wasn't from Dylan.

It was from Austin.

Ohmigod.

Hi, she texted back, laughing at herself for how much time and energy it took her to settle on that one word, two letters, no punctuation reply.

Thanks for last night!!!!! he responded almost immediately.

Zoe noticed all the exclamation points. She started to type back *You're welcome* but erased it before she even had time to consider using exclamation points of her own.

Before she could come up with a better, flirtier response, she got another text from Austin: *We should do it again sometime . . .*

Zoe noticed the dot dot dot. She loved all three of the dots very much. And then promptly freaked out, running around her bedroom, doing a full-on happy dance, until she realized Austin had no clue how happy she actually was, because he couldn't see her victory dance and she hadn't managed to respond to either of his last two text messages.

So far all she'd *actually* said was *Hi.*

One word. Two letters. No punctuation.

That was it.

Zoe really was just horrible at texting.

Yes! she typed as quickly as possible, pressing send before she could overanalyze anything.

Then, even more quickly, she added a bunch of extra exclamation points—*!!!!*—as their own separate text message.

Then she wished there were a text erase button so she could get rid of all those extra exclamation points, but it was too late. She'd already sent them.

Whatever.

Honestly? She didn't even care.

Alex would've said she was disrupting the delicate "flirting power balance" between them or something, which might've even been accurate, but Zoe didn't want to play games right now.

Luckily, Austin didn't either. He quickly sent back a smiley face.

Zoe very much appreciated that Austin was also a beginner level flirt and added her own smiley face to the conversation.

Then she also added: *But only if your dad doesn't drive this time.*

Deal, Austin texted back.

She took a screenshot of their conversation, mildly embarrassed by all the exclamation points and smiley faces, but mostly too proud to care. As soon as she sent the Austin screenshot to The Chat, she received another incoming text.

This one was from Dylan: *Caroline and I broke up.*

At least that explained why he hadn't responded to her sooner.

Wanna talk? She texted back, already certain the answer was no.

As anticipated, Dylan didn't respond to Zoe's text, but the truth was his silence didn't bother her nearly as much as it might've in the past. Zoe had seen Dylan go through enough breakups to know that he was hurting right now and just wanted to be left alone. In a couple of days, or weeks, he'd snap out of it and wonder how he ever let himself get so consumed by Insert-Ex-Girlfriend-Name-Here and all of her stupid bullshit. Then, maybe a couple of days or weeks after *that*, he'd be back to his cheerful self — and ready to move on to the next skinny blond girl.

At least once all that happened, Zoe and Dylan could go back to their regularly scheduled phonefalls. For now, she had Austin and his exclamation points, and a fresh batch of excited text messages pouring into The Chat from her girls. For now, that was more than enough.

153 days until graduation . . .

EMMA was only really happy in the yearbook room.

Lately, it was the only activity that managed to distract her from herself, so she'd been spending almost all of her free time there. She might not be able to give Layla a progress report on the sex pact, but at least she could make progress on something worthwhile. Today she was working on the layout for the Senior Superlative page. They hadn't voted on the Superlatives yet, but Emma knew they would soon and they'd need a layout. Might as well get a jump on it now. Someone would be voted Most Likely to Succeed. Someone would have the Best Eyes and the Cutest Smile. Emma thought she should nominate herself Most Likely to Have a Nervous Breakdown Slash Panic Attack Before Graduation.

"Your photo layout looks good," Savannah said as she sat down at the computer next to Emma.

"My photo layout looks *excellent*, thankyouverymuch," Emma confirmed playfully. "It's just . . . it's the rest of my everything that's all over the place."

"I swear you don't *look* like you're all over the place."

"Yeah, well, you can't see or hear any of the thoughts inside my head."

"Yeah, *well*, I think if I *could* really see or hear them, we'd have some sort of intense medical emergency on our hands," Savannah said with a laugh.

Emma loved Savannah's laugh.

It was substantial and unapologetic and always the perfect pitch.

Savannah flipped open her notebook, and Emma couldn't help but notice an impressive collection of doodles and scribbles interspersed with a smattering of notes about the boys' soccer game. "I'm sports news editor," Savannah explained.

"Really? Sports?"

"Yes. *Really.*"

"I mean. You just *look* like such a huge sports fan . . ."

"Little known fact: The sports section is the busiest beat on the paper. There are dozens of sports teams, and they all have dozens of games. There's always something to write about." Emma nodded, sensing there was something more to the story. "Anddddd, yeah. I didn't get my shit together fast enough at the start of the school year, and all the other editorial beats were already taken."

"So, we're saying my judgments are quite accurate?"

"If we must."

"Oh, we must." Emma laughed again.

Savannah laughed again too. Emma appreciated her laugh more and more each time.

"What's so funny?" Nick asked on his way into the room.

"Sports," Savannah said in a deep voice that made Emma laugh even harder.

"All right," Nick said, clearly missing the inside joke. He grabbed his binder off the counter and then noticed the Superlative layout on Emma's screen. "Oh, whoa . . . ," he said as leaned down, right over Emma's left shoulder, to get a better look. He didn't need to be quite so close to see it, but Emma would've been lying if she said she didn't like that he was standing there. "It's *brilliant*," he concluded after another long look. "Em, your layouts are *always* worth geeking out about. Every single time . . ." Emma smiled, trying not to blush. Nick squeezed her shoulder and then hustled out the door. The girls watched him leave.

"I officially nominate him for Best Butt," Savannah announced.

"Unfortunately juniors don't get to vote for superlatives."

"What. Ever. You should add his butt to your layout. It's that good." Emma hadn't really noticed his butt before . . . His lips? All the time. But never his butt.

Savannah's lips cracked into an embarrassed smirk. "I'm actually the weirdest," she blurted out as if she simply couldn't keep the words inside for a moment longer. "Butts aren't even my thing, like, sexually speaking or whatever. It's not like the thought of them turns me on or anything, but I always feel as if I want to put my hand inside people's back pants pockets. It's not even that I really want to *touch* their butts or anything, but I just, like, need to know what my hand would feel like inside their pocket. Don't worry, I'm super normal . . ."

"'The only normal people are the ones we don't know very well,'" Emma replied. Layla had sent that quote to The Chat one time. Emma loved it so much she wrote it down on a Post-it note and stuck it on her bathroom mirror.

"So then you agree that I'm weird?"

"Oh, totally. But I am too."

"You keep it together pretty well."

"God no. I told you," Emma insisted. "*My thoughts . . .*" She considered how much crazy she was willing to unleash into Savannah's world before deciding to open up a little bit more. "Okay, so you want to put your hands in people's pockets? Fine. That's weird. No question. But my weirdness is that I literally want to kiss everyone I meet."

"Everyone?"

"Yup. Everyone."

"By 'kiss' you mean, like, a peck on the cheek or you actually want to stick your tongue inside their mouth?"

"Tongue in mouth," Emma said with a giggle, but she was entirely serious. "It's not really even sexual, either. I just have this urge to know what it'd be like."

Emma had never said that out loud before. She didn't know what it was exactly, but something about Savannah made her want to say it.

"All right. I feel good about that," Savannah said.

Emma did too.

150 days until graduation . . .

ALEX still wasn't quite sure how she felt about Oliver.

"It's complicated," she explained between bites of her chopped salad.

"Obviously. It *has* to be complicated or you would've gotten bored forever ago," Layla said without judgment.

"True," Alex agreed. "Sometimes I think he's a misunderstood nice guy. Other times I think he's the asshole everyone thinks he is. I can't tell. This morning he finally asked if he could see me somewhere besides his car."

"Wait, w*hat*?!" Layla asked excitedly.

"Yeah. He said he wants to take me out somewhere," Alex explained as if it weren't a big deal. "Act-u-a-lly he said he wants to go somewhere sexy with me, which sounds ridiculous, but I swear it came out of his mouth."

"It's only 'ridiculous' if you actually mean 'hot,'" Layla said.

"It was hot, too, I guess, but who just *says* that?" Alex asked.

"A guy with a lot of confidence in the size of his penis," Emma quipped.

"You know," Layla said seriously, "penis size is actually *not* the most important factor in determining the amount of pleasure a woman has in any given sexual experience."

"Are you quoting the Sex Doc?" Zoe giggled.

"O-kay. I'm not having sex with Oliver. At least not on our first date," Alex clarified.

EMMA thought it was weird that Alex was even *having* a first date in the first place.

But, then again, maybe she was the weird one since everyone in The Crew seemed to be dating, too: Zoe and Austin were about to go on their second date. Layla and Logan had an official *sex* date on the calendar. And now Alex and Oliver.

"It's cool," Emma said, tucking her hair behind her ears. "You guys go ahead with all that . . . I'll just hang out by myself. It's fine. Totally fine."

"You *sound* totally fine," Alex teased.

"Let's find you someone to date," Layla said excitedly. "Or maybe someone you might want to hang out with. Like, for the pact . . ."

"I don't want to 'hang out' with someone just because of the stupid pact."

"Emma. The pact is not *stupid*," Layla defended.

"You're obsessing about it. It's all you want to talk about anymore." Emma directed that statement mostly to Layla, but she meant it for the other girls too.

"Em, it's just supposed to be fun," Layla said, trying to calm Emma down.

"I think it'll be a lot more fun if we stop making such a big deal about it."

"I swear I'm not trying to stress you out," Layla insisted, "but I *am* trying to say that I think it matters. Or that I think it *should* matter. But it's obviously not something you *have* to do—"

"No, I know I don't *have* to," Emma replied. "but school ending is already stressful enough, and now you decided that this has to have the same due date—"

"Emma!" Layla said, finally getting exasperated. "You're the one who's mushing it together with graduation"—Emma flinched at Layla's use of the G-word—"but for real if you don't want to do the pact, for whatever reason, just say so."

"I want to do it!" Emma declared. But she knew there was a "but" somewhere inside of her too. She paused for a moment, trying to find the right way, or at least the right words, to best explain herself to her best friends. "*But,*" she finally managed to add, "there's nothing more frustrating than a feeling you can't quite explain." The girls all nodded. Emma was relieved to see that they seemed to understand what she was saying even if she didn't quite understand it herself. "I'm starting to think that something is seriously wrong with me," she added.

"Nothing is wrong with you," Layla insisted. "And we always want to know what's going on, even if it's confusing, or hard to explain, or whatever."

"I'm just, like, frustrated all the time and I don't know why . . ."

"Sounds like you need to get laid," Alex teased, like only she could.

"Ha. Thanks," Emma said, finally cracking a real smile.

"Oh, look, there she is," Layla said, seeing Emma's grin.

And Emma felt more like herself again, at least for a moment.

And she really *did* still want to get laid.

Or at least she still liked the idea of the pact.

Mostly, she liked that the girls were all in it together.

A few hours later, after Emma's last class of the day, she walked into the yearbook room, and was glad to find Nick, sitting by himself, working on the copy for the Superlative page.

"Lookin' good," she said.

"Just trying to keep up with you . . ." Nick smiled. Emma slid a chair up next to his computer and watched him work for a minute. He didn't seem to mind. "So . . . what's up with you?" he asked after some time had passed. It was an innocent enough question, but Emma couldn't help but hear the weight of all her frustrations inside of it.

"Ohhhh . . . ," Emma started, but before she could finish, she heard Alex's words from the lunch table echoing in her head: *Sounds like you need to get laid.*

"*Ohhhh,*" Nick echoed back to her when she failed to say anything else. "I know you, Em, and I know *something's* up. Tell me what's bothering you."

Emma shuffled through her bothersome thoughts and

ultimately decided to play it safe: college applications and grades and the end of high school and all that, she answered.

"Yeah, it blows." Nick nodded. "*Especially* when you don't know what you're doing next."

Yep, Emma thought.

"My early application got rejected from NYU," he added after another moment.

"Oh, that sucks," Emma said before she could filter herself.

"Thanks," Nick said, chuckling.

"Sorry, I mean—"

"No, you're right. It does suck. And basically everyone I've told so far just wants to say sorry and talk to me about things 'happening for a reason' or finding a 'bright side' and all that bullshit. But it's like, what if I don't want a bright side? Maybe I just need to sit in the rain cloud for a little while, you know?"

"I do," Emma said, appreciating Nick's honesty.

"And what if things *don't* happen for a reason?" Nick asked, picking up steam. "What if it's all just random and the time we spend trying to make sense of everything is actually time that we're stupidly wasting because there is no meaning?" Nick looked up from the screen, catching Emma's eyes. She couldn't seem to take them off him. "I'm glad you get it," he said.

Emma did get it. She totally, *totally* got it . . .

. . . just as long as she didn't have to define what "it" actually was.

"I feel like there's something more you're not telling

me," Nick said intuitively. "I can practically see the thought bubbles floating up out of your hair."

Emma shook her head no.

"Really? No? I put all *my* lameness out on the table and you still don't want to share?"

Nick licked his lips.

They looked particularly kissable.

"It's not that I don't *want* to share . . . it's just . . ." Emma could hear Alex's words echoing in her head again: *Sounds like you need to get laid.*

"Come. On." Nick pushed one more time. "What's on your mind?"

"Sex."

"Ha. Right."

Emma had answered so quickly and without hesitation that it took Nick an extended moment to realize she wasn't kidding.

"Wait, *actually*?" he asked, his eyes popping a little. Emma focused her attention on her fingernails. "Oh, all right, well, I didn't mean . . . ," Nick bumbled, still surprised by Emma's boldness. "You know, sex is just, like, basically in my head a hundred percent of the time while all my other thoughts attempt to exist in front of it, so . . ."

Emma nodded, finally looking up long enough to make eye contact.

"Can you keep a secret?" she asked. Emma knew it was against protocol to talk about the pact with anyone outside of The Crew, but telling Nick felt right. She knew he'd think it sounded cool. He'd probably say it was "awesome sauce" or something nerdy cute like that.

"Wow," Nick said after she brought him up to speed. "That's amazeballs."

"It is," Emma said, smiling at his nerdy cute word choice—she was impressed with herself for calling it, "but now the girls are making a big deal about it."

"Your girls make a big deal about everything. No offense."

"None taken." That was Emma's point exactly. "But the pact's not, like, *binding* or anything," she clarified. "There's no pressure, or whatever, but I don't want to get left behind . . . I'm sure I'll figure it out."

Nick nodded, maybe a little too enthusiastically. "Well. Hey . . . ," he said with a chuckle, "if you end up needing any help with that . . ."

"Help with what?"

"The . . . the pact," Nick said, suddenly turning into a jumble of nerves. "I've . . . you know I've had sex before. Not, um, a lot. But a few times. Probably a decent amount. And we've . . . you know, I think we kiss well, together, and, so, I just want you to know that I'm . . . I'm *here*."

"Thanks . . . ," Emma said, unsure exactly what he was getting at.

"I'm just saying if you ever need, like, a hand . . . or . . . or a penis . . ." Nick laughed before the word "penis" even came all the way out of his mouth, "I'm happy to help."

"Aw," Emma said. "No one's ever offered me their penis before."

"Ha. Yeah. So. That's all. I'm here, and I *have* a penis . . .

and that's, like, half of the whole sex thing right there, so, yeah."

"Nick."

"Yeah?"

"Are you saying you want to have sex with me?"

"Mostly I'm saying, um . . . well, no pressure, but if . . . if *you* wanted to have sex with *me* . . . then . . ." Nick finally cut the bullshit. "Yes, Emma, that is what I'm saying. I would very much like to have sex with you . . . but, now, looking at your face, we should probably just. . ."

"Yeah."

"Yeah. Okay. That's what I . . . can we just please forget I said any of that?"

"No," Emma said, feeling as calm and confident as she had in a very long time. "I mean: *yeah* as in yes. I would very much like to have sex with you, too."

149 days until graduation . . .

EMMA didn't believe it was actually going to happen . . .

. . . until she heard the doorbell ring.

Her parents had a weekly Saturday night date night. They were always out of the house and on their way to the movies or some charity function or something by 7:00 p.m. at the latest. Nick had been over to her house at least a dozen times before, mostly to work on the yearbook or other assignments for class. He had met her parents quite a few times. but this time, since he was coming over for a very specific and completely non-school-related purpose, Emma felt like it made sense to avoid any unnecessary or potentially awkward parental interaction by telling Nick to come over at seven fifteen.

He rang the doorbell *exactly* on time.

She opened it.

And he was standing there.

And that was it.

She knew it was going to happen.

Yesterday, before Emma had left the yearbook room, she'd told Nick that she would have the house to herself all night and that he could come over and they could watch a movie or whatever. They both knew that the "or whatever" clearly meant "have sex," but it was just *a little bit* too awkward for Emma to actually say out loud. It occurred to Emma that if it was too awkward to say out loud, then maybe it would also be too awkward to *do* in real life, but she decided not to dwell on that thought. Especially since there were so many other more important questions to take its place, like: (1) Would it hurt? (2) Did she have a condom? And (3) When was the last time she'd shaved her legs? The answers were: (1) Hopefully not. (2) Nick would bring one. And (3) Absolutely no clue.

Emma made sure to shower that afternoon and shave her legs, armpits, and bikini line. Then she tried to figure out what to wear. Normally, she was a jeans and hoodie kind of girl, but that outfit seemed rather casual for the occasion. Emma reminded herself that one of the upsides of sleeping with Nick was that it *would* be casual.

But still.

There was a fine line between being laid-back and being lazy, and even though she definitely didn't want to *obsess* about this moment or stress about it . . . she still wanted it to be significant. Ultimately, Emma decided to just be herself and wear her favorite dark blue jeans and her softest, most perfectly worn-in purple hoodie. It felt right, so Emma went with it.

Nick had apparently also showered and shaved since the last time Emma had seen him. She appreciated the effort, as well as the fact that he also seemed to be hanging out in the space between "casual" and "significant." He showed up wearing too much aftershave on his baby face and too much gel in his hair, but he had the perfect mixture of sweetness and nervous excitement in his smile.

"Are you hungry?" Emma asked as she led him inside her house. Mostly the question was just a way to fill the silence.

"I ate dinner at home, but if you're . . ."

"No, I ate too."

"Okay. Cool."

And then there was more silence.

"I was thinking I'd make some popcorn," Emma said after another moment.

"Yes!" Nick said enthusiastically. Making popcorn seemed like a safe warm-up activity, and, since they'd technically talked about watching a movie together, it made sense.

"Beer?" Nick asked, as they waited for the popcorn to pop.

He pulled three Sam Adams Christmas edition beer bottles out of his backpack, explaining that was all he could take from his dad's refrigerator in the garage without getting caught. "Hopefully they're still good or whatever."

Emma took a sip, realizing that she wouldn't be able to tell if they were good or not. Beer always just tasted like beer, and she didn't particularly *like* the taste, but the bubbles felt good on her tongue.

Emma and Nick took the popcorn and went into the den, where there was a big flat screen TV. Apparently continuing the we're-just-here-to-watch-a-movie narrative felt good for both of them. To that end, Emma's parents had a very extensive DVD collection. Her mom had taken all the discs out of their cases and arranged them alphabetically in oversized three-ring binders. Nick started flipping through the first book, which contained all the A–G movies.

"What do you want to watch?" he asked before looking up and catching Emma's eyes. He seemed to know what her look meant. "You don't actually want to watch anything, do you?"

All Emma wanted to do was kiss him.

She wasn't sure exactly how many times they'd kissed before, but she knew they'd made out on four or maybe five different occasions, which made her wonder how many kisses there were in a make-out session: a hundred? A thousand? She had no clue. Emma realized that they'd never really planned any of their kisses before. They were always drunken or spontaneous, usually at a party in an upstairs bedroom or a guest bathroom or something. One time they made out for an hour on the trampoline in Layla's backyard. Emma couldn't help but think that out of all the hundreds (thousands?) of kisses they'd shared, this very next one would be the most important one of all . . . and so now, thinking about all that, all Emma really wanted to do was put her lips on Nick's lips and stick her tongue in his mouth.

That was it.

That was literally all she could think about, as if that one thought was filling her entire head and pushing everything else to the edges of her skull. The one kissing thought was so strong and overwhelming that she was worried it might *ultimately* pop all the other thought bubbles inside of her and somehow smush her brain up against her skull and destroy her entire capacity to function.

Emma shook her head no.

"Do *you* actually want to watch something?" she asked back.

Nick shook his head no too.

Clearly, Nick had come over (with beer and lube), planning to have sex. But judging by his quickening breath and the sweat on his forehead, he was still nervous about it . . .

Weirdly, Emma *wasn't* nervous.

Excited? *Sure.*

Awkward as hell? *Always.*

But not *nervous.*

Emma tried to tell herself that was a good thing, and she almost managed to believe herself too. Then, she looked at Nick again and absentmindedly licked her bottom lip. Suddenly, she was extremely aware of the all blood flowing through her body, especially the part that was pulsing past her hips and up between her legs like a not so subtle reminder that she had hormones and hands and boobs and a vagina, and they were all demanding attention, all at once.

Emma's lack of nervousness, combined with the foam

at the bottom of her beer bottle and all the buzzing in her body, pushed her head forward until her lips slipped onto Nick's lips and her tongue pushed into his mouth, and finally all of the thinking stopped and the bubbles and biology just took over and that next, first kiss, the newly crowned most important one, was the perfect combination of sloppy and sweet. It was casual but also special all at once . . .

. . . and the next ten, twenty, *one hundred*–something kisses that followed soon after were similarly enjoyable. And the best part wasn't *just* that Nick knew exactly what to do with his tongue, which he did, or that he knew *exactly* how hard to press his lips against hers, which he also did, but that Nick's kisses seemed to have the ability to listen to her kisses. They knew when to speed up or slow down, pushing harder or softer, always perfectly in rhythm with Emma. And then Nick pulled back, catching Emma's eyes, as if to ask, one more time, *Are we really doing this?*

Emma smiled back at him. *Yes, we really are.*

The next two, five, ten-ish minutes felt like they happened all at once.

Emma and Nick moved off of the floor and up onto the couch.

Nick's kisses moved to Emma's neck and then onto her chest.

Emma's bra came off.

Nick's pants slid down.

Her hands moved to his waist and then between his legs.

She got up to turn off the lights, but, then again, Emma might've done that before any of the kissing even started . . .

Even as it was all happening, she couldn't quite remember the order.

It all felt like a series of jump cuts, moving from one moment to the next. From fumbling to closeness to nakedness. It was all cold and hot and the whole thing made her want to giggle and cry at the same time, not because she was happy or sad, but because she was entirely, completely, 100 percent in the moment. She was so *in* her body and *out* of her head—a rare feeling for a champion overthinker like Emma—that she did everything she could to embrace it. And she could tell that Nick was appreciating all of it just as much as she was, in the same way she was, and the truth was that it was actually way more special than casual, which felt like a good thing. And then Nick pulled away for a minute to put on a condom. He opened the packet with his teeth, rolled it on rather quickly, and then squeezed some lube on top of it. As Emma watched him from the couch, feeling naked and exposed, she greatly appreciated the fact that he'd done this before.

Then he climbed back on top of her with a big, boyish grin on his face. Emma made sure to take a mental picture of him and the muddy green glint in his eyes, and his accidental half-Mohawk, and the palpable glow that seemed to wrap around his entire face, his entire being. . .

And then, finally, without much fanfare he slid inside her.

"Pushed" was actually probably a more accurate word.

It didn't hurt.

Not really.

Or, not exactly.

But it wasn't all that comfortable, either.

"Are you okay?" he asked softly. She nodded. She was. Nick pulled out a little and then slid back inside, slowly at first and then faster, finding a rhythm . . .

It was all sort of sudden and mostly clumsy.

As it was happening, Emma kept having the urge to remind herself that it was, in fact, happening.

This, she kept thinking.

This is sex, and this is real, and it's all really happening.

Emma was losing her virginity right now, at this very moment.

And then the moment ended, just as quickly and awkwardly and sincerely as it had begun.

And that was it.

148 days until graduation . . .

LAYLA did not expect it to happen quite so fast.

Obviously, the whole point of the sex pact was to actually have sex, but Emma's sexie more or less came out of nowhere.

"What's a sexie?" Zoe asked as they waited in line at The Bigg Chill.

"An after sex selfie, a sexie," Layla explained.

"Oh, is that what we're calling it?" Alex asked.

Yes it was. Layla was very proud of her new name.

After Nick left Emma's house last night, not too long after they'd had sex, Emma snapped a picture of herself and all her postcoital afterglow and sent it to The Chat. She added a text message saying that she *nailed it*.

The (not-yet-named) sexie as well as Emma's text message came as a complete surprise to Alex and Layla and Zoe, who didn't even know Emma was *hanging out* with Nick, let alone sleeping with him. Once the girls realized that Emma wasn't joking, and that she had, in fact, just had sex with Nick—and therefore lost her virginity *to* Nick— they sent an avalanche of texts, full of expletives and exclamation marks and emojis. Layla was pretty sure they'd sent more texts per minute than ever before in the history of The Chat.

"I haven't even managed to *kiss* a boy since we started the pact, and Emma's already done with it." Zoe laughed.

"She's not done," Layla corrected with a big smile.

"True," Emma admitted. "Still waiting on the fireworks . . ."

"Shhh," Zoe said as they reached the front of the line, where Bigg Chill Aaron was waiting to take their order.

"What are we shhh-ing about?" he whispered.

Surprising no one, his question made Zoe blush— and that was even before Layla honestly answered, "Fireworks."

Of course Bigg Chill Aaron didn't really know what that meant, but it still made his lips curl up into a sideways smile. There was always something memorable about his smile, Layla thought. His bottom teeth were slightly crooked, not in a bad way, but just enough to be interesting, and he had a little scar right below his bottom lip. The girls had known him only since September, when he started his freshman year at UCLA, but they'd seen him every single Sunday since, and now he was by far their favorite Bigg Chill employee. They always made small talk as they placed their orders, but the truth was they didn't know all that much about him other than the fact that he grew up in Philadelphia and was always incredibly generous with his frozen yogurt and topping portions.

Today everyone collectively decided to order large sized cups instead of their usual small servings, because Emma lost her virginity last night, and it was just that kind of day.

"Tell. Me. Everything," Layla insisted once the girls had settled at their usual table.

"I texted you most of it . . ."

"Yeah, but I still have so many questions," Layla said. "Like, did you like it?"

"The sex?"

"Yes, duh, the sex."

"Yeah. It was good. I told you it was good. Why do you keep asking like you don't believe me?"

"Maybe it's the tone of your voice. It keeps creeping up at the end of your sentences."

"I don't know what to say about the 'creeping,' but as far the sex goes—"

"Ohmigod-I-still-can't-believe-you-had-sex," Zoe blurted out all at once, causing the whole table to erupt into a round of giggles. "I'm sorry," Zoe said as soon as she could manage words again. "I'm just . . . it's like . . . *wow.*"

"Yes, it's definitely wow . . . ," Layla confirmed playfully for Zoe, "but we're still trying to get the full mental picture of whether it was good or not."

"I swear it was good," Emma said, still laughing, "but I guess, maybe if you really want the *full* mental picture maybe we have to define what 'good' actually means. And possibly also 'it,' too."

"Okay, so *it* would be sex," Layla offered.

"Yep. It happened. Nick put his penis inside my vagina."

"*Ohmigod* . . ." Zoe squealed, managing to put a napkin in front of her mouth so as not to spit rainbow sprinkles across the table. Her squirmy, sex pact–related reflexes already seemed to be improving.

"And *good* means you liked it," Layla said in a way that made it sound more like a question than a statement.

"I *did* like it," Emma insisted, "but, it wasn't . . ." She paused, as if she were trying to listen to her own thoughts. "I think the truth is that it didn't last very long. Like, it was happening, and I knew it was happening, but then it just sorta *ended.*"

"Right. No fireworks," Layla said definitively.

"Guys, it's okay. You can just say the word 'or' . . . 'org' . . ." Zoe melted into a puddle of giggles before she could get the entire word out of her mouth.

"Zoe, can *you* say the word 'orgasm'?" Alex teased.

ZOE apparently could not.

She also felt red, and rashy, and *ridiculous*, but even she had to admit that this was fun.

The conversation made her feel mature, even though she was still anxious and sweating in strange locations, like behind her knees.

"Was Nick on top of you?" Layla asked.

"As opposed to . . . ?"

"I don't know. Like. Some other position . . . ?"

"Oh. Ha. No," Emma said quickly. "We barely got through *one* position . . . I mean, we got *through* it, but then he finished and that was basically it."

"Hmmm," Layla said, looking a little bit like an inflated balloon.

"Also, it got a little messy, so I had to deal with that afterward," Emma explained. "We probably should've just put a towel down on the couch or something. I had to put one of the cushion slipcovers in the washing machine. It got wet . . ."

"Oh, from the . . . ?" Zoe started to ask before realizing she had no clue how to even begin to finish her question.

"Didn't you use a condom?" Layla asked.

"We *did*, but there's, like, fluid," Emma tried to explain. "*You* get wet and so that's . . . it gets all over. And there was a little blood, too," she added. "Not, like, a lot, but . . ."

"So it *did* hurt?" Layla asked.

"Not really. 'Hurt' isn't the right word . . . It's hard to explain. Sorry, I keep saying that, but maybe it's just something you have to do to totally understand."

Zoe wished she understood a little bit better, but, like Emma said, the only way to do that seemed to be to do it—and that wasn't happening. Not yet, anyway.

Wow.

Did Zoe really just think about herself and then also about sex and then *also* about all of it actually happening, but just not "yet"?

She did. She smiled, feeling good about herself and her place in the pact.

* * *

EMMA began to notice there was something distant about Alex.

As the other girls chatted and laughed and squirmed a bit too, Alex seemed more focused on how many chocolate covered gummy bears she could pile on her spoon at once.

Emma decided not to say anything.

"So then what happened afterward?" Layla asked, still curious.

"First I cleaned up, and then we thought about watching a movie, but we never really picked one, so Nick just went home. I called my sister Heather, 'cause she's the oldest, and I knew she'd be all excited, which she was . . . but then she got a little sentimental, too, and then she told me that I needed to pee *immediately* and then shower, so I did both of those things . . ." And then Emma explained that she had been left alone with all of her thoughts and feelings, but they were all jumbled and cluttered with hormones and questions and she wasn't sure if she would ever be able to recall all of it in the future. She felt a thousand feelings all at once that she just couldn't define, which is what led her to snap the first sexie. At least that way she could capture the moment. "Also, I wanted to share the moment with all of you," she added.

"I can't wait to see the next three sexies," Layla said.

"The next two, *technically*," Zoe clarified. "Alex would've had to have already taken hers. At camp."

"You didn't, did you?" Layla asked, only half joking.

"No," Alex said quickly. "No cell phones . . ."

"Right, duh. Well, that's too bad. But you can take one next time."

"Sure . . . ," Alex said.

Emma smiled at Alex. Now that they'd both had sex, Emma thought she understood Alex a little better than she had before. But even though Alex forced a smile back at Emma, Emma got the sense that something wasn't right. Emma wasn't going to ask Alex to explain herself, especially not right here and right now, but Emma was certain there was something more that Alex wanted—or even needed—to say.

ALEX was "technically, actually, completely" still a virgin.

She said it to Layla as plainly as she possibly could, but Layla seemed to be having trouble wrapping her head around the new information.

"Wait, wait, wait," Layla said, rubbing her forehead. "You're saying you did *not* actually have sex with Cameron at sleepaway camp two summers ago?"

"Correct. I did not," Alex confirmed.

She rolled over onto her stomach, propping herself up on her elbows so she could get a better look at Layla. The two girls were lying side by side on Layla's trampoline, and Alex felt like she needed to *see* Layla's face in order to finish the conversation.

She wanted to make sure that Layla understood.

"Okay . . ." Layla continued. "But here's the bump for me . . ."

"Bump away," Alex said, bracing herself.

"If you didn't do it at sleepaway camp, then why did you come home and tell us that you did?"

"I didn't. I mean *technically* I didn't tell you that."

"Why do you keep saying 'technically'?"

"Because . . . well . . ." Alex couldn't seem to find the right words to explain. Maybe the problem was that she wasn't even sure she had the right answer.

"Hey, if it makes you feel better . . . ," Layla started.

"Nothing is making me feel better," Alex said sharply.

"Don't get pissy. You're the one who's been lying to all of us."

Ugghhhh.

The last thing Alex wanted to do was lie, but the truth felt complicated.

Most simply, she had been trying to protect Cameron.

And maybe she was trying to protect herself, too.

At the very least she wanted to save them from the embarrassment of failure, but now, looking at Layla and seeing the hurt in her eyes, it just felt like Alex's best intentions had backfired.

"Can we maybe pretend I didn't say anything?" Alex asked.

"Nope."

Alex could see that Layla and her half smile were doing the best they could not to get mad. Alex smiled back at Layla, but she still didn't know quite what to say . . . so she just kept on smiling. And then she remembered that this whole mess actually started with that little Mona Lisa smile in the first place. It's what made the girls in her cabin jump to conclusions. They all knew that she had snuck out in the middle of the night to meet Cameron at make-out ledge. And—because there is no such thing as a secret at sleepaway camp—they knew she was planning to have sex with him. But, as Alex's mom liked to say, "Man plans and God laughs." It was her way of explaining that expectations can often lead to disappointments. Alex had heard her mom use the expression hundreds of times before, but she hadn't really understood what it meant until that night with Cameron on make-out ledge.

They'd planned to have sex.

But then they didn't.

And then, the next morning, Alex had just simply smiled.

Understandably, the girls in her cabin had all just assumed that the smile meant she'd sealed the deal.

It didn't.

Alex knew she should've spoken up right then. She should've just said, *No, we did not have sex. Not technically. Not actually. Not completely. Not at all.*

But she didn't.

Because Alex knew that the girls would've inevitably asked, *Why?* And then she would've had to tell them that even though she wanted to do it and Cameron wanted to do it, and even though they tried—and tried and tried—to make it work, they simply *couldn't.*

Now, all these months—and many other make-out sessions—later, Alex understood that there simply hadn't been enough foreplay. Now she knew that attempting to go from zero to "doing it" in almost no time for the very first time on a chilly summer night was a recipe for disaster, but in the moment, the whole thing just made Alex feel like a failure. And there was nothing—*nothing*—Alex hated more than failing, especially when it was her fault.

And that's exactly what the whole thing felt like: her fault.

Like she wasn't attractive enough or desirable enough or good enough.

Cameron tried so hard to reassure her that wasn't the case—she was perfect, he told her, over and over again, everything about her was perfect—but Alex didn't believe him.

She could still feel the tears from that night welling up in her eyes—and her Converse tennis shoes sinking into the grass—and the goose bumps on her arms—and the lump in her throat. And then, when their best laid "get laid" plan fell apart, it really did feel like the kind of thing that God or mean girls, or just about anyone, might want to laugh at.

It was awful.

"What happened, Al?" Layla asked softly, pulling Alex out of her head and back onto the trampoline.

"You want the full mental picture?" Alex managed to tease.

Of course Layla *always* wanted the full mental picture.

And so Alex told her.

Everything.

She told her about that cold night and Cameron's warm breath. About the sharp rocks. And the soft grass. And her sinking sneakers. And the way Cameron's embarrassed eyes had glowed in the dark. "But then, after all of that . . . he just couldn't get it in."

"Is it really that hard?" Layla asked.

"Well. It is if he can't *stay* hard . . . ," Alex explained, using her right pointer finger and left hand to demonstrate the problem.

"Ohhhhh, okay," Layla said, finally wrapping her head around the mechanics. She let out a big laugh. Alex laughed too.

And then it got quiet again.

"But that's camp," Layla said softly. "What about us?"

Alex knew that question was coming.

"I guess . . . ," Alex said, trying to explain it to Layla and maybe also to herself at the same time " . . . by the time I got home, Emma had already seen some stupid posts online from the camp girls, and then you and Zoe just couldn't stop giggling. And you were all asking what it felt like to do it, and the thing was . . . it basically felt like we *had* done it. We decided to. And I *wanted* to. And . . . I let him try. So. If he *could've*, we would've. And the more I thought about it, the more it felt like saying we *didn't* do it was just as much of a lie as saying that we did."

"*Technically*, you're still a virgin, but . . . ," Layla said, still wrapping her head around it.

"Yeah. There's a 'but.' I know it sounds strange, but I had a feeling you'd understand."

"It's different, obviously, but I feel like that with Logan sometimes too," Layla said after a bit of time had passed.

"Like, we've thought about having sex so much and talked about it so many times that it almost feels like we've done it already. Not *actually*, of course, but . . . sometimes I find myself wondering, what's the real difference, you know?"

"I do know," Alex said. "But I think the 'difference' might actually be everything."

147 days until graduation . . .

EMMA always saw things more clearly in the darkroom.

The irony wasn't lost on her, but the whole point of a darkroom was to give film the time and space it needed to develop. It occurred to Emma that high school, in theory, was sort of like a darkroom for teenagers, a time to find out who you really were and a space to turn into the kind of adult you were supposed to be. Or wanted to be. Or something.

The problem, Emma realized, was that in order to turn into the adult version of yourself, you sort of already had to know who that person was. And how could you know without meeting them first? It was a vicious cycle of epic proportions. It was simply impossible to know what should come first: who you wanted to be or who you'd turn out to be. All Emma knew was that there were only about five months left of senior year, and she felt farther away from figuring herself out *now* than she did on the first day of high school.

Everyone in Emma's life—her friends, her parents, her older sisters, even her teachers—*everyone* was expecting her to already be fully developed. They wanted superlatives. They wanted answers. They wanted college acceptances. Basically . . . everyone wanted fireworks. But the process of getting there, of lighting the fuse or whatever it was that made the fire actually *work*, seemed to be undervalued or maybe even just lost completely.

Emma was so deep in her own thoughts that it took her a second to realize that someone was knocking on the darkroom door.

"Em?" Nick called from outside. "You still here?"

"I'm here, yeah," Emma responded. "One sec!"

Emma finished developing her last photo, hanging it on the line to dry, and then told Nick it was safe to come inside. Maybe it was because (almost literally) the last time she'd been alone with him he'd (*actually* literally) been inside of her, but when he walked into the dark room, there seemed to be something even more adorable than usual about Nick's lips and his bed-head hair and the sweet expression on his face.

Emma could feel Nick—and all of his attraction—from across the room, and all she wanted to do was feel all of him again. She stepped forward, pulling him close and pushing her lips on top of his. It was a big, sloppy kiss, all hormones and anticipation. Nick kissed Emma back with just as much intensity, and all of a sudden his hands were everywhere. On her chest. And then unbuttoning her shirt buttons. Her hands rushed to keep up with his, moving to his zipper and then into his boxers.

Emma didn't know how long they'd been kissing before Nick pulled back just long enough to say the word "yes."

It was a statement kind of question.

Emma nodded, *definitely* yes.

And so Nick pulled her back in closer, grabbing her thighs and lifting her up so she could sit on the counter. He pulled his jeans and boxers down to the floor as Emma slid her own cords and underwear off too. She was thankful she was wearing a simple black thong and not a pair of granny panties or something with polka dots or the days of the week on it or any other equally embarrassing options that were currently sitting in her underwear drawer.

"You good?" Nick asked as he pulled a condom out of his pocket and started to roll it on.

"Yeah," Emma said, her whole body tingling. "You?"

"Yeahhhh," Nick said like an exhale.

"You're adorable," she said.

"And you're sexy as hell."

No one had ever said that to Emma before.

She mostly thought of herself as weird. Or smart. Or maybe pretty if she was in a particularly good mood. But sexy? That was new. "Thank you," she said.

"No, thank *you*." Nick chuckled and then took a step toward Emma.

With Emma sitting on the edge of the counter, and Nick standing in front of her, their hips were at exactly the same height. Nick pushed inside of her with far more confidence than he had the first time. Everything seemed to fit better this time around . . .

It maybe even felt good, Emma thought.

But the fact that she still had to *think* about the way it felt and also that her thoughts still included the word "maybe" made her wonder if she had any clue what "good" actually felt like.

When it was over, Nick slid down onto the floor. He was close enough that she could see the little beads of sweat on his forehead, and his chest rising and falling with each heavy breath. He was close enough that she could tell he was still processing what had just happened. She liked everything about the way he looked right now in this moment, all honest and vulnerable. All she wanted to do was take a picture of him. She probably would've, too, if her camera wasn't so far away and out of reach and his pants weren't still down around his ankles.

She didn't want to take *that* kind of picture.

"You still good?" Nick asked again, looking up at her.

Emma nodded, noting his use of the word "good" again. "You?" she asked.

"Ye-ah," Nick said quickly.

Emma could hear the implied "duh" in his voice.

He took off the condom, concealing it inside of a paper towel before dropping it into the nearby trash can. Nick leaned forward, pulling his boxers back on and then his pants, too . . . but *then* it seemed to occur to him that he may have forgotten something.

"Ohhh," he said, with another implied "duh" afterward.

He slid over to the counter where Emma was still sitting and rocked up onto his knees.

His head was now exactly the same height as Emma's waist.

"What are you doing?" Emma asked, even though she was *pretty* sure she already knew the answer to her question.

"I want you to . . . finish."

For a brief moment, as the *f* of the word "finish" started to come out of his mouth, Emma thought he might be saying "firework," and she had to bite down on her lip to keep from laughing. "Unless you don't, um, want to?" Nick asked, misreading her lip biting for hesitation.

"No. I . . . I do," Emma said softly but quickly, as if she were trying to take up as little space as possible with her words. And she really did. But she must've looked nervous, because Nick asked if she trusted him. Which she did. And so she told him that she did. And then he looked up at her with his big green eyes, holding her gaze as he pulled her underwear back down to her ankles. "I'm gonna . . . kiss you," he added, as if to make sure there wouldn't be any confusion.

Emma nodded again, this time with a smile.

Maybe that's what Nick had been waiting for, her smile.

He smiled back and then leaned forward into Emma's legs.

Between her legs, actually. . . .

And she felt his tongue against her body. *Inside* her body. And that definitely felt good—no question about it. Just like there was no question that her entire face was turning bright red, Zoe style. And she was sure her whole face got even redder as she suddenly thought about where

Nick's face was and exactly what he was doing with it—and also with his lips and his tongue and then also his fingers . . . and all of it together, all of it at the same time. And it all felt so good that Emma would not have been surprised if her entire *body* somehow turned bright red.

After a minute or two Nick pulled back. His face was flushed and his lips were slightly wet. "You okay?"

"Yeah. Why? Do I not *seem* okay?"

"No, no, you do," Nick assured her.

What Emma really wanted to ask was if she looked weird or smelled weird or tasted weird or anything like that. She wanted to ask if her *parts* measured up to any other parts Nick might have seen or smelled or tasted before. But that would've involved far too much talking and way too many questions for this moment. Still, Emma couldn't keep the words "no one's ever . . ." from escaping from her lips. Nick raised an eyebrow as he waited for Emma to finish her sentence. "This is my . . . I mean, no one's ever done what you're doing before. I just . . . I want you to know that."

"That's cool," Nick said sweetly. "I sorta figured." Emma wanted to ask him *why* he "sorta figured" and also a dozen other anxious questions, but before she could ask any of them, Nick found her eyes again and simply said, "Thanks."

"For telling you?" she asked.

"For letting me."

Then he moved forward, leaning back into her again . . .

. . . and she leaned back against the wall, letting herself

get totally lost in the moment with Nick and his tongue and all of her feelings . . .

. . . and it was *good*.

And then pretty soon it was even better than that.

And then . . . it was everything, all of the things at the very same time.

So.

Many.

Fireworks.

LAYLA had never blushed at a text message before.

She'd laughed at them.

She'd cried at them.

She'd gotten nervous and excited and maybe even turned on by them.

But she'd never actually *blushed* . . . until she saw Emma's texts about Nick's tongue and the massive fireworks display they'd set off in the darkroom earlier this afternoon.

Layla was already sitting at the dinner table with her family when Emma texted The Chat. Her little sister, Maxine, was lobbying their mom for a spring break trip to the beach. Her little brother, Avery, was discussing the incredibly important and rapidly approaching fantasy basketball trade deadline with their father. And Layla did everything she possibly could not to choke on the piece of mustard chicken that was already in her mouth. She coughed and coughed, causing enough mild alarm to be excused from the table.

She ran upstairs and closed her bedroom door, scrolling back through The Chat as quickly as she could. There were already dozens of old texts to read, but new texts from Emma and Alex and even Zoe kept pouring in too.

WAIT, Layla texted. *I want to hear all of this . . .*

SCROLL UP, Alex texted.

No no I want to HEAR it. Trampoline in ten?!?

Layla knew it was a long shot to get the whole crew together in person after dinner on a school night—they all had rules and curfews and all that—but she figured it was worth asking. Zoe said her parents had already turned on their alarm, which meant that unless she wanted to pull a Joey and climb out her window and down the tree, she was stuck inside for the night. Alex said her parents were still out to dinner, which meant she was hanging with Max. Emma texted that she *totally woulddddddd* come over, but she was about to put on her pajamas.

Okayyyyyyy, Layla texted. *Do I have to mention that there are only so many more times we're actually going to be ABLE to all meet in person before the-day-that-hurts-Emma's-heart?*

NOT UNLESS YOU WANT ME TO FREAK OUT AND HAVE A PANIC ATTACK, Emma texted back in all capitals.

A panic attack AND an orgasm seems like a lot for one day, Layla teased.

HAHAHA, Emma texted. *Jealous?* she added.

YES, Alex responded immediately.

It's fine, Emma texted. *I got you and your mental picture. OH and Layla now I've even got your progress report: Sex twice, once with an orgasm.*

OMG, Zoe texted.

Now you all need to get your shit together . . .

TRYING, Layla texted.

What happened to no pressure?! Zoe texted.

There's still no pressure, Emma teased. *You're all just missing out . . .*

Oh now look who's cocky! Alex texted.

Thank you, Emma. Thank you so much, Zoe added.

You're welcome. But seriously, now what do I do?

Do it again. Do it better, Layla texted.

HA! That's basically what you said when there weren't any fireworks.

Guess that's how it works. You do it again when it's good and you do it again when it's not as good, Layla texted, feeling like there must be a metaphor in there somewhere.

Emma, you did say sex was like pizza, Zoe managed to add.

IT IS LIKE PIZZA, Emma texted back, again in all capital letters.

Layla actually laughed out loud at her phone screen. The texts paused for a moment, and Layla was pretty sure everyone else was laughing too.

Em, that still makes no sense, Layla insisted.

IT ACTUALLY MAKES SO MUCH SENSE.

OK, OK, Layla texted. *Start from the beginning . . . mental picture ready go.*

Alright. Emma obliged. *So. I was in the darkroom after school . . .*

I like this already, Alex texted.

Ohmigod.

Guys. Let Emma type.

And they did.

And she did.

She described all the details, especially the fireworks—and the way that they *felt . . .*

Is this turning anyone else on? Layla finally had to ask, disobeying her own instructions to let Emma type. She couldn't help it. It was all too good.

YESSS, Alex texted back quickly.

Really?! Ohmigod.

OHMIGOD YES, ZOE, Alex teased.

Layla's face hurt from smiling and her chest hurt from laughing and her heart felt full and her whole body felt warm . . .

I couldn't possibly love you more, Layla texted. *ALL OF YOU.*

SAME, Alex and Emma texted back at exactly the same time, one right after the other. It looked like Zoe had maybe also tried to text the word "same" at the exact same time as the other girls, but it ended up showing up in The Chat as *SMALL* instead.

Small what, Zo? Layla asked, knowing she was being an asshole.

Damn autocorrect, Zoe texted. Then she tried again: *SMAEE.* And again: *SEMA.* And one more stupid time: *SMALL.*

Layla couldn't stop laughing as she thought about Zoe's adorable little fingers, struggling with the touch screen keys.

Ohmigod . . . Whatever, Zoe texted. *I told you, this keyboard sucks and autocorrect hates me. At least you all love me . . .*

THE MOST, Layla, Alex, and Emma all texted at the very same time.

145 days until graduation . . .

EMMA sat at her usual computer in the yearbook room.

She was the first one there, and the rest of the computers were still empty.

It wasn't like Emma to be early, ever, but she'd woken up a full hour before her alarm clock this morning. Apparently, Emma still couldn't sleep, but at least now it was from excitement and contentedness and not fear.

"Hey!" Savannah suddenly appeared in the doorway.

"Hey . . . ," Emma replied. Something about the look on Savannah's face told her to proceed with caution.

"Heard you had a good night last night. Or afternoon maybe."

"You *heard*?"

"Well, *over*heard. I was being nosy," Savannah said as she sat down at the computer next to Emma's and flipped open her notebook.

"Uh-oh. Why do I feel like I'm not gonna like this?"

"Sure *sounded* like you liked it," Savannah teased a little, knowing it would get under Emma's skin.

"You're the worst." Emma smiled, shaking her head. She liked Savannah's playful demeanor, but she didn't like the sinking feeling that Nick was spreading rumors about her.

"Not rumors, exactly," Savannah clarified. "His locker's near mine, so I just heard him talking to a couple of his friends."

"About *me*?"

"Well, yeah. Specifically, you and him . . . in the darkroom."

"Oh God," Emma said, burying her head in her hands. "I'm gonna die . . ."

"Don't die. He said you were great . . ."

"Too late—I'm already dead."

"No. Stop. Come back. It's not a big deal. I swear I only listened for a minute or two—"

"A minute or two? How long was he talking about me?" Emma asked, mostly embarrassed, but maybe the littlest bit proud, too. "Why is he telling people?"

"Because he's excited. You told your girls, didn't you?"

"Yeah, but that's different."

"Is it?"

"I tell them everything."

"Maybe he tells his boys everything."

"That's not exactly making me feel better."

"I'm just saying, I don't think we can blame him for bragging about you . . . You're way out of his league."

"Thank you," Emma said with a laugh. That *sounded* like a compliment, but she wasn't entirely sure.

"You're welcome." Savannah laughed back. "Whatever. Good for you."

"Yeah." Emma nodded. And then she couldn't help but add, "It was my first time. Well, my *second* time, but the first one was with Nick too, and it was just this past Saturday, so . . ." Emma could feel the blood rushing into her cheeks. She pushed her hair behind her ears just to give herself something to do.

"Lucky guy . . . ," Savannah said with a strange sort of bite in her voice.

Emma couldn't help but think Savannah sounded a little bit, well . . . *jealous.*

LAYLA could feel Logan's phone buzzing in his front pocket.

Layla and Logan were in the midst of a particularly heated afternoon make-out session. They'd gone off campus during their common free period to get lunch at the sushi restaurant at the bottom of the canyon near school. Off-campus privileges were one of the biggest perks of being a senior, and Logan and Layla liked to take full advantage, but today Logan's phone would just not stop buzzing—and it was killing Layla more and more with each new vibration.

"Do you need to answer that?"

"Answer what?" Logan managed to ask without taking his tongue out of Layla's mouth. Layla shook her head and refocused her attention on their kisses . . .

. . . until another buzz interrupted them.

And then another.

Layla couldn't take it anymore.

They were in the backseat of his car, and she was sitting on his lap, and his phone was in his front pocket, and all the buzzing was just too close for comfort. "It's nothing," he insisted. But before they could resume their kisses, another flurry of text messages came pouring in.

"Logan. Really. I need that to stop," she said, squirming off him.

"You don't like the vibrations?" Logan teased.

"I can only get so excited, knowing they're from Vanessa," Layla grumbled.

"How do you know it's her?" Logan asked as his phone buzzed yet again.

"*Seriously?* There'd better be, like, a giant fire or something . . ."

"No fire, she's just . . ."

"Oh, so it *is* her?" Layla said, thoroughly annoyed but also vindicated.

"They're printing the posters for the food drive," Logan explained, "and they can't decide if they should be vertical or horizontal, but Vanessa wants it to be in the shape of a can. She needs approval from the school board."

"Is that your problem?"

"Not exactly, but I know what they'll be expecting. Layla, I don't know if you're aware, but I'm actually president of the *entire* student body . . ."

"Are you trying to tell me you're important or something?"

"*Very* important." Logan smiled, flashing that dimple of his, but Layla still shook her head, not quite ready to let the Vanessa thing go. "*Really?*" Logan asked, recognizing the look on Layla's face. "Don't be mad at Vanessa. It's my fault. I offered to help."

And there it was.

Of course he had offered to help her.

Logan was way too nice like that. He was always extra-offering and overextending himself, which was all fine and good for friends and teachers or whatever, but not for Vanessa.

Layla knew that Vanessa didn't want his help.

She wanted *him*.

"Look. It's off." Logan held up his phone for Layla to see. "Okay?"

Layla nodded, even though she honestly didn't *feel* okay.

And then they went back to making out in the backseat of Logan's car, but Layla couldn't stop thinking about Vanessa, and, even worse, she couldn't stop thinking that Logan might still be thinking about Vanessa too.

ALEX had apologized to Zoe almost a hundred times.

She didn't know what else to say.

"There's nothing *to* say," Zoe said sharply, poking her California sushi roll with a chopstick.

Alex looked over at Emma, who had just joined them and was now biting into a slice of pizza. She didn't seem to be nearly as upset as Zoe was. Alex had called both of them last night and told them the truth about camp and Cameron and her virgin status. She'd been planning on telling them at school, but then after Emma's fireworks and all the text messages that followed, Alex didn't feel right about waiting any longer.

Again, Alex had planned and God had laughed.

Luckily, Emma had laughed a little bit too when Alex told her the truth.

"You're telling me *I* was actually the first one of us to lose her virginity? I totally would've lost that bet," Emma had said. And then Alex apologized a few (dozen) more times, and Emma accepted all of her apologies, and the whole phone call was more or less painless.

Zoe, on the other hand, didn't take the news nearly as well.

The first problem was that Zoe was hoping for a call from Dylan that still hadn't arrived, so, admittedly, she was in a bit of a mood when Alex called. The second problem was that she was confused as to why Alex was calling in the first place. Alex said it just wasn't a text message kind of conversation. Honestly, it wasn't really a phone conversation either, more of an in-person sort of thing, but it was already past Alex's curfew, and she didn't want to wait until morning now that Emma had already had sex twice and orgasmed once.

ZOE was confused as to what Emma's orgasms had to with anything.

But, before she could ask for clarification, Alex had

launched into a long apology slash explanation that started with: "I did not have sex at sleepaway camp."

Alex explained that it was all just a misunderstanding. She described all the technical difficulties. She insisted that she was just trying to protect Cameron and something about a Mona Lisa smile or whatever, and then she finished by adding that sometimes the truth feels more like a lie than an actual lie.

Zoe could tell that the whole story made sense in Alex's head.

But to Zoe it mostly sounded more or less like bullshit.

Zoe didn't care about the other girls at camp. And she didn't care about Cameron's feelings either. Or Alex's ego. Or any of that. All Zoe cared about was The Crew. And their friendship. And the balance that existed among the four of them . . .

. . . but now she knew that Alex had been lying to them.

For *years*.

Alex said she was sorry.

And all Zoe could say was "all right."

And then Dylan was finally actually calling, so Zoe got off the phone with Alex pretty quickly to talk to him. She honestly didn't want to talk about it anymore, but now she and Emma were sitting at lunch with Alex, and Layla was off campus with Logan, and Alex wouldn't leave the whole thing alone.

"I just wish you weren't mad at me," Alex said, trying not to get frustrated.

"I'm not mad—"

"Or hurt. Or whatever you are—"

"I don't know what I am!" Zoe said more loudly than she expected. "You lied to all of us for two years. I think I should get more than twenty hours to process the situation."

"I swear I never meant to lie," Alex said after a bit of silence. "I just need you to know that."

"That's fine. And I do know that. But that's still what ended up happening," Zoe said sharply. "I spent the past two years believing something that wasn't true. We all did. Whatever you *actually* meant to do, that feels shitty to me now."

"I'm sorry," Alex said more softly this time. "But it was . . . a year and a half."

"What?"

"Camp was only a year and a half ago. Not two years."

"Ohmigod, *really*? *That's* what you want to fight about—"

"I don't want to fight about anything!"

"Cool. So, what then? *Now* you're worried about the accuracy of your story—"

"Jesus, Zoe, I'm sorry! I should've told you what really happened as soon as it really didn't happen, but I can't exactly go back and change it now. And I know it sucks, but honestly, what happened with Cameron sucks for me too. I have these dreams about it, over and over, and they make me feel shitty every single time . . . but I guess I just figured there'd be another boy right away, and it would happen with him for real, and then the camp thing just wouldn't matter—"

"Of course it matters!" Zoe said, raising her voice. She could see that Alex wasn't expecting such a big response from her, but she couldn't help but get emotional. "*What?* Do you want me to say I wouldn't care if I spent forever thinking you lost your virginity to someone when you actually didn't? I care about everything that happens to you, Alex. And to Emma. And Layla. What you eat for lunch. What color running shoes you're wearing. What kind of punctuation you use at the end of your text messages. Whatever it is, whatever you do—as long as it's about you, I care. You don't think I'd care about something as important as the first time you had sex?"

"No, I know you would . . . ," Alex said quietly.

Zoe was sorry to have to be so forceful about it, but this was important to her.

She could tell it was important to Alex, too.

"Look," Alex said after a quiet moment. "I've spent a lot of time since that night wondering why it didn't *actually* happen with Cameron. And maybe the truth is that it didn't happen for me then so it could happen for me now, along with all of you . . . Maybe we really were always supposed to do this together."

"But not *together* together . . . ," Zoe managed to tease.

"You know what I mean."

Of course Zoe knew what she meant.

And the more she thought about it, the more she thought Alex might be right.

144 days until graduation . . .

LAYLA and Zoe stood at their lockers, packing their backpacks.

It was Thursday afternoon. The girls were rushing— Layla was going to be late for the student council meeting, and Zoe should've been at musical rehearsal five minutes ago—but Layla still managed to notice a pack of senior boys walking down the hallway. They were loud and impossible to ignore.

Right in the middle was Dylan.

Layla nudged Zoe and nodded in his direction. She figured Zoe would be happy to see him, but instead, Zoe got shy and dropped her eyes down to her shoelaces. Layla looked back at Dylan and then back to Zoe again, feeling like she was watching the moment unfold in some sort of strange slow motion, and she couldn't help but wonder if he was even going to say hi to Zoe, let alone stop and have an actual conversation with her. Dylan managed to throw Zoe a sideways "hey" as he walked past, but he didn't even break his stride. It was lame, as if he'd hurled the stupid little word across the hallway, and literally the least he could do.

Zoe nodded back along with a nervous little half wave, which was similarly lame. "What was that?" Layla could feel the frown forming on her face.

"Hm?" Zoe asked, playing dumb. She was still looking down at her feet, seemingly consumed by the ugly tile pattern on the floor.

"Is Dylan always like that at school?"

"Like what?" Zoe clearly wasn't going to make this easy on Layla.

"I don't know . . . like . . . you don't actually exist?" The words came out of Layla's mouth before she fully realized how mean they must've sounded.

"No, it's . . . I think we just work best on the phone," Zoe explained. Layla believed that *Zoe* believed that, and it might even be true, too, but Layla didn't like it. Not one bit. "I know you all think that I must like him or he must like me or something since we spend all that time talking at night, but you can see it's just . . ." Zoe gestured down the hallway. "It's just not like that."

Layla could hear a dozen little emotional cracks in Zoe's voice.

She knew it wasn't worth pushing back any harder, and Layla made a mental note to tell Alex and Emma to back off about the Zoe and Dylan stuff too. They all gave her a hard time about their phonefalls, but as long as Zoe was happy and being honest about what she really wanted from Dylan, Layla was going to support her in that.

Layla and Zoe closed their lockers and walked down the hall together. As they rounded a corner, Layla was thrilled to see that Austin was waiting for Zoe at the entrance to the theater.

She caught a glimpse of Zoe's freckled face as it lit up.

It was absolutely adorable.

The only thing even more adorable than Zoe and all of her excitement was that Layla could see the very same glow on Austin's face too.

141 days until graduation ...

ALEX decided that the blotchy bruise on Zoe's neck was fifty shades of purple.

Zoe and Austin had gone on their second date last night, and apparently there had been a lot of sucking involved.

"I just do not understand the point of a hickey," Alex insisted.

"Oh, me neither," Emma agreed, "but then I also kind of like that there is no point ..."

"You would ..." Alex laughed. "But, like, seriously ... *kiss* my neck if you want to, sure, but why all the sucking? If a boy really wants to suck on something I can think of at least twenty other body parts that would appreciate it so much more ..."

"*Twenty?*" Zoe squeaked, clearly trying to wrap her head around that number.

Layla pressed Zoe for more details about her date with Austin.

They had gone to dinner and a movie at The Grove.

He paid.

And held her hand all night.

But Zoe said that the best part happened on their way back to Austin's car. (The girls were all relieved to hear that they had ditched the dad chaperone this time around.) Zoe and Austin had gone out of their way and ridden all the way up to the top floor of the parking garage, which had an absolutely magnificent view of the city. Austin wanted to be a lighting designer, so he appreciated a view like that more than most people did. And as they stood up there together looking at the view with his hands wrapped around Zoe's waist, he had asked if she wanted to officially be his girlfriend.

"Aw," Layla said in her very Layla way.

"Look at that . . . Zoe has a boyfriend." Alex smiled.

Zoe also had a happy glow on her face.

The girls were all thrilled to see it.

"How about you, Layla?" Emma asked. "Where's *your* progress report?"

LAYLA was hoping someone might ask.

She didn't exactly have any *progress*, but there was a bit of a report.

"Well, I, actually . . . I attempted to, um . . ." Layla swirled her spoon in her froyo and then realized that the visual might be a good way to communicate what she was trying to say.

Zoe and Emma didn't seem to notice, but Alex got the message loud and clear.

"You *masturbated*?" Alex asked way, way too loudly.

"Aaaaand we're totally in public right now . . . ," Zoe whispered.

"Whatever. She didn't *masturbate* in public."

Emma and Layla laughed.

Zoe turned chartreuse.

"How was it?" Alex continued, pressing Layla for details.

"I don't know," Layla admitted, "and, honestly, I feel like a loser saying this, but it's almost confusing. Like, what am I even supposed to really do?"

"Well, you . . . you touch yourself," Alex said matter-of-factly.

"Yeah. *That* I understand, but . . . where? I mean where *exactly*?"

"That's *exactly* what you have to figure out," Alex explained.

"It's just sort of wherever feels good," Emma offered more sincerely.

"Okay, but that doesn't help me," Zoe piped up. "Like, rubbing my *shoulder* feels good."

"I promise you're not gonna get off from touching your shoulder." Alex snickered.

"*Clearly*, but that's why I agree that it's confusing." Zoe returned her attention to her frozen yogurt, but then felt the need to add, "Not that I've tried . . ."

"Just keep it simple," Alex said. "Touch your boobs. Vagina. Butt."

"Butt? What? Do you touch your butt?" Zoe squeaked, looking to Emma.

"No." Emma laughed.

"For the record, me neither," Alex said. "I'm just saying: erogenous zones."

"I don't even know what that means," Zoe admitted.

"An area of the body that has heightened sensitivity," Layla said, explaining that she had just read an article in the Sex Doc about it. "It said to mostly focus on the clitoris."

Layla realized that might've been the first time she'd ever said "clitoris" out loud and officially decided it was the most awkward sounding word in her vocabulary.

"Sounds awkward, yeah . . . but feels *amazing*," Emma whispered.

"Yeah . . ." Layla grinned. "Apparently there are all these different *techniques*, like for rubbing or stroking or tapping it or whatever . . ."

"Tapping?" Zoe asked.

"Yeah, I dunno . . ." Layla said. After reading the article, Layla had concluded that the masturbation options were endless, and intimidating—all of it was nearly enough to stop her from trying before she'd even gotten started . . . but, she somehow managed to get over her fear of embarrassing herself *in front of herself* and had attempted to masturbate last night.

But . . . there were no fireworks.

"Not even close," Layla added.

"Well, A for effort." Emma laughed.

"Honestly, probably more like a C for effort." Layla laughed back.

Another article Layla read in the Sex Doc said it might

take *weeks* of experimentation before even getting close to fireworks, and that it was a good idea to allow about thirty to forty minutes of time per session, so as not to feel rushed. Layla only lasted about five minutes before she'd given up.

"Ohmigod." Zoe squirmed.

Layla laughed. She was impressed how long Zoe had managed to go without squirming.

"Zoe, I'm sure you'd figure it out if you tried," Alex said sincerely.

"It's really just like pizza, I swear," Emma said, causing everyone to laugh.

"No, pizza is way less confusing." Zoe giggled.

"Yes, but there are so many toppings."

"And it can be thick crust or thin crust," Alex added.

"Guys, wait, Zoe is gluten free," Layla teased.

"I love/hate this so much right now," Zoe said as The Crew got lost in another epic fit of laughter. It was the best, as always.

ZOE wasn't expecting to get a text message from Dylan at five thirty in the afternoon.

You home? it said.

Yeah . . . , she replied. She'd just gotten home from froyo a few minutes earlier.

K, he texted back quickly.

And then three dots popped up on his side of the conversation, indicating that he was typing something else. Zoe watched the dots closely. She also watched as they disappeared without producing a new message. Then, almost immediately, the dots came back again. More typing, but still no message. Those three dots and their constant disappearing act were two of the many reasons that Zoe hated texting.

Finally, Dylan managed to send a new text: *I'm coming over.*

It wasn't a question. It was a statement. And he texted it as if it were totally normal behavior. Like the kind of thing that happened all the time.

It did not.

This would be the first time Dylan had ever come to Zoe's house.

About an hour later Dylan rang the Reeds' front doorbell, and the chimes rattled throughout the whole house. Zoe scampered down the stairs, hoping to be the first one to the door, but, unfortunately, her dad beat her to it.

"Hi, Mr. Reed," she heard Dylan say. "Is Zoe home?"

"Yes! Hi . . . ," Zoe said loudly, sliding up behind her dad. "I got it," she added, mustering up as much "chill" as she possibly could. She was hoping her dad would just nod and walk away, but she knew that was wishful thinking.

"Who's this?" he asked as if Dylan weren't standing right in front of them.

"I'm Dylan," Dylan said, extending his hand for a handshake.

Good move, Zoe thought. Her dad always appreciated a good handshake. Still, he felt the need to look Dylan up and down. Zoe couldn't quite tell if he was trying to be intimidating or just genuinely confused by the hand-some water polo player standing in front of him. After a moment, Dylan added a "nice to meet you," and Zoe's dad finally shook his hand.

"Come in," Zoe said, shooting her dad another be-cool kind of look.

But "being cool" wasn't her dad's style. "It's a school night," he said.

"Yessir." Dylan nodded.

"We just have some homework to finish," Zoe offered lamely.

The fact that Dylan wasn't holding a backpack or any books wasn't lost on Zoe's dad, but thankfully he didn't feel the need to push the issue anymore. Instead, he simply told them to be quick about it and went back into the den to watch the rest of the Lakers game.

Zoe led Dylan upstairs and into her room and closed the door behind them. Immediately, she felt weird about it. They weren't going to do anything that required a closed door, and now that it was closed, all she wanted to do was open it again, but then that just felt like it would be even weirder, she thought, so she let it be. Besides, Dylan hadn't seemed to notice the location of the door. He was too busy getting a good look at Zoe's bedroom.

"Wow, Z," he said, taking in all her decorations.

Zoe's entire wall, the one above her bed, was covered in pictures and postcards and magazine clippings and things she'd printed out and collected over the years. There were quotes and song lyrics. Doodles and tickets. Awards. Blue ribbons. The whole wall was bright and extremely well curated. Zoe was very proud of it. She was always adding to it and changing it. She felt like it was a pretty accurate reflection of who she was at any given moment in time. She noticed that Dylan took an especially long look at The Other Team ticket stub from her concert with Austin, which was prominently displayed in the center of the wall.

"I feel like I'm inside of your head right now," he said.

Zoe hoped that wasn't true. Her head felt like a giant jumble. There may have been a lot happening on her wall, too, but at least the layout was meticulous and the composition was balanced and everything was more or less color coordinated and, finally, and probably most important, everything was stuck in place and couldn't move. In real life the thoughts in Zoe's head would not stop moving. Ever. They were jumping from Dylan and his wandering eyes and the fact that he was currently sitting on the edge of her bed, to Austin and his kissable lips and the fact that he put a hickey on her neck last night, to her hair and its constant frizz and the fact that right now she couldn't stop herself from thinking every thought she'd ever had over and over again . . .

"Nice scarf," Dylan said, noticing Zoe's accessory.

"Yeah . . . ," Zoe said, pulling it off.

"Oh shit." Dylan smirked, getting a good look at the hickey.

Zoe had texted him about it, but the visual was even more impressive. "Too bad it's purple and not red," she said. "It would blend right in with my face."

"Surprisingly, your redness is mostly in check right now," Dylan admitted.

"Good," Zoe said as she sat down in her desk chair, attempting to get comfortable. Dylan certainly was. Now he was sitting on her bed and leaning back against all of her pillows.

"Is it weird that I feel like you've been here so many times before?" Zoe asked, knowing that it wasn't actually all that weird but trying to find a way to make more conversation.

Their silences felt far more natural on the phone.

"Not weird at all. I probably should've, but it's nice to see where the magic actually happens. Now I don't have to imagine."

If they'd been on the phone, Zoe would've pressed him about the details of his imagination, forcing him to let her deeper inside his head. She could say almost anything to Dylan on the phone, but now, in person, it just seemed like too much. It was almost as if it were too real. It wasn't as if what happened on the phone *wasn't* real, but the distance between them and the lack of visuals made it all seem safer somehow.

After another mostly awkward silence Dylan finally stopped stalling and pulled a CD out of his jacket pocket. "I made this to commemorate your big date night. It's a mix CD," he added, as if he were worried Zoe wouldn't know what it was. "It's a little old school, but there's this whole stack of them in my brother's room from when he used to DJ, and I figured it was more substantial than just sending you a playlist. Also, I had to see the hickey for myself." Dylan handed Zoe the CD. On the front, in blue Sharpie, he had written *ZOE GOT SOME*. He'd also drawn a little awkward smiley face with squiggles around it. "That's your hair," he explained.

"Thanks," Zoe laughed. She was touched and also a little bit overwhelmed by the sweetness of the gesture.

"I, um . . . ," Dylan started. Zoe waited for him to find the right words. "I just want you to know that I'm really happy for you. You know, and Austin."

Zoe looked up, catching Dylan's eyes. He really did look genuinely happy for her—as he should be. But still, Zoe felt like there was something more he wasn't saying. It felt like there was a "but" missing from the "I'm happy" part of his statement . . . *but* Zoe couldn't prove that, and Dylan certainly wasn't going to just come out and say it, so that seemed like the end of the conversation right there.

"Well," Dylan said after a few moments, "I should probably get going before your dad notices we didn't actually have any homework to do."

"He's harmless, but yeah, that's probably a good idea . . ."

"I'm sure he's on high alert with all the boys who've been hanging around these days." Zoe rolled her eyes. "You know what I mean . . ."

Yes. Zoe knew exactly what he meant. In the past couple of weeks, both Austin and Dylan had shown up on her doorstep. Both of them had nervously rung the doorbell. Both had given her dad an awkward handshake. But only Dylan had gotten an invitation upstairs. And only Dylan had gotten to sit on her bed. Partially because he didn't ask for permission, but mostly it was because Zoe knew there was no chance of anything happening between her and Dylan. But with Austin . . . *Ohmigod.* Last night they'd been sitting in the middle of a crowded movie theater, and Zoe still ended up with the world's largest, purple-est hickey on her neck. She couldn't even fully imagine what might've happened if she and Austin had been on a bed instead . . .

"What?" Dylan asked, seeing Zoe's smile. "Thinking about your boyfriend?"

She was. And Dylan already knew that she was. If they'd been on the phone, Zoe would've been able to ask him if he was jealous. Dylan probably would've laughed and said no and then made some stupid comment about how many more boyfriends she would need to have—four? five?—in order to even the score between them.

But they weren't on the phone.

They were still in real life. In Zoe's bedroom. Sitting eight feet apart. And Zoe could see Dylan's face. And the look in his eyes. And she could see that even though he was her best guy friend, and even though he had shown up with a thoughtful present in order to celebrate her first hickey with her first real boyfriend, and even though he was clearly doing everything he could *not* to be jealous . . .

. . . Zoe had a pretty strong feeling that he most certainly was.

She could see it all over his face—and she couldn't help but like it.

136 days until graduation . . .

ALEX didn't know exactly how many boys she had made out with.

She suspected it might be approaching triple digits, but she wasn't sure. What she did know for sure was that she could count on one hand the number of boys she'd gone out on a real, honest, he-makes-a-plan-and-picks-you-up kind of date with.

Alex tried not to make a big deal about too many things, but tonight's date with Oliver was certainly a bigger deal than her normal Friday night.

In the past hour and a half, she had pretty much tried on every piece of clothing in her entire closet. Now, every inch of her boring, beige carpet was covered with all of the bright or black or flirty clothes she owned. She was annoyed at herself for spending so much time and energy trying to pick out an outfit, but she wanted to get this right. She wanted to send the right signals, and she knew her outfit was an important place to start. She wanted to wear something not too serious or dressy. Something with the perfect amount of cleavage right in that sweet spot where her shirt was low enough to see more-boobs-than-not, but still high enough that the view of said boobs might just be a happy accident. The point was to try as hard as possible to look as good as possible while also looking like you didn't try at all.

But all of that was way easier said than done, which was why all of her clothes were sitting on the floor of her bedroom.

"Way to make a mess," Max said as he walked in without knocking.

"Hello to you, too . . ."

"Where are you going?"

"Minigolfing."

"Cool." Max pushed a couple of Alex's skirts onto the floor, making enough room for him to sit down in Alex's rolling desk chair.

"Excuse me," she said, laughing.

"It's too much," he said simply.

Alex knew that Max was literally talking about all of the clothes, but, because he always talked literally like that, it also seemed like he was talking about how much time and energy she had been wasting trying everything on—and all the obsessing and overanalyzing. She agreed that it was too much too, but she still needed to make a decision about what to wear. Showing up to the date naked definitely wasn't going to send the right signal.

"Final question: This one or this one?" Alex held up two options.

"I dunno." Max shrugged.

"Can you please pretend to care?"

"No," Max said sincerely.

"Okay, fine. Thanks for nothing." Alex laughed.

"You're welcome." Max laughed back.

Alex wasn't sure if Max understood *why* she was laughing, but she loved when they laughed together. It made her feel a strong connection to him. And she appreciated the brotherly reminder that Oliver probably wouldn't really care what she was wearing either. He would be able to pretend that he cared better than Max could, but still.

Alex finally settled on a white crop top and a blue flannel shirt. It made her feel cute, but it was also comfortable, too. She didn't want to come on too strong. She wore her hair up in a casual high ponytail and wore extra lip gloss. Alex felt really good about her outfit and the way she felt in it and the purposefully mixed signals it might be sending. She snapped a picture of herself in her full-length mirror and sent it to The Chat.

Please tell me that's a sexie, Emma texted back quickly.

Ha, Alex responded. *Not even close.*

About an hour later Alex and Oliver found themselves on a minigolf course in Sherman Oaks, in the midst of a heated battle. Alex was impressed with Oliver's choice of date location. The golfing provided enough activity to fill the quiet spaces in their conversation, but also left plenty of room for talking and flirting and competing too.

Unsurprisingly—but true to form—Alex and Oliver were both taking the game far too seriously, doing everything they could to win.

They were all tied up going into the second-to-last hole.

Alex took a few practice swings before hitting her ball under a bridge and watching it land about two feet from the hole. Alex tapped the ball into the hole for an impressive score of two.

"Nicely done . . . ," Oliver said. Alex got the feeling there was something he wasn't telling her. She wanted to ask what it was, but she held her tongue. Oliver also took a couple of practice swings, but then, instead of hitting his ball under the bridge like Alex just had, he sent it rolling through a seemingly hidden passageway at the bottom of a stone covered wall. This secret shortcut allowed his golf ball to roll *directly* into the hole for an automatic hole in one.

"Wow," Alex said, feeling dumb. "Way to make me look bad."

"Only on the scorecard," he said, flirting.

"Only on the . . . Did you really just say that out loud? *Only on the scorecard*?"

"I did."

"Okay, cool. Just checking. I think I just also heard you say it to every other girl you've ever brought to this golf course, but I wanted to make sure."

Oliver shook his head, but he didn't take his eyes off of Alex.

He had a Mona Lisa smile of his own.

A few minutes later, Oliver ended up winning the

minigolf match by two strokes, but he didn't gloat. "Gotta act like you've been there before," he said.

"You mean like you've been on this date? 'Cause, *clearly*," Alex teased.

"I mean in the *winner's circle*," Oliver said as they dug into burgers and fries and chocolate shakes. They shared a booth at the diner, which was connected to the golf course and nearby arcade. "I promise I don't get around any more than you," Oliver insisted.

"Ouch . . . and here I thought things were going so well."

"Oh, like you haven't kissed half the guys on my team?"

"You know I've only kissed *two* of the guys on your team . . ."

"And Trevor Morgan," Oliver added, somehow knowing Alex had forgotten about him.

"Right. Okay. *Three* of your boys, but that doesn't mean—"

"I know," Oliver interrupted. "I'm trying to say you don't have to explain it to me. I know what it's like . . ." *To be mislabeled. To be called a slut. To have everyone jump to their own conclusions about you all the time*, Alex thought as Oliver searched for the right way to complete his sentence. " . . . to be able to kiss anyone you want," he said finally.

"You know, it's those sorts of comments that make other people think you're an ass."

"Luckily, I don't care what 'other people' think," Oliver said in a way that made Alex actually believe him. "I'm here with you, so."

"Well. I *also* think you're an ass, so . . . ," Alex said without missing a beat.

Oliver laughed. "I know you wouldn't be here with me if you didn't like me at least a little bit. And *I* wouldn't be here if I wasn't interested in kissing you."

"Right. I figured that had to be the reason."

"It's not the *only* reason."

"It's fine. We've already clarified that you can kiss anyone you want . . ."

"I can. But that doesn't mean I don't think kissing's a big deal."

"You really expect me to believe that?"

"It's true," Oliver said. It took a lot of self-control for Alex *not* to roll her eyes. "If there's something you're not going to believe, it's that I think that kissing is actually a bigger deal than having sex," Oliver added.

Alex couldn't stop herself from letting out a quick, loud, snort-filled laugh.

"I'm serious," he insisted.

"So then you've slept with more people than you've kissed?"

"Hell no. But I swear I haven't slept with as many people as you think. Whatever number you're thinking, I promise my real one is less. *Way* less, probably. Everyone assumes about me, too . . ." Alex shook her head slowly. "What? You don't believe me?"

"It just sounds like another line."

"It's not a line," Oliver insisted. "I mean, of course, yeah, I've kissed more girls than I've slept with, but I still think kissing is *bigger* than that . . ." He trailed off, finally sounding unrehearsed. "I'm not saying sex *isn't* big. But it's . . . like, at some point, all the attraction takes over, and it's . . . *biological*. But when it's just kissing? I don't know, but that feels like something I can control. Like it's a choice I have to make. It's more intimate, maybe? Whatever it is exactly, I just know I have to feel it."

"So basically you *feel* like your tongue is more precious than your penis?"

"Oh, hell no. My penis is way more precious."

Alex laughed.

She didn't really want to, but she couldn't help it.

"Maybe what I'm really trying to say is that I have way more control over what I do with my tongue," Oliver said as he leaned in closer to Alex. His face was only a few inches away from her, but he was already all the way inside her head. At this moment the only thing Alex could think about was Oliver's tongue and all the things he was saying with it—and then all the things he might be able to *do* with it . . .

After dinner Alex and Oliver spent a couple hours running around the arcade, playing as many games as they could. Alex was particularly good at Skee-Ball and Whac-a-Mole. Oliver racked up tickets on the basketball shot game. It was all fun and playful, and more or less innocent. They had their flirty moments, of course. And, as always, there was a lot of sexual tension between them, but they managed to make it all the way back to Oliver's car without so much as a kiss on the cheek.

Oliver drove them home, winding his car along Mulholland Drive. The radio played softly, filling the silence between them as Alex replayed all the moments in her head where they had *almost* kissed. She counted seven just on the golf course alone . . .

Then her thoughts wandered and she noticed that Oliver's right hand was resting on top of his right leg, while his left hand steered the wheel. Alex suddenly had the urge to slide her hand over and slip her fingers into his, but if Oliver thought *kissing* was intimate, she couldn't imagine how he'd feel about holding hands.

He would probably prefer a hand job, she thought.

Of course he would . . .

But then she couldn't help but think that maybe she'd prefer that too.

If she held his hand, that would raise all sorts of intimate questions. A hand job would raise his blood pressure, but then it would be over. It felt like that might just be simpler. Not that Alex was *actually* trying to do either one. The truth was, she didn't want to hold Oliver's hand *or* give him a hand job, but she couldn't stop thinking about both options.

Without warning, Oliver veered off Mulholland and pulled to a stop at one of the lookout points with a glistening view of the San Fernando Valley down below. He turned off the car.

"What are we doing?" Alex asked.

"I have something for you," Oliver said.

"And you want to give it to me here? Now?"

"What's wrong with here and now?"

"I thought the whole point was to hang out somewhere *besides* your car . . ."

"We did that already."

"Oh, okay. I get it."

"You get what, Campbell?"

"You spent the whole night putting all of your charm points into my kindness machine, and now you're done and . . . expecting sex to fall out."

"I don't know what a kindness machine is"—Oliver smirked—"but I think it's fair to say that I'm hoping more than expecting."

"I think it's fair to say that's not how it works," Alex smirked back.

"I know, I know. I swear that's not what I'm doing. You brought it up, not me. I just . . . I know you're nervous about breaking the state record," he said as if they'd talked about it before. They hadn't. They'd barely even talked about the record itself, let alone all the pressure that came along with trying to break it. "But I want to say I believe in you. And I think you're going to do it." Oliver pulled a small box out of his glove compartment. He handed it over.

"I almost don't want to open it," Alex said, trying not to sound emotional. She couldn't help but feel like the thoughtfulness of the box would be better than whatever was actually inside. But she knew Oliver wasn't going to let her get away with that. She took a moment to breathe before pulling off the lid. Inside was a small silver star charm.

"It's for your shoes," Oliver explained. "You're always lacing them up in here in the morning and sometimes you even remember to bring two of the same shoe . . ." He trailed off for a moment. "I don't know. I just figured you could put it on your laces, and then we'll both know it's there when you break the record like the . . . star that you are." Oliver waved his hand toward the windshield as he said the word "star," gesturing to the view as if to say: *See, this is why we're up here in my car. It's so we can see all the stars.*

"Are you gonna say something?" Oliver asked after a quiet moment. For the first time all night, Oliver seemed unsure of her answer.

"I love it. Thank you. I just . . . I had no idea that you were such a giant cheeseball."

"Campbell. No. Take that back now."

"It's cool. No one will believe me anyway . . . ," Alex said, finding Oliver's gaze. His eyes actually looked sincere. Alex could hold his eye contact for only so long before she had to look away. She knew if they looked at each other any longer they would start kissing.

"Is that your way of saying you don't want to kiss me?" Oliver asked, totally inside Alex's head again.

"I didn't say that . . ." She could feel his gaze practically burning a hole in the side of her head. "You were right," said added. "Kissing is more special."

"Too special?" Oliver asked. It sounded like he was hoping for a no.

"I'm not sure yet," Alex said truthfully.

"So . . . just sex, then?" Oliver teased.

"Ah yes. That *is* what you were hoping for after all . . . ," Alex teased back.

"Can you blame me?"

Alex shook her head no. Then, she couldn't help but ask, "How many?"

"What?"

"How many girls have you slept with?"

"Oh, okay . . . ," Oliver said as if he expected they'd get here sooner or later.

"You don't *have* to tell me—"

"Two."

"Really?" Alex asked, trying to hide her surprise. That was about ten fewer girls than Alex had been expecting.

"I told you not to believe everything you hear," he said, smirking. "Your turn . . ."

"Well, speaking of not believing everything you hear . . . I actually *haven't*."

"At all? What are you waiting for?"

Alex was surprised Oliver didn't make a joke. He waited patiently as she considered her answer: *The right person* sounded corny. *The right place and time* sounded lame. Anything else she could think of to say felt like it would be a lie . . . until the truth snuck up on her. "I have to feel it," she said, taking Oliver's words about the intimacy of kissing and using them as her own.

It was a simple thought, but entirely true: Alex was waiting to feel it.

135 days until graduation . . .

LAYLA did not understand why Alex hadn't just kissed Oliver in his car.

I can feel the sexual tension all the way from here, she texted The Chat the next morning.

That would've ruined everything, Alex texted back.

She attempted to explain that there was a delicate power balance between her and Oliver. She texted that she couldn't let him get the upper hand or everything would be ruined. Layla wanted to text and ask what *exactly* it was that would be ruined (since it wasn't clear what was going on between Alex and Oliver anyway), but that seemed like too practical of a question.

How blue were his balls? Layla asked instead.

I dunno. I didn't look, Alex texted back. After a few seconds she added, *Do you guys want to go to Trevor's party with me tonight?*

Layla didn't really know Trevor except that he was the

starting center on the basketball team. The party would probably be a lot of athletes and those sorts of kids she didn't really know. Layla still might have gone anyway, but she already had plans to see a movie with Logan.

Emma texted that she had a family dinner but would try to meet up when she was finished.

Zoe said she was in. Actually, she texted *We're in*—the "we" being herself and Austin, of course. Apparently they were a package deal now.

ALEX's mom dropped her off at Zoe's house around eight o'clock that night.

"Be home by midnight," Alex's mom said, as always, as if she were going to turn into a pumpkin or something if she didn't make curfew. Alex wasn't worried about that. She was glad to have someone to go to Trevor's party with. Oliver had invited her to come, but that didn't mean he wanted to go *with* her. He wanted to see her there, which meant she had to show up with someone else. Someone who wouldn't mind being ditched almost immediately. Zoe and Austin were the perfect wingmen. Zoe even found them a ride to the party since her brother Joey was home from college for the weekend and already planning on going. A bunch of his friends from the track team would be there too. He offered to be the designated driver.

Alex walked up the front lawn toward the Reeds' front door, but she made it only as far as the forest green Ford Explorer sitting in the driveway, because Joey was already in the front seat and ready to go. He was fiddling with the rearview mirror.

"Well, look who it is," Alex said.

"Hi, Lexi," Joey said, breaking into a grin.

Alex rolled her eyes. "No one calls me that anymore."

Back in Joey's junior year, when Alex was a freshman on the track team, some of the older guys had taken to calling her Lexi—as in *sexy* Lexi—because that rhymed, and teenage boys can be really clever like that sometimes.

"That's a shame," Joey teased.

"All the boys who thought I was sexy must've graduated already . . ."

"Oh, I'm sure *that's* not true . . ."

"How's the bay?" Alex asked, changing the subject.

"The best. I'm sorry to hear you're going to school on the wrong side of it, but I imagine you'll manage." Joey ran his fingers through his reddish-brown hair as he launched into a whole love letter to college. As he spoke, Alex watched him closely: the way his lips moved and his deep brown eyes sparkled, the sweet way he pushed his thick plastic glasses back up onto his nose whenever they slipped down. Joey's glasses were round and teal, and Alex couldn't help but think that he was the only person on the planet who would look good wearing them.

The truth was that Joey didn't just look good, he looked *effortlessly* good.

Back in high school his features had been softer. His face was rounder and his cheeks were fuller. His chubbiness was adorable, but now, all of his baby fat had given way to a more angular jawline and a longer, thinner face. It was as if he'd grown into his own appearance, like he'd gotten rid of the parts of his body he didn't need. Now, Joey managed to look hot and also completely comfortable in his skin and his clothes and even his glasses without being cocky about any of it. And as a bonus, Joey's good looks matched his sparkling personality.

"What's happening, guys?" Zoe asked as she walked out of the house.

Alex realized that Zoe meant the question rhetorically, but the truth was she wasn't entirely sure of the answer. Honestly, something was happening between her and Joey. Alex was leaning up against the car listening to Joey talk about life and college and everything, and she felt like she could've existed in that moment for the longest time. If Zoe hadn't walked outside, and they didn't have a party to go to, Alex couldn't imagine why she would want to do anything else.

ZOE wasn't oblivious to the situation.

And she certainly wasn't an idiot. She saw the matching grins on Alex's and Joey's faces. But, rather uncharacteristically, they didn't concern her.

In the past Zoe might've been insecure about her brother flirting with one of her best friends, but not anymore. She couldn't blame him for looking at Alex that way—boys always did. And she couldn't blame Alex, either. Zoe imagined that's what she probably looked like whenever she looked at Austin. She felt funny admitting it, even only to herself, but the whole boy-girl attraction thing made so much more sense now than it had even just a few weeks before.

Zoe jumped in the backseat of the car and let Alex sit up front next to Joey. They were going to stop at Austin's house in a couple of minutes to pick him up, so it made more sense for them to sit in the back together.

"Zo, you have the shortest little legs," Joey said, adjusting the settings on the driver's seat.

"Oh yeah. Thanks for letting me use your ride."

"I'm just glad the car's still in one piece," Joey teased.

Zoe was a decidedly bad driver and avoided getting behind the wheel as much as possible. Normally, she rode the bus to school, but every day this week—ever since Sunday night when Dylan showed up on her doorstep and sat on her bed and handed her a mix CD—she'd been driving Joey's car instead. Her laptop didn't have a CD drive, and she didn't want to listen to Dylan's mix on her parents' desktop computer in the living room, so the Ford Explorer was her only option.

The 'ZOE GOT SOME' Mix CD started playing as soon as Joey turned the car on.

"We don't have to listen to that . . . ," Zoe started to say, but it was too late. Joey was already turning the volume up.

"We don't have to listen, but we most certainly will. This Mix has to be good, if it's the reason you've been stealing my car all week."

"Well, it's perfect," Zoe explained, "but that doesn't mean you're gonna like it—"

"'Bootylicious,'" Joey said, laughing as the first song filled the car. "Dylan's a Destiny's Child fan?"

"It's actually a genius first song choice. It's a modern classic. The intro is perfect—and then the whole thing builds and crescendos in all the right places."

"You've obviously thought about this quite a bit," Joey said.

Yes, Zoe had thought about it.

And she knew Dylan had too.

And it was that precise combination of thoughtfulness that made Zoe appreciate the mix so very much. Even though Zoe mostly listened to pop songs and show tunes and Dylan liked rock and rap and EDM, he managed to pick twenty songs that he knew they would both love. And, as far as Zoe was concerned, he had put them all in exactly the right order from start to finish.

It had been only a week since Dylan gave her the mix, but Zoe had already listened to the whole thing on repeat so many times that she'd lost count of the exact number. Zoe felt like you could tell a lot about a person by the music they listened to. It was like a window into their soul. She knew she wasn't going to be able to stop Joey from shuffling through all the songs on the mix, but she couldn't help but feel like he and Alex were sitting inside her head—and heart and soul and all that—as they listened to the music Zoe loved so much: "Man in the Mirror." "Walking in Memphis." Andy Grammer's "Kiss You Slow." Paramore's "Ain't It Fun." "Wait for It" off the Hamilton Broadway cast album. And of course "Wonderwall" by Oasis.

Joey seemed rather impressed by the selection.

Then, he came across a track he hadn't heard before.

"That's this band Arkells. The song's called '11:11,'" Zoe said, knowing Dylan put it on the mix as a shout-out to her strange habit of kissing the clock and making a wish whenever she saw that time on her cell phone. She didn't explain that part to Joey and Alex. That was just for her and Dylan. "If you skip ahead a couple of songs, there's an amazing acoustic cover of Mariah Carey's 'Dreamlover' I've been geeking out about."

"No one geeks out better than my little sister."

"Hey, you can turn it off at any time," Zoe said, hoping he'd take the hint, but he kept shuffling. He didn't let any of the songs play for more than a few seconds, but he paused for a little while longer on "I Know Things Now," the one from *Into the Woods* about being excited and scared that had been stuck in Zoe's head for months. It meant a lot to her that Dylan had included this one, because she knew he'd never heard it before she mentioned it to him.

Finally, Joey got restless and turned off the mix, switching to the radio instead.

Then, Zoe's phone and Alex's phone vibrated at the same time.

Try actually kissing Oliver this time, Layla texted The Chat.

No promises, Alex texted back.

Zoe giggled.

"You guys talking about me?"

"Oh no. Alex's boy . . . ," Zoe explained.

* * *

ALEX caught Joey's eyes in the rearview mirror.

"That's not really an accurate description," she said.

"Only 'cause he's an idiot," Zoe exclaimed. "I still don't understand why you didn't make out all over his car last night."

"I would've kissed him back if he kissed me first. But I'm sure he knows that, which is probably why he didn't make a move in the first place."

"Wait. You think he didn't kiss you because he knew you'd kiss him back?" Zoe asked.

"No, he didn't kiss me because he wanted *me* to need to kiss *him* more than he *actually* wanted to kiss me in the first place," Alex explained.

"Your flirting ability is so far above my skill level I don't even really know what any of that means."

"I don't either," Joey said, chuckling.

Alex appreciated Joey's sincerity. And his ability not to take himself too seriously. Oliver was so calculated about everything, always playing games.

Once they got to the party, Zoe and Austin took off pretty quickly, joining some of Austin's friends at the beer pong table. Joey and Alex walked into the kitchen together, looking for something to drink. She spotted Oliver across the room, setting up a boat race with Trevor and some of the other guys from the basketball team. He waved her over.

"Thanks for the ride," Alex said to Joey.

"Have fun with your boy," he said, smirking.

"He's not actually my boy . . ."

"Then Zoe's right. He is an idiot."

*   *   *

ZOE might've been the worst flip cup player in the history of flip cup.

The game was simple enough: Drink all your beer. Flip your cup over.

But Zoe simply could not do any of it.

The first problem was the fact that she didn't like beer. The second problem was that Zoe wasn't good at drinking quickly, no matter what the liquid happened to be. The third problem was the flipping, which was the entire point of the game. If the objective had been to flip the cup over and *not* have it land upside down, Zoe would've won every single time. As it was, she was a complete and total failure.

"You are so far away from doing this right, I think you might be close," Austin teased before pulling Zoe in for a big kiss. Zoe's heart skipped a beat every time Austin kissed her, but it skipped twice whenever he did it in public. Austin would kiss her anywhere: in the hallway at school, in the senior parking lot, or right now, in the middle of Trevor Morgan's party. *As he should*, Zoe could hear all her girls saying, but this was new for Zoe.

"Wanna go upstairs?" Austin whispered in her ear.

That kind of question was new for Zoe too.

Zoe nodded and Austin grabbed her hand, interlacing their fingers, and together they made their way up the staircase. Halfway up, Zoe turned back, glancing down at the party below. She caught the gaze of a girl she didn't know for a moment, but then the girl darted her eyes away quickly, not wanting to make it look like she had been staring. Zoe had never seen this girl before, but Zoe had definitely *been* her before. So many times. The girl watching another couple walk up the stairs and not wanting to be caught. The girl longing to trade places but not wanting to admit it. At least for now Zoe didn't have to long for anything. She was with Austin, holding his hand, and heading toward an empty bedroom.

The first door Austin pushed on at the top of the stairs was locked, no doubt already occupied by another happy or drunken couple. After trying a few more locked doors they found the last one at the end of the hallway unlocked and unoccupied. Austin pulled Zoe into the room, kissing her as soon as he shut the door behind him. It occurred to Zoe, as they moved toward the twin bed, that maybe he had more on his mind than just kissing. . . .

They could've made out downstairs or outside in the backyard.

Here, now, they had a bed and a dark, quiet room.

Here, now, they could get naked if they wanted to.

Austin pulled off his shirt. Clearly, *he* wanted to . . .

Zoe pulled him in for another kiss. She could taste the beer on his tongue, which made her wonder if *she* tasted like beer too. And here, now she was drunk enough to ask him.

"Do you taste like beer?" Austin repeated back to her as if he were seriously considering the question. "I don't know, but I know how to find out . . ."

He leaned in for another kiss.

And then another one after that.

He never answered Zoe's question, but it just didn't seem to matter anymore.

After a few more minutes of kissing, Austin reached for Zoe's shirt, pulling it off. Honestly, Zoe had wanted to do that herself, but she hadn't been able to get up the nerve to take it off. Austin was more than happy to help. Zoe noticed that the sheets on the bed were pink and ruffled. There was a white floral pattern around the edge. They looked like the sheets she had on her bed when she was in elementary school, which made her feel small and also more drunk than she'd been even just a few moments before. She pushed her attention back to Austin and his kisses. He moved his lips down to her breasts and then even farther down onto her stomach. She moved her hands along his chest and up onto his shoulders. She couldn't help but giggle as she thought about how good it felt to have your shoulders rubbed. *Obviously,* it was not the same kind of good that caused orgasms . . .

Zoe and Austin kissed for a while longer, hovering right around second base, and just when it started to feel like it might be time to make a move toward third, the door swung open and a bright light flooded into the room.

At first Zoe couldn't see who had opened the door, but she heard the drunken giggles . . . And she could recognize that laugh anywhere—at least the male half of it.

Once Zoe's eyes readjusted, her suspicions were confirmed and she saw Dylan standing in the doorframe.

And he saw her, too.

This was not how Zoe had imagined Dylan would see her in her bra for the first time.

Not that she had ever really imagined that sort of thing. Or maybe she had?

It was hard to tell what was just the beer in her brain talking and what she was really feeling.

The truth was, right now, it didn't matter either way. She was with Austin. And Dylan was holding the hand of a girl who Zoe didn't recognize. She was probably a sophomore or maybe even a freshman. She was thin and blond. Her hair was too long and her skirt was too short. Zoe didn't necessarily *care* about any of those details, but they were impossible not to notice.

"You mind?" Austin finally managed to ask.

"No, sorry, buddy . . . ," Dylan stammered before stepping back out into the hallway and closing the door behind him.

It was only after he was gone and Austin's tongue was back inside her mouth that Zoe realized Dylan had been stuck staring at her for all that time.

Now she was the one stuck *thinking* about him.

His eyes had been glassy and his cheeks were flushed, probably because he was drunk, but maybe from embarrassment, too. But either way, it didn't *really* matter. Zoe was kissing Austin. And Austin's hand was under her skirt. And anything else she had been thinking about—Dylan or the awkwardness or his new girl of the moment—*all of it*, was overshadowed by the way Austin's fingers felt inside of her.

It was exciting . . . and also scary.

But mostly Zoe just *liked* it.

And she liked that, too.

133 days until graduation . . .

EMMA was still the reigning champion of mixed emotions.

She liked hooking up with Nick, especially that second time in the darkroom, but she wasn't particularly excited about the idea of doing it again. Of course, Emma being Emma, she wasn't entirely sure *why* she wasn't excited, but she knew Nick was very excited, and for some reason that contrast wasn't exactly helping things between them. She wasn't cocky enough to think Nick was falling in love with her or anything, but it was clear that his feelings for her were stronger than her feelings for him. His initial friendly offer to "lend her his penis" had already been more than accomplished, but Nick still seemed to want more.

He was waiting for Emma at her locker when she got to school.

"Hi you," he said, pulling her in for a hug and a quick kiss on the cheek.

A public kiss, even just on the cheek, was a pretty bold move at any time of day, but *especially* at 7:55 a.m. on a Monday morning. It took a lot of self-control to keep Emma from wiping off her cheek. She turned down the hall, heading toward the yearbook room. Nick followed closely behind her, which wasn't really evidence of anything as much as a by-product of the fact that they had their first period class together. "What are you up to this weekend?" he asked eagerly. "'Cause it's . . . you know, Valentine's Day . . ."

"Oh yeah, I don't know," Emma said, trying to stop him from asking anything else. "I don't usually make a big deal about that."

"Me neither," Nick said. "But I guess it's also, just, you know, *Saturday*, so if you want to hang out or whatever . . ." He said "hang out" as if he were putting quotations around the words. He might as well have just said, *If you want to have sex on Saturday, let me know.* Emma couldn't help but think that if he *had* actually just said that, she would've probably been down.

Nick stayed right on Emma's heels as she made her way to her computer station in the back of the yearbook room. Savannah was already seated at the computer beside hers. "All right, well, just let me know what you're thinking," Nick said rather awkwardly.

"Sure, yeah." Emma nodded. And then she made sure to smile at him. She knew Nick well enough to know that he needed a little positive reassurance from her before he would feel like it was all right to walk away.

Cherry

Once he left, Savannah leaned in close. "He looooves you . . ."

"No. He doesn't. Not even close. He just . . . has a lot of expectations about the whole thing."

"Yeah. You're super weird about expectations."

"To be fair, I'm super weird about a lot of things, but, in particular, *yes*, expectations freak me out." Emma got lost for a moment in all of the thoughts swirling around her head. She didn't know *why* expectations freaked her out so much or if Nick's expectations were actually real or if she was just projecting her own feelings onto him or whether it was normal for high school kids to think about "projecting their feelings" or if that was only something Emma thought about because her father was a therapist . . . and all her thoughts started to blend together until Emma couldn't tell where one stopped and the next one began . . .

Finally, Savannah's smile caught her eye.

"What?" Emma asked uncertainly.

"Just trying to figure out how many thoughts you're having at the same time. I can practically see all the gears moving in that pretty little head of yours."

"Then you must know that the inside of my head is anything but pretty . . ."

"Well, aesthetically speaking, the brains and blood are rather gross, but they're also incredibly complex and beautiful, so I think 'pretty' is a totally accurate description."

"Twelve," Emma answered. "I think it's safe to say that

I'm always having twelve distinct thoughts at any one time, give or take."

"I'll take it," Savannah said, still smiling.

Good, Emma thought.

She'd take it too. Whatever *it* was.

132 days until graduation . . .

LAYLA had never been particularly good at falling asleep.

Once she fell asleep, she had no problem staying there, but turning her brain off in the first place was nearly impossible. This past week had been even more problematic than usual. She simply could not keep her head in the moment. Her thoughts would get so far ahead of her actual life, racing into the future, that she constantly had to remind herself to return to reality . . .

Her phone buzzed.

There was a new text from Logan: *4 DAYS!!!!*

Four was Layla's lucky number, and their V-card/V-day date was now only four days away.

Under normal circumstances, Layla would've loved everything about the text message: the number, the symbolism, the way Logan used the appropriate number of exclamation points. But tonight all her thoughts and fears and hopes and dreams were running on overdrive.

She didn't know what to text back exactly, but she wanted to say *something*, so she responded with a red heart emoji. Normally, Layla didn't like emojis, because she thought they were easily misinterpreted, but in this moment she could see the upside to ambiguity, to allowing the other person to interpret the communication in their own way.

Can't. Wait. He texted back *Can't stop thinking about it . . .*

Layla couldn't stop thinking about it either, but she was pretty sure that her thoughts and Logan's were remarkably different.

She was thinking about emotions and logistics and ramifications.

Last time I fingered you, you got so wet . . . Logan texted.

Clearly, he was thinking about that.

Layla couldn't exactly blame him.

She realized it might've been stranger if he *weren't* thinking about that sort of thing . . . but it made her realize that all the sex stuff was just different for boys.

Logan imagined it would feel good.

Layla was worried it would hurt.

Logan had good reason to assume that there would be fireworks.

Layla had already lowered her expectations accordingly.

Logan knew his friends would be impressed that he finally did it.

Luckily, Layla knew that her friends would be supportive of her, too, but if any of the other kids at school heard about it, they'd probably look at them both differently, even though they were doing the exact same thing together at the exact same time.

You're the hottest and the best and I love you!! Logan texted when Layla didn't respond to his last message about the last time he fingered her.

Same and same and I love you too!!! Layla texted back, adding a bunch of exclamation points—but not so many as to look like she was overcompensating. Layla obviously spent a ton of time thinking about anything and everything, but she laughed at herself as she tried to calculate what percentage of that thinking time was dedicated to typing and/or analyzing her text message conversations. Far too much, she concluded.

Then Logan texted that he was going to sleep.

Layla wished she could say and do the same, but her brain still wasn't tired yet.

Actually, her brain was *exhausted*, but it wasn't ready to turn off. Layla couldn't stop thinking about the importance of the number four and the V-card/V-day and the sex and the fireworks and how those last two thoughts were very much not the same thing. And *then* all she could think about was how her first time was going to be anticlimactic and firework-less, which was an extremely unhelpful and unsexy thought to be having before it even happened.

It was literally the opposite of orgasmic.

Layla knew that the odds of setting off fireworks the very first time she had sex were about as likely as spotting a unicorn in the wild, but she still hated the unwavering feeling that the outcome had already been decided for her. Like, no matter what happened, no matter what she did or what Logan did or what they managed to do together, it wouldn't be as good as she wanted it to be. Not even close.

Maybe the truth was that *nothing* would ever be as good as she wanted it to be—but that couldn't possibly mean that she shouldn't try. And Layla wasn't just thinking about sex, of course. Life was full of expectations and failures, but Layla knew she still had to try.

But, at the very same time, she also had to be prepared to fail and try again and fail again no matter what she was doing or when she was doing it . . . and then just like that, as always, her thoughts were racing off into the future.

She was powerless to stop them.

She could barely even keep up with them.

131 days until graduation . . .

ZOE hadn't spoken to Dylan since he saw her in her bra that night at the party.

He'd been sick, apparently, and going to bed early, and she'd been distracted by Austin, but that didn't mean she didn't want to talk to Dylan, too. She couldn't remember the last time they'd had a real phonefall. "Why aren't we talking?" Zoe asked Wednesday night once she finally managed to get Dylan on the phone.

"What? We're talking. We're literally talking right now."

"I mean, for real. The phonefalls . . ."

"Oh. I don't know . . . ," Dylan said as if he hadn't even noticed. But Zoe was sure he had. The last time she saw him, she had only been wearing a bra, and she was very sure he'd noticed *that* as well. "I don't want to get in Austin's way," Dylan added.

"You're not. I swear. He goes to sleep early. And I really don't think he would care anyway." Dylan didn't respond right away. "What am I missing?" Zoe pushed again. "How many girlfriends have you had since Chem? Six? Seven?"

"Five."

"Five, right, and I—*we*—outlasted all of them." Dylan didn't respond to that right away either. "You had no problem making me talk to you then—"

"Okay, Zoe, I'm so sorry I *made* you talk to me—"

"Stop it. You know that's not what I'm saying—"

"I don't, actually . . ."

Zoe took a breath, forcing herself to pause for a second. "Look. I like falling asleep on the phone with you. And maybe *that's* weird, but it's how we've always been. Ever since we became friends. And that doesn't have to do with Austin. Or it shouldn't, anyway. But if you don't want to do this anymore . . . I mean, obviously you're *allowed* to say that—"

"Am I? Thank you for the permission," Dylan said, sounding like an asshole.

"Whatever, Dylan. I'm just saying, be honest with me—"

"I am being honest—"

"No, you're not. You're blaming Austin. You're blaming me. If *you* don't want to talk to me in bed anymore, then you need to just say that."

"I don't want to talk to you in bed anymore."

Dylan's words were quick and sharp. Zoe let them hang on the phone line for a moment, engulfing the entire conversation in silence. But it wasn't their normal, comfortable kind of silence. This felt decidedly different, and Zoe didn't like it at all.

"Why not?" she asked, even though she could sense that Dylan wasn't ready to answer that. "Is it just because I have a boyfriend?"

"I don't know." Zoe could hear the honesty in Dylan's voice. He was just as confused as she was, but it still hurt. "But I know I don't want to do this right now," he added.

And that hurt even more.

"Okay," was all Zoe could manage to say before she hung up the phone.

She didn't give Dylan a chance to backtrack or say "sorry" or even just soften the blow. She knew him well enough to know that he wasn't going to, and she didn't want to waste any more time waiting for him to say something she wanted to hear.

She'd spent too many years doing that already.

129 days until graduation . . .

LAYLA was in charge of the senior class's red carnation table.

Every year the student council sold red carnations on Valentine's Day in order to raise money for a local food pantry. Each flower cost a dollar. Students could buy as many flowers as they wanted, and then student council members would deliver them to the lucky recipients in their classes throughout the day. The whole thing was a giant undertaking requiring lots of organization and careful planning. Basically, it was Layla's dream come true.

Layla spotted Zoe as she got off the school bus. Zoe waved at Layla but seemed hesitant to come over to the carnation table and actually say hi. Layla knew why. Zoe wasn't a big fan of Valentine's Day. She was scared from too many years of adolescent disappointment. Too many years of not having a valentine. But Layla already knew that this year was going to be different.

"What's up, Zo?" she asked loudly, giving Zoe no choice but to head over. As Zoe approached, Layla held up one red carnation. "For you . . ."

"Aw," Zoe said, mimicking Layla's standard response to anything even mildly cute or sentimental. "You shouldn't have."

"I didn't. There's no pink slip, but it's not from me, I swear."

Whenever someone bought a flower, they had the option of filling out a pink slip of paper to go along with it. They could write a note, simply sign their name, or choose to remain anonymous. Most people went the anonymous route. Layla wasn't going to break protocol, not even for Zoe, but she hoped Zoe would suddenly be able to read her mind and figure it out.

Zoe's entire face lit up as she realized that—for the very first time—a boy had sent her a Valentine's Day carnation. "Thanks, Lay!" Zoe cradled the flower and ran off.

"Don't thank me . . . ," Layla called after her, knowing Zoe would think it was from Austin.

Layla glanced over at the crew of water polo players sitting at a nearby table. She wanted to make sure Dylan saw Zoe get the flower.

His flower.

A few minutes later, as Dylan walked by on his way to his first period class, he nodded at Layla as if to acknowledge what had happened. Layla could tell that he wanted to keep walking, but she couldn't keep quiet. "You should've written her a card."

"I'm not really a writer . . ."

"Just a late night phone talker?"

That made Dylan stop in front of her table. This was already the longest conversation they'd ever had, but Layla already felt like she knew him because she'd been hearing about him from Zoe for years.

"I just remember how bummed she was last year when she didn't get a flower. It's been bothering me, so . . ." Dylan trailed off.

"But you don't want her to know?" Layla wasn't just talking about the flower.

"As long as she's happy, mission accomplished . . ."

Layla didn't realize Dylan cared quite so much.

ALEX jogged down the hallway carrying two *dozen* red carnations.

She appreciated all the Valentine's Day love, but now having all these flowers just felt excessive, especially since they were slowing her down as she hustled through the crowd on her way to class. She turned a corner and ran smack into Oliver, who had been racing in the other direction with his gym bag on his shoulder. The impact caused Alex to drop all of her flowers, which made it look like a small garden had sprouted on the tiled floor.

"Sorry," he said with a grin.

"No, *I'm* sorry. It's not like you have a big game tonight or anything . . ."

The boys' varsity basketball team was playing in the first round of CIF playoffs against a school up in Santa

Barbara. It was a big win-or-go-home kind of game.

"Yeah, no pressure," Oliver said as he bent down to help Alex pick up her flowers. "Wow, you must be breaking records with all of these . . ."

"How many are from you?"

"I can't take any credit."

Alex raised an eyebrow. She could've sworn at least *one* flower would be from him.

"Don't take it personally. I didn't throw any to anybody," he added, clocking her facial expression. "Besides, Campbell, you can't just put charm points or, you know, like, *flowers*, into a girl's kindness machine and just expect sex to fall out."

"Is that so? Who told you about the kindness machine?" Alex asked.

"Oh . . . just this girl."

"*Just*, huh?"

"I drive her to school."

"Lucky you." Alex smiled. She liked the playful banter between them, but she was finally noticing just how calculated it all really was, as if they were putting on a show for each other.

"Are you actually mad?" Oliver asked, breaking their rhythm.

"About the flower?" Alex asked impulsively. If she'd thought about it, maybe she would've realized that he was asking about Trevor's party last weekend. They'd spent most of the night playing drinking games and hanging out with the other guys on the basketball team, which was *fun* and all, but they didn't even come *close* to kissing this time. "I don't care about the flower," Alex added, hoping it sounded believable.

"Good. I know you think Valentine's Day is bullshit—and so do I."

"Is that your way of saying you don't have any plans tomorrow?"

"I'll text you," Oliver said with a smirk before he took off down the hallway.

"That's not what I meant," Alex yelled after him.

"But it's what you wanted me to say," Oliver shouted over his shoulder without breaking his stride or looking back at her. Alex shook her head. Mostly she was annoyed that he was right.

LAYLA helped carry the crate of leftover carnations to Logan's car after school.

Logan had the brilliant idea to donate the extra flowers to a nearby retirement center. Logan was always having ideas like that, ideas that were so thoughtful that you couldn't help but be impressed by his kindness. Layla *was* genuinely impressed but, at the moment, she couldn't help being annoyed with him too.

"Layla. I got every single person on the student council a carnation," he tried to explain. "Even the boys."

Layla didn't care about that part. The problem was Logan had gotten one for Vanessa, too.

"So what? Was I supposed to get one for everyone *except* her?"

"I don't know." Layla exhaled. Now she was annoyed at herself for even starting the conversation. "I'm sorry I brought it up, but I saw the carnation hanging in her locker, and now she, like . . . she has it forever, this romantic thing from you—"

"Layla, it's not *romantic*—"

"Okay, but *she* doesn't know that. She thinks it's special."

"Lay, come on. Can we please just forget about Vanessa?"

"I'm trying."

"All I can think about is you," Logan said, which made Layla smile but also made her feel more petty and stupid, too.

Of course Layla *wanted* to forget about Vanessa and her shameless advances toward Logan, but that wasn't Layla's nature. She couldn't just pretend to be something she wasn't. But she *could* stop complaining to Logan about it. And she would. Starting now.

"Thank you," she said sweetly. "I'm sorry."

"Love means never having to say you're sorry." Logan smiled.

"So, I'm *not* sorry?" Layla asked, laughing a little.

"No, I don't know . . . that's from a movie. My dad says it sometimes."

"What movie?"

"I don't know, but it's older, and black-and-white maybe. He's always trying to rewatch it with my mom, but she says she doesn't like the movie as much as he does, and whenever he says the you-don't-have-to-say-sorry thing, my mom says it's the stupidest thing she's ever heard about love, so . . ." Logan always talked just a *little* bit faster than normal when he got nervous.

"Love also means never having to ask *Did you get my text?*" Layla offered, hoping to ease Logan's nerves.

"Oh. Did you text me?"

"No. That's a quote I found online. Makes more sense now that I realize it's probably making fun of your movie."

Logan smiled as he pulled a small red envelope out of his pocket and handed it to Layla.

It was the first clue.

My Layla, the letter started. The words were written in blue pen in Logan's boyishly sloppy handwriting, and just those first two words were enough to make Layla's heart melt. She almost didn't want to read the rest. Right now everything was perfect: the card, the handwriting, the blue ink. She didn't want to ruin it. But, practically speaking, she also didn't want to stand in the parking lot forever, so she kept reading: *I want to start by saying that you are the absolute best. Pack an overnight bag—and I'll take care of the rest. Be ready tomorrow for a bright and early start. I love you with all of my big, silly heart. To the moon and back, always, Logan.*

"I wish I were better at writing or rhyming," Logan said.

"Nope. You're perfect. The card is perfect."

"If you think *that* was perfect . . . ," Logan said as his lips curled into a smile. His dimple was on full display, popping out of his cheek as he laid out the plan for their Valentine's Day. He explained that there would be thirteen more clues (for a grand total of fourteen, obviously). The clues would take them all over the city. He'd made plans and reservations and had mapped out a whole schedule. "It's going to be the most 'Layla day' that's ever existed," Logan said, pulling her in for a big kiss. "Get excited."

ZOE had stopped making excuses to sneak into the tech booth during rehearsals.

When she and Austin first started hooking up, she would pretend that she needed some more spike tape. Or she needed to ask him a question about the spotlight. And then she'd make her way back to the booth, and they'd make out for a few minutes, or for many minutes, or for as long as they could go without getting paranoid that anyone was getting suspicious.

Other times Austin would be the one making up excuses, finding reasons to come visit Zoe backstage. He'd say he needed to adjust the focus on one of the lights, for example, and then walk back to the utility closet where the ladder was, and Zoe would meet him, and they'd make out there for a while.

Now they were both getting far bolder and cockier about their make-out sessions. They'd meet in the tech booth or backstage and make out, for longer and longer each time. And they didn't even really care if anybody noticed anymore, because it was simply too much fun. Today, Austin had pulled her behind the curtain, which was bunched up on the right side of the stage and provided the perfect hiding spot. Zoe wasn't sure how long they'd been kissing during this particular make-out session, but she was pretty sure that in the past couple of weeks, she'd spent more time kissing Austin than she had kissing anyone else in her entire life *combined*.

To be fair, Zoe hadn't kissed all that many people before him, but still, this seemed like an achievement worth celebrating. She'd read somewhere that in order to be a master at something you had to do it for ten thousand hours. She wondered if it were possible to be a master of kissing (whether you kissed for that many hours or not). She wondered how many make-out sessions she and Austin would have to have before they'd even get close to that number.

Then, her thoughts returned to another familiar question . . .

"Am I sexy?" she asked between kisses.

"Do you really even have to ask?" Austin asked, pulling back for a moment. "I guess you do, since you just did, but *yes*. The answer is obviously yes. You are *so* sexy. *Beyond* sexy."

He looked into Zoe's eyes, and she could see her image reflected in them, and she felt strangely and wonderfully beautiful. It was like she could feel his attraction to her pouring out of his pupils and into her soul. And she knew his feelings were strong, and real, and . . . *hard*.

Or.

He was hard.

Zoe was almost embarrassed to admit, even just to herself, that she liked turning him on like that. She liked the fact that her kisses made him hard and that she could feel him between her legs as they kept kissing . . . but it made her nervous, too—and also excited and scared and all that—but mostly it just made her want to kiss him more and touch him more, so that's exactly what she did.

LAYLA's version of "getting excited" also meant being prepared.

As soon as Layla got home from school, she climbed onto her bed, opened her laptop, and read her entire Sex Doc from start to finish. Ultimately, all of the "oh my God I'm having sex tomorrow what do I need to know?" advice more or less boiled down to three key points: make sure you're ready, pick the right person, use protection.

Layla knew they were using a condom. *And* she was on the pill.

She knew she'd picked the right person.

And she knew she was ready . . .

But.

She was still nervous.

She wasn't nervous about having sex with *Logan*, but, if she were being entirely honest—with herself or the universe or whatever—the truth was that she *was* nervous about having sex in general.

Layla decided that maybe a little nervousness was actually a good thing.

It meant that it mattered.

Yes, tomorrow with Logan would be a big deal, a *very* big deal, even, but it would only be one time. The first time. And the whole point of having a first time in the first place was that there would be many more times to come. Layla giggled at her thoughts and the thematically appropriate use of the word "come"—or "cum."

There'd be more time for that, too.

She clicked on another article in the Sex Doc, called "How to Have Better Sex," which provided tips like "talk dirty" and "undress slowly" and "use the reverse cowgirl position."

Layla didn't know what the *regular* cowgirl position was, let alone the reverse version. A Google search revealed some pictures that quickly cleared up any confusion, but now all the preparedness was just stressing her out. Even though Layla had endless amounts of information, literally at her fingertips, there was still so much more that she wanted to know.

Like, about her actual fingertips, for example.

Where was she supposed to put them during sex?

And where was she supposed to put her *hands* for that matter? On Logan? On the bed? How would she know? How would she know what to do with *any* part of her body? Like her eyes, even. Should she look at Logan? At the ceiling? Would he be on top of her? She read in the Sex Doc that it generally felt more pleasurable for the woman to be on top, but that seemed rather ambitious for her first time. Emma said there probably wouldn't be time for more than one position, but Layla wanted to know how long it would last. Or at least how long it *should* last. She realized that the answers to those last two questions were probably not the same thing. And then what about everything else afterward? Would she feel different? Or look different? Would there be any sort of aftertaste? Or whatever . . .

Layla felt silly for wanting to ask these questions, as she realized that they were all basically things you could only know by actually having sex with someone, which made the little hairs on the back of her neck stick straight up. She could feel her blood pressure rising and some sweat pooling on her forehead . . . She recognized this feeling. It was basically the one she'd get before a big test at school. She knew she was as ready as she possibly could be, and now the only thing left to do was take it already.

Or in this case, "do it" already.

Luckily, Layla didn't have to wait much longer.

Twenty-four hours and counting . . .

EMMA watched the minutes slip into seconds as the game clock wound down.

59 seconds, 58 seconds . . .

Emma could feel a pit of nervous excitement growing in her stomach. She really wasn't a sports fan, but she'd spent the last 47 minutes and *46 seconds, 45 seconds* watching the boys varsity basketball game from the stands and getting swept up in the intensity of it all. The team's entire season was on the line: win and advance to the CIF semifinals or lose and go home.

The tension was real and palpable, and Emma could feel it all pulsing through her entire body as she sat in the stands next to Savannah, who was covering the game for the school newspaper. Emma was supposed to be snapping pictures for the yearbook, but she kept forgetting to watch through the viewfinder, which was a rarity for Emma.

There'd already been more than a dozen lead changes in the game, and now, as the seconds fell off the clock, the Wolverines were still losing by one. Oliver controlled the ball, dribbling down the court. Beyond Alex's Oliver car pool stories, the general rumors that existed about him, and all the whispers in the hallway, Emma didn't actually know him very well. Regardless of what was true about Oliver, he was, without a doubt, the most impressive thing Emma had ever seen on a basketball court. To be fair, Emma hadn't actually seen all that many things on a basketball court, but still . . . even she knew he was special.

With *22 seconds . . . 21 seconds . . .* left on the clock, Oliver threw the ball off his defender's foot, causing the ball to go out of bounds and stopping the clock.

After the inbound play there would be time for only one more shot. Oliver would take it. He knew it. His teammates knew it. The other team knew it. Every fan in the stands knew it. And yet. When Oliver dribbled right and faked left and finally pulled up for a fadeaway jumper with no time left on the clock there was absolutely nothing anyone else could do . . .

Emma held her breath . . .

And Savannah squeezed her hand . . .

And then entire sold-out, maximum capacity crowd watched with baited breath . . .

. . . as Oliver launched the winning shot up into the air

and through the rim—swishing perfectly—nothing but net!

Oliver did it!

He won!

Technically, the whole team won, but every other guy on the court knew it was almost entirely Oliver, which is why they wasted no timing mobbing him at center court. "We woonnnnnnnn!" Savannah yelled, twirling around in a circle as she and Emma ran out on the court to join the celebration.

"THIS IS SO COOL!" Emma yelled back as her shoes squeaked on the sweaty hardwood floor and her heart pounded against her chest and her brain took a mental picture, managing to turn the magical, adrenaline-filled moment into a memory even while it was still happening.

Luckily, Emma also managed to remember to grab her real camera too, and she snapped a few dozen winning pictures of the celebration. She'd taken more than a hundred shots during the actual game, but these victory pics were by far the best. Especially when Trevor Morgan hoisted Oliver up into his shoulders and carried him around the court in a giant victory lap.

After all the cheering and twirling and screaming finally died down, everyone, including the team and the cheerleaders and Emma and Savannah, made their way back to the school bus. The girls shared a seat up front near the coaches and trainers and members of the staff, who had clearly given up on trying to keep any sort of order on the ride home. Savannah pulled out her green notebook and scribbled down a few notes for her article, while Emma pulled out her camera again, hoping to snap a few more candid shots. Mostly she focused her lens on Oliver. And his blue eyes. And his cheekbones. And perfect jawline. He made her job easy. "He's like a joke," she said, looking at his face in the viewfinder.

"What?" Savannah asked looking at this picture.

"His face . . . I mean, the eyes alone . . ." Emma couldn't help but smile.

"Yeah," Savannah said playfully, "if you're into that sort of thing."

Emma turned around to snap more pictures and saw that Oliver had moved up a few rows. Now he was sharing a seat with Caroline. She was still wearing her cheerleading uniform, her midriff and thighs and cleavage all showing. Oliver was wearing a mesh practice tank top, his arms and abs and jawline all perfectly visible too. Even from twelve rows away Emma could see the attraction simmering between them.

"Uh-oh," Emma said. "That's Caroline. Dylan's ex-girlfriend."

"The cheerleader?"

"Yeah."

"And?"

"*And.* Alex and Oliver have been . . ." Emma stopped, realizing that they hadn't actually *been* anything, and they hadn't actually *done* anything either. "Well . . . I don't know exactly *what* they're doing, but they're neighbors and they car pool, and they went on a date and played flip cup at a party last weekend. I don't know. There's a lot of mind games . . ."

"And Alex is Dylan's best friend?"

"No. That's Zoe."

"Okay," Savannah said, putting the pieces together. "So. The girl Dylan *doesn't* date anymore is sharing a seat with the guy Alex *isn't* really dating at all."

"Well. Yes."

"Is it possible I'm missing the point?"

"There's no point," Emma admitted, "but I have a feeling Alex won't be very happy if they hook up right now."

"Because she likes Oliver?"

"Technically, she's not *sure* yet how she feels about him, but I think she does."

"And does Zoe like Dylan?"

"No. Well. I don't know. Zoe's dating Austin."

"I give up," Savannah said, laughing. "Your friends are complicated."

"It's one of the many thing I love about them." Emma laughed.

She and Savannah spent the next hour of the ride home talking about everything and anything. Their conversation were always so easy and effortless. After a while Emma turned around, stealing another glance at Oliver and Caroline.

"Are they kissing yet?" Savannah asked.

"No. Just sitting all close . . . but it looks like any minute now . . ."

Savannah turned backward to look too. Oliver and Caroline were both sitting with their heads pressed again the bus seat, their foreheads only a few inches apart.

Savannah turned her attention back to Emma, pressing her forehead against the seat only a few inches from Emma's forehead, just like Oliver was doing to Caroline. "Looks like they're having a bad case of basorexia."

"Basorexia? That's supposed to be a real thing?"

"It's *your* thing," Savannah explained. "I've been meaning to tell you I looked it up. Basorexia is the feeling of having the overwhelming urge to kiss someone. Urban Dictionary said it could also be defined as a strong craving for kissing, or a hunger for it . . ."

"Oh well, if Urban Dictionary says so . . ."

"It's real, I swear."

"Awesome. My weirdness has a word and a definition," Emma said.

"I feel pretty good about all your weirdness," Savannah replied.

Emma smiled. Honestly, at this moment . . .

128 days until graduation...

... **EMMA** actually felt pretty good about all her weirdness too.

"Happy Valentine's Day," Emma said as she realized that the time on her cell phone had just switched to midnight. They'd been on the bus back from Santa Barbara for almost two hours.

"Hey, yeah, you too," Savannah said, realizing it was officially tomorrow. And then she asked, as if she just remembered, "Did you get my carnation?"

"Your what?"

"I sent you a carnation today. Or yesterday I guess."

"You did? Just one?"

"Ha, yeah, *just one*. Sorry. I'll make it a dozen next time."

"No, no, one is great. Like, so nice. I got it. I got two, actually. But I thought they were both from Nick, since the one he sent me had a card." Emma didn't know what else to say, but she got the feeling Savannah was waiting for something more. She finally managed a "Thank you."

"You. Are. Welcome," Savannah replied. "Sorry about the lack o' card. I'm pretty good with words usually, but I didn't quite know what to say."

Emma totally knew the feeling.

"Actually—that's a lie."

Emma caught Savannah's eyes. *What was a lie?*

"I think I knew what to say," Savannah explained, "but it was, like . . . it was like there was just too much."

Emma nodded. She totally knew that feeling too.

And then suddenly Emma felt like there was a reason to turn around.

And she was right.

Oliver and Caroline had finally given into their basorexia—into all the urges and cravings and hunger or whatever it was—and were now in the midst of the inevitable make-out session. Their lips and hands and hormones were more or less everywhere.

Emma snapped a quick picture on her cell phone.

"Is it just me or does it look like he's trying to swallow her entire head?" Savannah whispered, so as not to disturb the horny couple.

"I guess this is unequivocal proof that two sexy people kissing is not an automatically sexy situation," Emma whispered back.

Savannah had to bite down on her bottom lip to keep from laughing.

Emma was more certain than ever before that the pink shade of Savannah's lips was actually the same color as her own. It was all she could think about for the rest of the ride home . . .

And she woke up the next morning thinking about Savannah's lips too.

But she wasn't thinking about their color as much anymore. Instead, now, she was thinking about the words that had come out of Savannah's mouth about that one carnation.

And all Emma could really think was *why?*

Why did Savannah send her a flower?

Was it a *friendly* flower?

It didn't *feel* particularly friendly.

As Emma wiped the sleep out of her eyes, she remembered that she hadn't sent the Oliver and Caroline make-out picture to The Chat yet.

She wasn't sure who would hate it more, Alex or Zoe.

LAYLA texted back to The Chat almost immediately: *Oh. Snap.*

She knew Alex and Zoe weren't going to be happy to see that.

She was sitting by her cell phone waiting for Logan to text her. His first clue had said to be ready "bright and early" but she knew that Logan wasn't actually a morning person, so that was a joke. Still, it was almost 10:45 now, and she was getting antsy.

Thankfully, her phone buzzed again almost immediately. And this time it was Logan: *Your chariot awaits.*

Layla grabbed her bag and flew down the stairs, yelling a quick good-bye to her mom on the way out the door.

"Call me from Alex's!" her mom yelled back. Layla didn't like lying to her parents, and she wasn't very good at it, but she had no choice. Even if Logan's parents had somehow been okay with some sort of sleepover situation, which they weren't, there was no way Layla's parents would've ever approved. She told her mom she was spending Valentine's Day with Logan, but she'd had to lie and say she was sleeping at Alex's house afterwards. Alex's parents were distracted enough not to notice, and Alex was happy to cover for her. Layla wasn't sure what Logan's actual plan was for their sleeping arrangements, which made her rather anxious and itchy, but she trusted he had figured something out.

Layla opened the front door. . . .

And there was Logan.

He was standing at the end of her front walkway, leaning against his car, holding a small bouquet of handpicked flowers.

Some people tried so hard to do so much, and none of it seemed to matter.

All Logan had to do was shift his weight and *lean*, even just ever so slightly, and something inside of Layla completely melted. Layla had felt this feeling before. This Logan-induced, full-body-meltage kind of feeling . . . but this time was different.

This time she could almost literally feel her heart drop out of her chest and all the way down into her feet, as if it were just too heavy, or too full, to stay suspended inside of her.

It felt like she needed to surrender herself—her feelings or her heart or whatever—to gravity.

"What are you waiting for?" Logan asked, all happy and playful.

Nothing. And also everything, Layla thought as she walked to greet him.

ALEX wasn't sure how long she'd been staring at the Oliver-Caroline picture of doom.

But she felt powerless to stop.

She wanted to respond to The Chat, but she couldn't seem to do that, either.

She'd started typing a few different responses: *screw him* and then *ouch* and then *loser* with lots of extra *r*'s tacked on and too many exclamation points, but none of that seemed quite right. Alex wasn't mad, exactly. She definitely wasn't surprised. "Disappointed" sort of—*kind of*—felt like the right word, but not entirely. Technically, Oliver was allowed to make out with whoever he wanted. He wasn't her boyfriend. He wasn't even a friend with benefits or anything like that. All things considered, he might not even be a friend at all. Oliver was simply her car pool driver. They'd *almost*—

̶t not actually—kissed in his car one time.

phone buzzed again. There was a new text. This one was from Oliver. It felt like he knew she was thinking about him or trying *not* to think about him. Either way, she closed her phone without looking at his text message. She didn't care what he had to say. But that defiant feeling lasted for only about two and a half seconds, and then her curiosity won out. She picked up her phone and opened Oliver's text.

Wanna hang out

UGH.

No.

She did not want to hang out.

And she didn't want to respond, either.

She put her phone back down again, but then, once again—almost immediately—it vibrated, signaling another text from Oliver. She didn't want to look but again—dammit, *again*—she couldn't help herself. She had to check.

That wasn't a question

Alex hated herself for ever thinking that Oliver's lameness had been cute. She also hated that he didn't use any punctuation. There were no question marks. No periods. He was literally the worst.

She started to type *No thanks*—but decided to

Instead she wrote: *Why d*

Ha, Oliver texted back almost immediately.

Alex waited for something more.

You spying on me now? he added after a minute.

Don't flatter yourself.

Don't try and tell me you don't want to hang out tonight

UGHHHHH, Alex thought to herself.

She wasn't sure what she hated more: the fact that she did, in fact, still want to hang out with him even though he had been making out with someone else the night before, or the fact that he—and all his stupid cockiness—somehow seemed to know that already.

Everything she could think to text back to him sounded stupid or lame or just plain petty. Instead, she turned off her phone without responding.

The only thing she wanted to give to Oliver right now was her silence.

ZOE attempted to remember all the tips the girls had ever told her . . .

Watch your teeth.

Don't forget to use your hands.

Make *eye contact.*

She remembered Alex had said something about sucking on an ice cube first in order to make the whole thing feel cold or something, but Zoe didn't have an ice cube, so that piece of advice wasn't really all that helpful.

Mostly, Zoe just followed her instincts, which seemed to be working well enough. Austin *seemed* to be having a good time. A very good time. But Zoe still wasn't sure whether or not she was doing it right. "You're doing it *so* right," Austin assured her. He was sitting on the edge of his bed with his feet on the floor and his pants and boxers down around his ankles. Zoe was kneeling down in front of him. "It feels amazing," he insisted, "like, really, the only thing that could even possibly be better right now would be if we were having sex."

Whoa.

Zoe stopped what she was doing again and sat back on her heels.

"You want to have sex?"

"Um. Yeah," Austin said as if that were the only possible answer. "But I know you haven't, so I didn't think . . . I wasn't sure if you wanted to."

"I do want to," Zoe said all at once. She was almost surprised how quickly and confidently the words came out of her mouth. Her voice wasn't shaking. Her body wasn't squirming. Her face was red, but not more than usual, and that was mostly because Austin's penis had been in her mouth until just, like, thirty seconds earlier . . .

She hadn't told Austin about the sex pact, but this felt like so much more than that now.

Zoe wanted to have sex *with Austin.* And she told him again that she did.

He could not have been more excited to hear it.

"Now?" he asked with a gigantic grin on his face.

LAYLA opened Logan's sixth red Valentine's Day envelope very carefully.

She didn't want to mess up her freshly painted nails. So far, the first few envelopes had led Layla to the Coffee Bean on Pico for an iced vanilla latte, to the small park near her house for a quick ride on the swing set, to her favorite nail place for a mani-pedi, and now they were just finishing lunch at The Apple Pan, an old-fashioned burger spot they both loved.

Layla read the sixth clue: *You wore a headband in your hair. I won a giant teddy bear. This was the site of our first real date. There are still quite a few hours until sunset—but I'm so excited I cannot wait . . .*

Of course Layla knew that their first date was at the Santa Monica Pier. The teddy bear was still sitting on top of the bookshelf in her bedroom.

"Don't worry," Logan said, chuckling, "the rhymes are only gonna get worse . . ."

"Not worried," Layla said, but even as the words came out of her mouth, she could feet a pit hardening in the back of her throat. Again, she could feel her heart drop down into her feet, overcome by gravity. This moment, this day, this scavenger hunt, this whole first time, was everything Layla could've hoped for. . . .

Logan was surpassing all of her wildest dreams.

And yet . . . Layla could feel the tears welling up in her eyes as she and Logan walked back to his car. She glanced over at him. He was being so cute and so natural, so effortless . . . and Layla felt so exactly the opposite of that, all calculated and forced. They climbed back into Logan's car and sat together for a minute. No music. No talking. Just their own quiet thoughts. And then a few tears rolled down Layla's face. Layla had never felt smaller.

"Talk to me," Logan said finally.

"This was my idea . . ."

"What was?"

"The scavenger hunt. The date. *Tonight.*"

"Yeah," Logan said, already reading between the lines. He knew Layla well enough to know what was coming next.

"I'm sorry." She tried to find more words to add to those first two, to find a good explanation for what she was feeling and why she wasn't ready to have sex, but Logan stopped her.

"Hey. It's okay," he said. "And it's still Valentine's Day. Let's go to the pier?"

"Please," Layla said, already feeling lighter.

Logan started the car. He pulled out of the parking lot and turned right on Pico Boulevard, heading west. "We have bomb dinner reservations tonight."

"Please tell me it's sushi . . ."

"Layla, *come on*, can you please not ruin everything?" Logan teased.

"Oh God . . ."

"Too soon?

"*Way* too soon," Layla teased back. "And I didn't ruin *everything*. There are still seven more clues, right? Six, I guess, since I know about the sushi."

"Right," Logan said with some heaviness in his voice.

Now it was Layla's turn to read between the lines . . .

She knew him well enough to know he wasn't going to give her any more clues.

"It's not that I don't *want* you to have them. But they start to get, like . . . sexy," Logan explained with a little smile, trying to make light of it. Layla nodded, letting that sink in. She tried to keep her face from looking disappointed, but she couldn't help it. "*Lay*," Logan said in a tone of voice that managed to be playful and honest and sincere all at the same time, "if it's okay for you to tell me you don't want to have sex tonight, then I think you have to be okay with me not giving you any more clues."

Layla nodded again. "I just wish the physical and the emotional weren't so tangled for you," she said as plainly as possible, but she could still hear a bit of sharpness in her voice.

"Of course they are. I think that's how it works. But that doesn't mean whatever's *not* connected isn't, you know . . . great." In Layla's head the word "great" basically sounded the same as the word "awful." "Come on, Layla, you know I love you, right? To the moon and back." Logan waited for Layla to nod before saying anything else. "And you gotta know I'm gonna love you even if . . . I mean, no matter what happens or doesn't happen tonight, but I wrote the clues when I thought we were gonna have sex, so . . ." Logan paused for another moment before asking, "We're . . . we're *not*, right?"

"I feel like you're holding out on me," Layla said, avoiding the question.

"Can I say the same thing? Or does that make me an asshole?"

"You're not an asshole, but you should tell me if you're mad—"

"I'm not *mad*, Layla, but I think I'm allowed to be, like, *disappointed* if we don't end up having sex." Layla could feel her face and all of its features sinking towards the floor. "I know you think I'm all perfect all the time, like this perfect boyfriend, but I'm really not . . ."

"No, stop that, you *are* perfect—"

"Then, why don't you want to have sex with me?!" Logan asked, finally allowing himself to get heated.

"I don't know!" Layla said loudly, filling all the space inside the car with her voice and her breath and her emotions. "It just feels like . . . *pressure*. All the clues and everything—"

"I only did all that stupid shit because you asked for it! I was ready to just do it in my car a month ago—"

"Jesus Christ, Logan, yes, I know, your *stupid* car," Layla yelled, annoyed they were even having this *conversation* in Logan's car let alone somehow still sort of entertaining the possibility of having sex in it. "I don't want to '*just* do it', but if that's what you really want, then maybe we should pull over right now—"

"Layla, stop it—"

"Why? We both know you have a condom in your glove compartment!"

"I actually have *two* condoms in my glove compartment!" Logan said, trying to calm Layla down, but the words came out of his mouth loudly—very, *very* loudly— which caused him to break into an unexpectedly big belly laugh.

Layla couldn't help but join in on the laughing too.

And before they knew it, their laughter had taken over completely, wrapping them both up in an uncontrollable fit and giving them a much-needed break in the conversation.

"What are we doing?" Logan finally managed to ask, far more softly.

"I hope we're still driving to the pier."

"Okay, good. Me too."

"I'm sorry," Layla said after a bit of a pause.

"It's called *Love Story*," Logan said after some more silence.

"What?"

"The movie with that quote, 'Love means never having to say you're sorry'? It's called *Love Story*." Layla couldn't help but think that maybe Logan had written that in one of the envelopes she wasn't going to get to read. She agreed with Logan's mom, it *was* one of the stupidest things she'd ever heard. She was in love with Logan, but she was also sorry.

Very sorry.

And she simply had to say it to him.

Then, the red light they'd been sitting at for a small eternity finally turned green, and Logan continued to drive west toward the Santa Monica Pier as if nothing had changed between them.

Even though, clearly, everything had.

127 days until graduation . . .

EMMA glanced at the stack of phones in the center of the table.

So far it was just hers and Alex's and Zoe's. There was no sign of Layla.

Normally, Layla was the first one to arrive and claim a spot in The Bigg Chill line, which was usually so long it went all the way out the door. The rest of The Crew would arrive before Layla reached the front, and they'd all order together. But today, it was Emma, Zoe, and Alex who made it all the way to the front of the line without any sign of Layla. Alex had already tried every flavor. And Bigg Chill Aaron had already filled their orders. And the girls had already claimed their usual table in the back corner. Now, the three of girls sat together, more or less in silence, picking at their yogurt, and blatantly stalling as they waited for Layla.

Just as Emma was about to ask if maybe they should

try texting or even calling, Layla came bounding through the door of The Bigg Chill, causing the welcome mat to make its familiar, happy ding-dong noise. "There she is!" Alex said, using an outside voice, "Layla Baxter, ladies and gentleman . . ." Emma applauded along with Alex, making a bit of a scene in the Sunday afternoon froyo parlor. Emma noticed that Zoe hadn't really joined in on the merriment.

LAYLA humored the girls with a bit of a wave and then beelined for the counter.

She knew she was late, but she desperately needed some froyo before she'd be able to talk to them. Luckily, Bigg Chill Aaron was waiting to take her order.

"Good timing," he said, remarking on the rare absence of the usually long line. "You want The Layla?" He didn't seem to realize that he'd called her order "The Layla" until he'd already said it. "I mean, uh, *the usual*," he corrected as quickly as he could. "Half peanut butter, half chocolate, Sno-Caps on the side?"

"Yes, please. And, for the record, I love that you just called it The Layla."

"Cool, yeah. Don't worry. I'm only, you know, *marginally* embarrassed . . ." Bigg Chill Aaron said as he flashed his sideways smile. Layla smiled back, holding his eyes for an extra moment before joining the rest of The Crew at their table.

She dropped her overnight bag on the floor.

She put her cell phone on top of the phone stack.

She pushed her bangs out of her eyes.

She stuck her spoon in her froyo and took a big bite.

And then, when she couldn't think of any more ways to delay the inevitable, she took a little inhale and finally just came out with it: "Still a virgin."

"Whoa," Zoe said softly, almost reflexively.

"Yeah." It was still sinking in for Layla, too.

"I kind of figured . . . 'cause you didn't send a sexie," Alex admitted. "Are you okay?"

Layla *was* okay.

More or less . . .

"You know I don't like it when the plan changes, even if I'm the one who changes it."

"Did . . . um . . . did you guys break up?" Emma asked carefully.

"What? No—*no!*" They hadn't broken up, and to be honest they hadn't even discussed that as a possibility, but Layla could feel the quick cadence of her words and the weight of her body language . . . she knew it was all over-compensating. The fact that Layla had to try so hard with her face and her smile and everything made her sick to her stomach or maybe even sick to her heart, which was sitting all the way down on top of her feet again.

Layla had hoped some of her heaviness might have disappeared now that she and Logan hit the snooze button on their V-card swap, but it felt like her emotions simply didn't work like that.

Layla looked over at Zoe, who looked like she was

about to burst into tears, so Layla managed to put on an even braver and happier face, so much so that her cheeks started to hurt from smiling. "I promise we're good. We still had a fun Valentine's Day—and night. We went to the pier and watched the sunset and slept at Logan's uncle's beach house in the marina, which was pretty cool. We'd never actually, like, *slept* in the same bed before."

"But he wasn't, like, mad?" Emma asked.

"Well. He wasn't *thrilled*. But I just . . . I don't know. I wasn't ready . . . He understood that."

"And then you gave him the best head of his entire life?" Alex asked even though it was more of a statement than a question.

"Duh. Twice," Layla admitted, which made her and Emma and Alex laugh.

ZOE wanted to laugh along with the other girls, but she couldn't.

Instead, a tear dropped down her cheek.

"Oh, Zo, don't . . . It's okay. Logan and I are gonna be all right. I promise."

Zoe nodded. She knew that they would. Or at least she believed Layla when she said it.

But that's not why her tears kept falling.

"What's wrong, Zo?" Emma asked.

"I, um . . . ," Zoe started to say, but a few more tears fell down her face before she could push any more words out of her lips. "I don't even know why I'm crying. I mean, *I know* . . . but . . ." The girls waited lovingly as Zoe took a deep a breath and then finally explained herself.

"Austin and I had sex yesterday."

"Whoa."

"What?"

"Zoe . . ."

"Yep." Zoe could feel even more tears bubbling up and then pouring down her cheeks. She hated that she was cry-ing. "Sorry I'm such a girl . . ."

"Hey. No. Do *not* apologize for being a girl," Alex said sternly. "Or for crying, either. You don't get any bonus points for pretending not to have emotions. Tears are so important. And totally underrated." It wasn't the sort of thing Zoe would expect Alex to say. Most of the time Alex protected her thoughts and feelings, bottling them up inside, which made her words seem even more true and important.

"Why didn't you tell us when it happened?" Layla asked.

The simple answer was that Zoe hadn't wanted to step on Layla's big day. She and Logan had been planning to do it for so long . . . and it all just happened so fast with her and Austin. She figured she would text The Chat after Layla did, but then Layla never did.

"I'm sorry," Zoe said again. "Not for crying," she clari-fied, almost laughing a little through her tears. She still didn't know exactly what was making her cry. She wasn't sad, exactly, but it felt like she was having a lot of emotions all at once. All of the feels, apparently. And they were all showing up in her eyes and then falling down her cheeks. She simply couldn't stop them.

"If you don't want to talk about it . . . ," Layla said.

"No, I do," Zoe replied. She could feel that *not* talking about it had actually been making her feel worse, as if having sex with Austin were some sort of secret, which it wasn't. Or as if she'd done something wrong, which she hadn't. Zoe told the story as completely as she could, giving Layla and the girls the "full mental picture." She started from the beginning, explaining how she had been giving Austin head and how he'd mentioned wanting to have sex . . . and how she said she did too. And how, even though they hadn't talked about it before, they couldn't think of a reason not to do it right then and there, except that Austin wasn't sure whether or not he had a condom. Zoe said she didn't want to have sex if he didn't have one, so literally he ripped his entire room apart until he managed to find one tucked in the back of a drawer on his nightstand. Zoe went to the bathroom to freshen up, and when she came out Austin had cleaned up his room the best he could and lit a bunch of candles to try and set some sort of mood. It was afternoon, so it was still light outside and the candles weren't all that effective, but it was a nice, sort of romantic gesture— except that one of the candles smelled like a pumpkin spice latte, and Zoe had to blow it out because it just kept making her think of Thanksgiving dinner, which was a decidedly unsexy thought. After they figured out the candle situation, Austin turned on some music on his phone. It was a song Zoe had heard before but she couldn't quite remember the name. It certainly wasn't a song that Zoe would've picked to listen to, especially not at a moment like this, but she'd been so particular about the pumpkin candle she decided to let it slide.

After that, everything felt like it happened at the same time. Zoe and Austin were kissing and then they were naked and then Austin put on the condom. The good news was that Austin seemed to know what he was doing, or at least what he was *trying* to do. He'd had sex a few times before, but it took him a minute to line everything up just right. . . . Once Austin found the proper angle and body position and all that, he managed to successfully push inside of her, but it wasn't very graceful. Zoe decided it was probably whatever the exact *opposite* of graceful is . . . Clumsy? Ugly? Awkward? Probably all of the above combined.

"Yeah, it's definitively not pretty." Emma laughed.

"Ohmigod, I can't even imagine what we actually must've *looked* like . . ."

"Whatever. The real question is did you like it?" Layla asked after a little bit more laughing.

Zoe had to think about that.

The truth was that it felt . . . well . . . it felt better once Austin found a rhythm.

After a little bit of time had passed, he had stopped to ask if she was okay. She was—and she said she was. And then he asked if it felt good. She knew he wanted her to tell him that it felt amazing or something all big and perfect like that, but that truth was that it actually kind of hurt. But she still told him it felt okay, which was more or less true—or at least true enough—and so Austin kept going. And then, after a few more minutes—or maybe just one more minute, Zoe wasn't sure exactly—it really did start to feel more painful than pleasureful, and Zoe felt like maybe Austin's penis was just too big for her vagina, which, under normal circumstances, might've made her giggle, except that right then whatever was happening really did *actually* start to hurt—*a lot, way* more than it had even just a moment before.

Zoe was about to ask him to stop or at least take a break, but before she could, he said he was gonna cum—and he did.

He fireworked.

Zoe, unsurprisingly, didn't.

But she did feel a whole rush of emotions. Predominately she was proud that she had just made Austin do that. She was proud that she'd made him look like that and feel that way, all primal and euphoric . . . but then she had two more overwhelming thoughts at the very same time. One was that she didn't feel that same way he did (even though maybe she wanted to) and the other was that she hadn't *actually* done much of anything at all. Austin had done most of it. He was the one moving or thrusting or whatever it was exactly. Zoe had just been on her back, lying on the bed, trying to figure out whether or not it hurt . . .

Afterward they'd cleaned up and Zoe'd snapped a sexie that she never ended up sending.

And that was it.

And it was only then, as Zoe got to the end of the whole

story, that she realized she hadn't answered Layla's original question: Did she like it?

Honestly?

She still wasn't entirely sure.

"That's okay," Emma reaffirmed. "It's a lot."

Yeah. It *was* a lot. Zoe certainly didn't *regret* what had happened, but the reality of it was more than she had anticipated.

"Do you want to do it again?" Layla asked rather carefully.

"Not today," Zoe said with a little laugh. "But, yeah. I do."

A few hours later Zoe found herself standing in front of her bathroom mirror. She was wrapped in a towel, freshly showered, staring at her reflection. She'd seen this same reflection a million times before, but tonight she wondered if she looked any different. Would anyone be able to tell that she wasn't a virgin anymore? Probably not, she thought. She looked the same to herself. Same pale. Same red. Same frizz and freckles and all that.

Then a new text message from Austin had just appeared on her phone: *Hi sexy*

Zoe looked back at her reflection.

She didn't *feel* particularly sexy.

It was ironic, she thought, to feel like she knew *less* now than she did before she had sex, or maybe now she just understood that there was still so much more to know. And it made her think about "I Know Things Now," the song from *Into the Woods* that had been echoing in her head. The very last lyric of the song said that it was "nice to know a lot . . . and a little bit not."

Now *that* is how Zoe felt: nice and also not.

Both, simultaneously.

Hi, she texted back.

Thinking about you, Austin responded quickly.

Aw, that's sweet, she thought.

But *then* she thought about what exactly he might be thinking about . . . and laughed as she realized that, yes, Austin really was a sweet guy, and yes, she was sure his intentions were good, but mostly, *yes*, she was sure his thoughts were most likely dirty, too.

And she liked that.

But, then again, she also did not.

118 days until graduation . . .

ALEX was running out of time.

Literally.

Lately she'd been spending as much time as she could on the track, but it still felt like there would never be enough runway to run as fast as she needed to run in order to break the record.

"You gotta believe!" Coach K said, or almost *scolded*, as Alex pulled off her track shoes after practice on Tuesday.

"I do believe . . . ," Alex grumbled.

"Then why don't I believe *you*?"

"I don't know!" Alex said.

At least that sounded like an honest answer.

More than anything, Alex wanted to clear her mind and just focus on her feet, but it didn't work like that. She had a whole body of parts in between that needed attention. And she still had to show up at school every day. And Oliver was still her car pool driver, and they were still riding to school together, even though they hadn't actually *spoken* since Valentine's Day. And it was fine, really. But then again it also really wasn't. And they were just both so stubborn, Alex was starting to think they might never speak to each other ever again.

But. As was the case with so many of her thoughts and plans, Alex was mistaken.

"Hi," Oliver said far too casually as she approached the parking lot. He was sitting on the hood of his car, his hair still wet from a recent shower.

"Hello," Alex replied with enough emphasis to let him know she was surprised to be *hearing* from him let alone seeing him here and apparently waiting for her.

"You need a ride?"

"I'm okay," Alex said, trying to give him a nice but firm brush-off.

"Are you though? Really?" Oliver pressed. "Are *we*?"

"We?"

"Obviously you're mad at me—"

"Why would I be mad at you? It's not like you said you wanted to hang out on Valentine's Day and then spent the whole night before making out with some other girl—"

"It was mostly *adrenaline*."

"That's a lame excuse."

"I wished it was you the whole time," Oliver insisted, sounding even lamer. Alex rolled her eyes. "I don't care if you think that sounds like a line. It's the truth."

"Yeah, well, the problem with you is that it's too hard to tell the difference."

Oliver nodded, absorbing that. It didn't seem like he was going to try to argue. "You sure you don't need a ride home?" he asked finally.

"I'm sure," Alex said as convincingly as she possibly could.

The good news was that her words and her feelings were actually one and the same. She didn't need a ride home—and she honestly didn't need Oliver, either. Right now she didn't *need* much of anything, and that was a phenomenal feeling. As she watched him drive away, she couldn't help but think that maybe this would be the first day of the rest of the year. Maybe now she was ready to wholeheartedly believe in herself and get over her fears and have enough faith and finally break the track record and all of that.

Or maybe not.

Maybe Alex should just get used to feeling more wrong than right.

Her phone buzzed. Oliver had sent her a new text message.

Two text messages, actually.

The first said: *it is bigger, I swear*

The second was a picture of his penis.

Alex understood dick pics even less than she understood hickeys. She didn't see the point. It seemed to turn boys on way more to send them than it did for her—or any girls she knew—to actually get them . . . *Ugh*. Now Alex couldn't help but wonder how many other girls had already gotten this very same picture from Oliver.

She deleted it without even really looking at it.

Well.

No.

That was a lie.

She looked at it for about ten seconds first.

Maybe twenty.

But the whole time she was looking, a jumble of thoughts raced through her head. She wondered why he had sent it to her exactly and what he was thinking about when he took it and what he thought *she* would be thinking about when she saw it . . . and then also what she was *actually* thinking, which was a two part answer mixed together as one: the first part was that his penis was larger than she had expected—not that she was expecting it in the first place, but still, it was—and the second was that she didn't think penises were particularly sexy looking. At least not in pictures. As far as pictures were concerned, she was far more impressed by abs or lips or maybe even just a piercing set of eyes. Alex could imagine that some other girls might *like* getting this kind of picture. Maybe some other girls would even be turned on by it, and that was all fine or good or whatever, but Alex knew she wasn't one of those girls.

After what could not have possibly been more then thirty seconds—*tops*—she finally deleted Oliver's picture. And she definitely did not text him back.

Of course, that didn't stop him from texting her again.

And again and again.

He wanted a picture of her in return.

Of course he did.

117 days until graduation . . .

LAYLA never got anything important in the mail.

Her parents got bills and junk and the occasional party invitation, but no one ever sent Layla anything important.

Until today.

The University of Southern California wasn't just Layla's first choice school, it was basically her *only* choice. Layla's parents had gone to school there. It's where they met and fell in love, and it was the only school Layla had ever wanted to go to. Now Layla sat on her bed looking at the envelope. It was big and thick and proudly stamped with an emblem from USC. Layla knew it was good news. You didn't get a thick envelope unless it was an acceptance. She knew her parents would be thrilled. And her siblings, too. And all her teachers. And The Crew, of course. The only person she wasn't entirely sure about was Logan. Things had been decidedly different between them since Valentine's Day.

"Obviously, I'm ready—whenever you are," Logan had said the next time they sat off campus after one of their usual off campus make-out sessions. Layla knew that. But she also knew she still wasn't, so they decided it would happen whenever it was supposed to happen.

"We're releasing the plan," Layla told the girls at lunch a few days later. They all nodded and laughed—and she knew they all only sort of believed her.

And then, as luck or the universe or whoever would have it, Layla ended up with an empty house that very same night. Her parents and siblings were all out and about and all she had to do was text Logan, and he could've come over, and they could've closed any of the doors—or all of the doors—and done whatever they wanted in any room or on any bed or anywhere . . .

. . . But she didn't text Logan.

And she felt guilty about not doing it, but not nearly as guilty as she would've if he'd driven all the way to her empty house, with the two condoms in his glove compartment, and then she still hadn't been able to do it with him. It seemed simpler to just avoid the situation altogether.

Today, however, she texted Logan to come over as soon as she got home from school and saw the big envelope waiting for her. Logan had to stay late. Something about a student council project. Layla wasn't really sure. She had been too consumed by the envelope.

The one that now sat between them on her trampoline. "This is it," she said solemnly.

"You might want to actually open it before you start

225

making too many big, emotional plans."

"Whatever it says, you're still gonna be in Philadelphia next year," Layla said.

"Please just open it," Logan pushed, not wanting to have that conversation again.

As Layla went to open the envelope, she noticed that the last remnant of her Valentine's Day manicure was still clinging to her nails. The coat of red polish that had looked perfect just a couple weeks ago was now all chipped and fading. Now it was all just a mess.

Layla couldn't help but think that was thematically appropriate.

"'Congratulations, Layla Baxter,'" she read out loud from the letter.

"Yay!" Logan cheered, interrupting her. "Victory!!" he yelled, holding up his fingers up in the shape of a V. "Is this what they do? That victory thing?"

"I don't know . . ."

"Layla, come on. Since I've known you, all you've talked about is going to school at USC. 'Congratulations' means you did it! Why do you look so miserable? Are you going to tell me what's wrong or do I have to guess?"

"Nothing is wrong," she tried to lie.

It didn't work.

"We've known we were gonna be on opposite sides of the country next year for *months*," Logan said. "What did you think was going to happen?"

Layla shook her head. She didn't know. She had done her best to mentally prepare for this moment. She knew

it was coming, but the reality of it still hurt. Now, officially: Logan was going to spend the next four years in
Philadelphia and Layla was not.

She could feel all of her emotions creeping up on her,
washing over her. She felt powerless to stop them. She felt
disconnected from Logan and all the things she thought
she'd wanted so badly even just a few weeks ago.

And so.

When Logan said he wanted to take a break, Layla had
no choice but to agree with him.

The words had blindsided her, knocking the breath out
of her chest and the blood out of her brain, dislodging the
tears from behind her eyes . . . but, deep down, Layla had
to admit she'd seen it coming. "Okay," she said.

"You agree?"

"No. But I understand why you're saying it." Actually,
she didn't. She didn't understand. That was a lie, and Layla
really was an absolutely horrible liar.

"I love you to the moon and back," Logan said the way
he always did. Layla knew that he meant it, he really did
love her, but maybe that just wasn't enough anymore. "I
just . . . ," he tried to explain, trailing off.

"I just won't sleep with you," Layla said, completing
his sentence.

"Stop," Logan said sharply.

"If I said, 'Let's go right now,' I don't think you'd be
walking out the door."

"Layla, *obviously* I want to have sex with you! Right
now? Tomorrow? Since the first day I laid eyes on you?

Yes, *please*, let's have sex. But. Clearly, I can't do it *without* you, and you don't want to do it *with* me, so . . ."

Layla didn't know quite what to say anymore. She wiped a tear from her eye before it could fall down her cheek, but Logan saw it. And he heard it loud and clear.

He took a break.

He took a breath.

He ran his fingers through his hair.

And then he softened his voice and started again as sweetly as he possibly could. "I'm not trying to make you feel worse than you already do."

"I know," Layla said.

She really did know that part.

"But don't you think it says something that you *didn't* want to sleep with me—and that you still don't? This isn't me trying to pressure you, I swear. This is just me. And I'm just saying I think there's a reason you aren't feeling it . . ."

Now all the tears were streaming down Layla's checks. She couldn't wipe them away fast enough. Logan watched her cry, giving her the time and space and silence that she needed. Layla appreciated him more in this moment than she had in a very long time.

"I'm sorry," she finally managed to say.

"I hate seeing you cry, but you're pretty damn adorable while you do it, so it's confusing . . ." Logan smiled a sad, little smile. For the first time ever even his dimple looked sad. And his face, too. It was full of appreciation. And love. And a little bit of loss.

Layla felt the same way.

"It's all the feels . . . ," she said, almost beginning to laugh through the tears.

She loved *and* hated this feeling so much.

"It is . . . ," Logan agreed, quickly trailing off before any more words could come out of his mouth. It was the first time Layla thought *he* might actually cry too. And then that made her eyes burst into a fresh, new set of tears. Fully explosive waterworks. And it wasn't *just* because of Logan. It was everything. The Crew. The end. The pact. The plan. It was all of it, and now it was all streaming down her face and staining her cheeks and causing a giant snot bubble to slip out from her nose. It was an ugly cry at its ugliest. And Layla needed it.

"I love you, Layla," Logan said again after enough time had passed. This time, his words sounded like the good-bye that they were. "And I always want to have love for you. But I'm worried if we don't break now . . ."

"Do you want to break? Or break up?" Layla asked.

"I don't want to let it get so bad that I feel like I'm going to really lose you."

"You don't have to lose me at all," Layla said after some silence.

But Logan had already made up his mind.

This was it.

After he left, it took Layla two hours and fourteen minutes to text The Chat. Layla didn't want to text them, but she knew that she had to. She knew that was the part that would make it feel real. That was the part that would hurt the most.

And it did.

She didn't text Logan again, though.

She couldn't.

She also couldn't eat dinner.

Or talk to anyone.

She couldn't do much of anything except watch the minutes tick off the clock. And listen to her sobs. And feel all her tears. And then the phantom tears too. The ones that didn't actually fall after all of the real tears had already rolled down her cheeks. Layla felt like there should still be more tears, but there just literally wasn't any more salt water left in her entire body. Layla didn't know there was a limit to that sort of thing. But apparently there was.

Apparently, maybe, there was a limit to *every* sort of thing.

Even love, she thought.

Maybe, she hated to think, *especially love*.

115 days until graduation...

EMMA understood the importance of a good distraction.

"Savannah is having a big birthday party tomorrow night," Emma said as they sat at their lunch table. "At her dad's. Her friend's gonna DJ. We should go. It's gonna be awesome and I'm sure Savannah would appreciate it." Emma hadn't really told the girls all that much about Savannah. They knew she worked on the yearbook and the newspaper, but besides the facts Emma hadn't shared all that much. Mostly it was because, Emma being Emma, she didn't know what to say *exactly*, but she knew that she wanted them to come with her to her birthday party. But Alex already had a *Star Wars* movie date with her brother, Max, and Zoe had an actual date with Austin. Layla tried to say she was going to stay in and watch a movie, but Emma shot that down really quickly.

"Nope," Emma insisted.

"Nope?"

"Friends don't let friends throw themselves pity parties."

"I'm not throwing anything . . ."

"Exactly. You're coming with me to Savannah's. You need to." It had only been about forty-eight hours since she and Logan broke up, but Layla was barely functioning. She was still referring to the whole thing as a "break" even though it was very clearly and definitively a breakup. It's not like any of the girls expected Layla to be all "okay" all of a sudden or anything, but this was worse than Emma had ever seen. She knew Layla needed a push in the right direction. "And the truth is I'm really not asking you to come with me, I'm telling you. It's time to get up, dress up, show up."

"Oh, look at you, using some of my favorite words against me . . ."

Yep. Emma knew exactly what she was doing. She rattled off a few more of Layla's favorite sayings for good measure. "Fake it till you make it. No one can make you feel inferior without your consent. Be gentle to your precious little soul."

"O-kay. Serenity now. I hear you," Layla said, finally cracking a smile.

114 days until graduation . . .

LAYLA did not want to go to Savannah's party.

At all.

But she also knew Emma was right. She had to do something. Moping wasn't going to get her anywhere and at least once she and Emma got to the party, and drank some beer, Layla stopped feeling so sorry for herself . . . she had to admit she was having a marginally good time.

At least a much better time than she had expected.

To be fair, most of the goodness was because of Wyatt, the cute boy she'd been talking to for the past ten minutes. Wyatt went to Venice High School. He owned a skateboard and a surfboard and a guitar. And he had longish blond hair that kept falling in front of his eyes. When Emma first saw him approaching, she made a joke that he could be the Ken to Layla's Barbie. Layla wasn't looking for a Ken—she wasn't looking for *anything*, honestly, and couldn't stop thinking about Logan—but Wyatt's grin had managed to occupy at least a little space in Layla's brain, and Emma forced an introduction and then had somehow managed to slip away, saying she needed a beer refill, and just never came back. So far it was all working out fine. Wyatt was easy to talk to and even easier to look at, and just as Layla began to think that this enjoyable moment might be a sign from the universe, a reminder that she needed to trust the timing of her life and accept that Logan was right about needing to take a break slash breakup . . .

. . . it happened.

It started simply enough.

Wyatt called her a cutie, which wasn't even all that remarkable as far as compliments go, but she couldn't remember the last time she got a compliment from a boy who *wasn't* Logan. She could feel the heat in her cheeks. And her heartbeat. It all made her look down at her feet and the floor and the Ping-Pong ball that just happened to be rolling down the hallway. It rolled under the kitchen table until it came to an abrupt stop next to *Logan's* sneaker. Her first thought was that she wasn't expecting to see Logan at the party, but then she couldn't help but think about the stupid Ping-Pong ball. She wondered why he wasn't bending down to pick it up . . . until her eyes drifted up *his* legs which led her to *Vanessa Martin's* legs and then to Vanessa's skirt and her hips, which were on top of Logan's jeans and his hips, and then to Vanessa's hands, which were basically *under* Logan's shirt, and Layla couldn't tell whose tongue was in whose mouth, but it looked like the answer was that both of their tongues were in each other's mouths at the very same time, and the whole thing was the absolute worst thing she had ever seen.

"You okay?" Wyatt asked, mostly oblivious to the situation.

Layla managed a little nod. She also managed to put her number in Wyatt's phone. But that was all she could do. She had to get out of there. Immediately. But just before she could make her way out of the living room, Logan pulled away from Vanessa and looked up just long enough to catch Layla's eyes. She could feel her her cheeks turning red and her lips begin to quiver.

Clearly Logan wasn't expecting to see her tonight either.

EMMA walked through the party, looking for Savannah.

She didn't really know anybody else here, but she recognized everyone's faces and knew most of their names. She'd seen all of their yearbook pictures. She knew which clubs they were in and what they wore to school dances and which Superlatives they'd been awarded, but she didn't actually *know* them. Before Emma could get lost in a drunken thought pattern about how hard it was to actually know anyone in this big, crazy world, her phone started buzzing.

The Chat was blowing up: Layla had just seen Logan with his tongue in Vanessa's mouth. It was very possible she was going to puke. Zoe and Austin had just sex for the second time. The whole thing was an upgrade from the first time even though Zoe still didn't feel any fireworks. And the *Millennium Falcon* had just been captured by the

Death Star's tractor beam. Alex felt like it wasn't going to end well. Alex had been live-texting the entire *Star Wars* movie. None of the girls had the heart to tell her they didn't really care about Han Solo and his new hope or whatever. Emma tried to contribute to the conversation, but the texts were pouring in too fast and furious: Logan's stupid lips. Zoe's lack of fireworks. Princess Leia's hair.

"Let's dance like no one's watching," Savannah said as she slid up behind Emma, "'cause, you know, they're actually *not*, since everyone's just on their phones all the time." Emma looked up. Her face had, in fact, been buried entirely in her phone screen. "How's The Chat?" Savannah asked knowingly.

"It's, um . . . *drama*," Emma said as she texted Layla, asking where she was.

"Dance with me," Savannah said. She grabbed Emma's hand and pulled her out into the backyard and onto the makeshift dance floor. "I like this song," she yelled over the music.

"Me too. What is it?"

"No clue."

Emma started to reach for her phone so she could look up the song, but Savannah stopped her, reaching out to touch her hand. "Or . . . how 'bout let's just appreciate that we don't know?"

Emma appreciated everything about Savannah all at once. And she felt like the feeling was mutual. And then all of a sudden Emma and Savannah lost track of time and space and got lost in the music and the moment, until everything else just seemed to slip away . . .

. . . and even though Emma was very tipsy, and literally slipping and sliding across the damp grass, she felt grounded in this moment. Her drunken thoughts were crystal clear as she thought about all of the times she'd thought about Savannah's lips and their particular shade of pink . . .

They were perfect, Emma thought. Savannah's lips are absolutely perfect.

There was really nothing left to do but kiss them.

113 days until graduation...

LAYLA speared a heap of Sno-Caps with her spoon.

"I don't care about Logan and Vanessa," she said, trying as hard as she possibly could to sound like she *actually* didn't care, even though she knew that the girls—or Bigg Chill Aaron or any other stranger in The Bigg Chill who might be able to overhear her overcompensating—could tell that was a total lie. Everybody always knew when Layla was lying. Zoe, Emma, and Alex had all turned their attention back to their froyo flavors—vanilla, strawberry, and salted caramel chocolate, respectively. It felt like they were all trying to come up with a new topic of conversation, but before anyone could say anything new, Layla had already freaked out about Logan and Vanessa again . . . "Do you think they had sex in his car last night?"

"No," Alex said certainly.

"How do you know? Logan has two condoms in his glove compartment, maybe he only has one now . . ."

"I don't know for sure that they didn't, but I really don't think so. It's way more likely that she gave him road head on the way home."

"Alex—"

"What?"

"Not helping . . . ," Zoe tried to whisper.

"No. It's okay, she's probably right," Layla agreed, "but they are probably *going to* have lots of sex, and I'm just *not*—and that's . . . that's fine, that's just how it is . . ."

"Wait, you're 'just not' what?" Zoe asked quickly.

"I don't know . . ." Layla exhaled, not wanting to say something she'd regret. She turned her attention to Emma. "Was Savannah upset we left early? I just couldn't deal."

"Oh no, she wasn't," Emma said. "I don't think."

EMMA hadn't really talked to Savannah since that moment on the dance floor.

That moment where she *kissed* Savannah on the dance floor.

By the time Layla walked over, with her cheeks all red and her lips still quivering, Emma and Savannah were done kissing and had mostly stopped dancing too. They were just standing and staring at each other. Emma hadn't been sure what to do next, and Savannah hadn't said or done much of anything, but Layla was saying and doing more than enough for everyone. Logan had followed her outside, and he wanted to talk to her, but all she wanted to do was leave. *Immediately.* So they did. Emma felt bad about the kiss-and-run, but she had to take care of Layla. It was her fault she was at Savannah's party in the first place.

Once Emma got home, after spending some time on Layla's trampoline, letting her ugly cry and angry jump, she texted Savannah to say that she was sorry and that she hoped she had a good birthday and a good night. Savannah had texted her back that it was *all good*—and that was it.

Since then, Emma estimated, rather conservatively, she'd replayed their dance floor kiss about a million times.

It's possible it was the very best first kiss she'd ever had.

Or it might've just been drunken and sloppy and confused.

But definitely one of the two.

Or possibly both.

Whatever it was—or wasn't—Emma didn't mention it at the froyo table.

After the girls left The Bigg Chill, Emma found herself driving over to Savannah's house. She didn't know what she was going to say or do exactly, but she knew she needed to go there. She had to. She pulled to a stop in front of the house and sat for a minute, still processing all of her thoughts. All of which were about Savannah. Most of them were about her lips. She could still taste her cherry ChapStick, and, *yes*, she could basically hear the girl-kissing pop song playing on repeat inside her head . . . but this wasn't just a song.

It was real.

The most real.

Most of the time when Emma kissed someone, she felt like she was giving something away to the other person.

And not just, like, her literal spit and saliva, but something beyond that. Something intangible. Like her emotions or her expectations, maybe.

But this kiss felt different.

Yes, it was only *one* kiss.

And yes, it was drunken and fast and maybe a little bit stupid . . .

But it also felt like . . . *more*.

Yep.

That was it.

Emma felt like she had pulled away from her kiss with Savannah with so much more than she had leaned in with in the first place.

But, then again, a lot of that "more" might simply be confusion.

Savannah knocked on Emma's window, disrupting her rambling thoughts.

Emma rolled down the window.

"What are you doing here?" Savannah asked. Before Emma could answer that, Savannah followed up with. "How was froyo?"

"Good. Really good."

"Yeah? What did the girls have to say?" Emma felt like Savannah was asking specifically what they said about their kiss or maybe what they said about her, but either way Savannah could see the answer on Emma's face. "You didn't tell them . . ."

All Emma could think to say was that she was sorry.

"For what?" Savannah asked with a laugh.

Such a good question, Emma thought.

For not knowing the answer exactly?

For feeling too many feelings at once?

For being an absolute mess of a person.

"I don't want it to be weird," Emma said after a moment.

"I think it's a little late for that." Savannah smiled.

"Yeah, no, I mean, obviously *I'm* weird . . . I just don't want you to think that every time we're, like, sitting at the computers in the yearbook room or on the school bus or wherever, I'm suddenly gonna lean over and kiss you . . ."

"Oh . . ."

"Or that I'm even *thinking* about kissing you . . ."

"I thought you were always thinking about kissing everyone."

Oh, yep.

Now, *that* was it.

Emma felt a strange sense of relief, as she realized that Savannah was absolutely right. She *was* always thinking about that. Always. So maybe the kiss wasn't just drunken and sloppy—and maybe it wasn't the best, either. Maybe it wasn't even really a kiss after all. Maybe it was just Emma and all her inside weirdness spilling out into the real world and onto Savannah's lips. That didn't necessarily mean that it was *about* Savannah's lips. Or at least not the fact that they were *her* lips. Whatever it was, Emma was really glad that she and Savannah had been able to talk about everything and straighten everything out. It wasn't until a few minutes later, once Emma had driven away and had a chance to replay the whole conversation in her head, that she realized they hadn't straightened anything out.

Honestly, they hadn't even had much of a talk at all.

ZOE was tired of talking about orgasms.

She wanted to have one.

Now that she'd had sex *twice*, she was absolutely certain that having sex and having an orgasm were *not* the same thing. Not even close, unfortunately.

Her second time with Austin had been better than the first. It lasted a little longer and hurt a little less, but it wasn't . . . well, it still wasn't as much *fun* as she wanted it to be—or as much fun for her as it seemed to be for Austin.

He looked like he was having a lot of fun. With his body . . . his face . . . his eyes . . .

Zoe wanted to look and feel like that too.

Apparently, she was going to have to take matters into her own hands.

Literally.

And so . . .

Zoe lay in bed that night—and laughed at herself. Zoe knew a lot about her body. She knew which foods tasted good or what gave her an upset stomach, but she honestly didn't have the first clue about what would make her orgasm. And *that's* what was making her laugh.

Okay, she thought to herself after the laughing had stopped. *How hard can this be?*

She put her right hand on right boob and her left hand on her left boob, cupping each one. She squeezed . . . and squeezed again . . . then simply had to laugh some more.

She wanted to ask if she was doing this right. And she *did* ask, in her head anyway. But that only made her laugh even harder, because she certainly didn't know the answer—she was the one asking the question in the first place!

Zoe realized pretty quickly that whatever she was doing with her boobs wasn't actually doing much of anything for her hope of future fireworks, so she moved her fingers onto her nipples . . . which got hard quickly when she squeezed and rubbed them, *so quickly*, in fact, that it seemed strange to Zoe that her nipples didn't get hard more often or that they weren't just somehow, like, automatically hard all the time. After a little more touching and rubbing and attempting to listen to her body, Zoe finally—*fi-nal-lyy*—felt like she was getting somewhere.

Zoe felt good. And soon her whole body felt good. And she could tell which parts of it wanted more attention than others. And right now, all of that "good" made her reach down into her pajama pants and then into her underwear and actually into her*self*, which seemed like an odd way to be thinking about what she was doing with her fingers, but it was also an entirely accurate description of the situation—and the more she did it, the better it felt, which was the whole entire point, so Zoe tried as hard as she could not to be critical of herself and her feelings. . . .

And then: her phone rang.

She ignored it.

She was far too focused for phone calls.

It was probably just Austin. Or one of the girls. Even

though . . . she couldn't help but think that none of them ever actually called her.

Whatever.

Whatever it was, it could wait.

But then, her phone rang again.

Zoe glanced at the clock.

It was exactly 11:11.

Of course it was . . .

She touched her hand to her lips and then to the clock and then back to her lips again, and that's when she realized, thanks to a slightly salty aftertaste, that the last thing she'd touched with her hand had been her vagina, and all of a sudden she was overwhelmed by a bout of giggles . . . and all the while, Zoe's phone was still ringing, and the clock still said 11:11, and her hand still smelled like her underwear, and life was totally strange and ridiculously amazing, and she was both proud of herself and embarrassed for herself at the very same time, and all the while she couldn't seem to stop laughing . . .

Somehow she managed to glance over at her phone and see Dylan's name on the screen, and she was already missing him and their phonefalls and everything, and so without overthinking it any further than she already had, she picked up the phone.

"Hello," she said with a giggle.

"Hey . . . ," Dylan said. "You okay?"

"Oh yeah . . . I'm . . ." Zoe tried to control her laughter, but her blood was all still pumping faster than usual.

"What are you doing?" Dylan asked, sounding as if he

had *almost* managed to put the pieces together.

"Um, you know, I'm just . . . ," Zoe said, focusing on slowing down her breathing. Deep breath in. Deep breath out.

Dylan heard the breaths, and the tone in Zoe's voice and suddenly it clicked. "Zoe. Reed," he said deliberately. "Sorry if I'm . . . *interrupting*."

"What? *No.* There's nothing . . . you're not . . ."

"You sure about that?" Dylan laughed.

No.

Zoe wasn't sure about anything.

She wasn't sure what she was doing or if it really felt good or even why she'd picked up the phone exactly. "I just . . . I'd been wanting to talk to you, and I saw you were calling."

"It's cool," Dylan said without any judgment in his voice. "And . . . whatever you're doing right now, I think you should know that I, um, I like it, and I'm gonna let you get back to it."

Zoe wanted to say that she didn't want to get back to it or need to get back to it, but that would've been a lie. She wanted to. And so she would. And a very small part of Zoe also wanted to ask Dylan to stay on the phone with her while she did, but she couldn't say that, either.

Extending that kind of invitation would mean crossing an uncrossable line.

She wasn't going to do that right now.

Not to Dylan. Not to Austin. And not to herself either.

110 days until graduation . . .

EMMA had expected things would go back to normal with Savannah . . .

. . . but they still hadn't.

She wasn't sure if it was the dance floor kiss itself or the conversation they'd had in front of Savannah's house the following afternoon that had thrown everything out of whack, but something between them just wasn't the same anymore.

It used to be all easy and effortless.

Now everything felt rather strained and calculated.

Savannah stayed after school on Wednesday to cover the varsity water polo match for the paper. Emma stayed too. To take pictures for the yearbook. The girls spent most of the match standing only about ten feet apart, watching the game and taking notes and snapping pictures, but the distance between them might as well have been a mile. Afterward, Savannah headed back to the yearbook room to type up her notes. Emma followed after her. "My HD card is full," she said out loud as an explanation.

"You don't have to make up excuses to keep hanging out with me."

"What?" Emma asked, hoping Savannah would stop and talk to her for a minute.

She didn't.

Instead, she kept walking and talking, forcing Emma to pick up the pace. "You have an open invitation to hang out with me. If you want to stay for the water polo match, if you want to come to the yearbook room, if you want to sit and do nothing, then fine, let's do it, but you don't have to make things up," Savannah said all at once. It wasn't her usual tone of voice or the usual kinds of words she used to talk to Emma, and Emma didn't like the way it sounded as it came out of her mouth. But when Emma opened *her* mouth to try and respond, all her thoughts just came out with the sound of a giant whistle. It was the whistle that finally made Savannah stop walking. She turned back to look at Emma. "What is happening?" she asked, clearly exasperated.

"What do you mean?" Emma asked just as sharply.

"I mean, what the hell are you doing right now?"

"I don't know! I don't ever know what I'm doing! Ever!" Emma shouted. "I don't even know why I was just shouting," she added, lowering her voice again.

Then.

After what felt like the longest silence in the history of

silences, Savannah finally managed to say what they were both thinking:

"It wasn't weird."

"The kiss," Emma whispered back. The two little words came out of her mouth so softly she wasn't sure Savannah would even hear them.

"You don't have to pretend you didn't like it," Savannah said, using her normal voice volume again.

"I'm not pretending. I'm here—"

"Yeah, you're here, but only because you're making excuses—"

"Okay, okay," Emma said, stepping closer to Savannah. She reached out and touched her arm, as if to make sure she wasn't going to walk away again. "I'm . . . you know, I've been having a hard time with senior year and everything . . ." Savannah waited for Emma to find some more words, but after a few moments she could only manage two more. "It's not . . ."

"What? It's not you, it's me?" Savannah teased. "You're such a giant, boring cliché, Emma O'Malley."

"So maybe I am. But high school is almost over, and I feel like I know even *less* now than I did when I started, even though it feels like everyone is expecting me to just, like, magically be this whole person all of a sudden . . ."

"Emma. Stop. Look . . . I hate to have to be the one to break this to you, but you're *already* a whole person. It's not 'all of a sudden.' It's *already* happened. Like, right now, in this *actual* sudden—"

"Actual sudden? That is not a real phrase—"

"Yeah, well, for actual and for real: You are already a fully formed human. You can still be in process or whatever. I think we all are . . . but you're still already you."

"Thank you."

"Do you hear me though?"

"I think so," Emma said, even though she wasn't sure.

"You're already you—and you're already magical, so can we agree that whatever *this* is . . . is already good too?"

"Yes." Emma nodded. Savannah's use of the word "magical" was still echoing inside her head. She didn't just *hear* that part, she felt it.

"Okay. So. Then. Are we . . . ?"

"Savannah. If you try to '*expectation*' me right now, I swear . . ."

"No, no," Savannah said quickly, "I wouldn't dare do that to you."

Good, Emma thought.

Right now, for the first time in a long time, all of her thoughts were mostly clear and genuinely good.

Now *that* felt like some actual progress.

ZOE was surprised to see Dylan standing in front of her house.

He had texted her about an hour ago, saying that he needed to see her. And now here he was, standing on the sidewalk at 9:00 p.m. on a Wednesday night.

"What's up?" she asked. "Another mix CD?"

"I can't stop thinking about you."

Zoe wasn't expecting that.

"And," he added, nervously biting his lip, "I can't stop thinking about the other night . . . and how you picked up the phone while you were—"

"Ohmigod, Dylan. I swear to God if you say it out loud—"

"Okay, I won't . . . ," Dylan said as his whole face turned into a smile. "But I do want to say that . . . I think there's a reason you picked up."

"I picked up because you were calling me for the first time in *weeks*—"

"Yeah, but . . . I know you're attracted to me—"

"Oh, okay. Thank you—"

"—and I know I'm attracted to you, too! That's it. That's why I'm here. I can't stop thinking about you."

Zoe let Dylan's words hang in the air for a moment.

She'd never heard him say anything like that before. Not even close. She waited for him to say something—*anything*—more . . . but he didn't. So she filled in the silence instead: "I have a boyfriend." Zoe could feel her temperature rising. "I don't want to do this right now . . ."

"But . . . I just . . . feel like I'm gonna lose you, Zoe," Dylan finally managed to say.

"That's a weird thing to say."

"Why?"

"Because you never had me. You could've, maybe, at some point, but you didn't want me all these years, so—"

"That's not true—"

"But it *is* true. It's painfully, absolutely true—and you're only saying this to me now because I have a nice boyfriend who isn't embarrassed to be with me in public—"

"No. Stop. Your nice, public boyfriend only started liking you once you got boobs!"

"Ohmigod."

"What?"

"That's not fair."

"Are we just supposed to pretend they don't exist?"

"I don't know! Why do you care about them so much?"

"That's kind of a stupid question."

"*You're* kind of a stupid question," Zoe said, wanting to laugh and scream at Dylan all at the same time. "I didn't really even know Austin *until* I had boobs, so your argument is also stupid."

"Whatever. I'm saying I knew you before all that—"

"And what . . . ? Do you want, like, friendship *bonus points* for being nice to the awkward, frizzy-haired charity case?"

"Being *nice*? Zoe, is that what you think we've been doing all this time . . . ?"

"Stop," Zoe said, surprised to hear the word come out of her mouth.

"Stop?"

"This isn't . . . I have a boyfriend."

"I know, Zoe, but that doesn't mean . . . I'm just trying to tell you how *I* feel—about you—"

"I don't care how you feel! About anything!" Zoe said, even though they both knew that wasn't true. She did care.

She cared about Dylan so much. Probably too much. And there was a time when she would've killed for a moment like this. She'd wanted it to happen for years. But not now. Not like this . . . She didn't know what else to say. "I'm with Austin, and we're having sex now, so . . ."

Dylan's face sank.

Zoe knew he wasn't expecting that.

And this was certainly *not* how she had envisioned telling him, but the words had come out of her mouth, and she couldn't take them back now. "I'm sorry. For just saying it like that—"

"No, it's—"

"—but we hadn't really talked in a while, so . . ."

"Yeah. It's . . . I mean that's . . . cool. I just . . . I feel like an idiot."

Zoe hated the look on Dylan's face right now, so disappointed and betrayed. Honestly, she felt like an idiot too. And she felt like there was so much more she wanted to say to him—but maybe there was also nothing at all. Dylan stood silently in front of her, avoiding her eye contact. All of their past conversations, all of the phonefalls, began to replay in Zoe's brain all at once, giving her a front row seat to relive them and over-analyze them at the same time. It looked like Dylan might've been doing the same thing. Or maybe he was just trying as hard as he could not to get emotional and therefore maybe he wasn't thinking about anything at all. Zoe couldn't quite tell. "I feel like you've been lying to me this whole time," she finally managed.

"Zoe. I never lied to you," Dylan insisted.

"I think it's time for you to go home."

"Zoe, please . . . ," Dylan said as sincerely and sweetly as he could. "The only lie I ever told you was that I only liked you when I already knew I was completely in love with you."

"Completely?"

"Maybe not the whole time, but—"

"Of course it wasn't the whole time! It couldn't've been! You were too busy dating a parade of skinny blond girls!" Zoe said sharply and loudly.

"Yeah. And falling asleep on the phone with you every night," Dylan said softly.

Zoe had wanted to hear Dylan say this sort of thing for so long, but now that he had, now that she was listening to the words actually come out of his mouth, it just felt forced. "I feel like you only want to be with me now because I want to be with someone else," Zoe said. She wasn't entirely sure she believed that, but was sure that she had to say it. And then there really was nothing left to say. Zoe turned around and left Dylan standing alone behind her.

109 days until graduation . . .

LAYLA couldn't remember the last time she'd had a new first kiss.

The only person she'd kissed for the past two years was Logan, and the painful truth was that he was still the person she wanted to be kissing, but he was no longer an option.

Instead she made a kiss list.

She took out a pen and a piece of paper and wrote down a list of people she wanted to kiss. It wasn't another to-do list, more like a wish list, and it made her feel silly and small, but she had to do *something*. She wished she had a better, more brilliant idea, but this kiss list was the best she could come up with considering the circumstances, mostly the fact that Logan was now (indefinitely) kissing Vanessa and there was absolutely nothing she could do about that.

So far Layla had written down five names: Wyatt (the cute boy from Savannah's party whose last name she didn't know) followed by Jackson Clark, Miles Roth, Tyson Marks, and Channing Tatum.

Obviously, that last name was more of a dream than a plan, but Layla always mushed those two things up in her mind anyway.

"Might as well shoot for the stars, I guess," she'd said to the girls at lunch a few days earlier. She was doing her very best to find the bright side and trust that things happened for a reason and all of that, but right now even the stars felt like they were tainted. Logan always said he loved her to the moon and back. And they'd spent oh-so-many hours out on her trampoline staring up at the moon and the stars, and she hated that even as she was talking about other boys, other boys she genuinely wanted to kiss, her thoughts were still drifting back to Logan . . .

"It'd be weird if you *weren't* thinking about him," Emma said.

"I'm not even thinking about *him*," Layla had tried to explain. "But he basically ruined all the stars so that's annoying."

"Okay, no," Alex said, her voice sounding way too reasonable for Layla's liking. "Let's not give him that much power. Or *any* power . . ."

Easier said than done, Layla had thought, but she trusted her girls, and also the power of step-by-step instructions, so she started at the top of her kiss list and texted Wyatt, and that's how she ended up sitting next to him near the edge of the Venice Beach skate park after school on Thursday.

"You *sure* I can't get you on a board?" Wyatt asked.

"Positive. Not happening. But it's cute of you to ask."

Layla wasn't sure she remembered how to flirt, but she was trying. Actually calling him cute seemed far too obvious, but he really *was* cute. And adorable. And uncomplicated. Right now Layla appreciated that about him most of all. There was so much complication with Logan, so much Layla didn't understand and couldn't quite explain. It was nice to sit with Wyatt and not be confused. He was attractive, and she was attracted to him. And that was it.

Wyatt was playful with his kisses, and Layla liked that. *A lot.*

The only thing that Layla didn't like about Wyatt's kisses was that she couldn't stop comparing them to Logan's. She tried to cut herself some slack, considering how many thousands of kisses Logan had pressed onto her lips compared to these very first few she was now sharing with Wyatt, but she didn't like that she could still somehow *feel* Logan's kisses even though it was Wyatt's tongue inside her mouth.

And then she couldn't stop thinking about Vanessa's tongue.

And what her tongue might've felt like inside Logan's mouth.

And whether or not Logan had thought about *her* lips when Vanessa's lips were pressed up against his.

And despite the distractions and unhelpful thoughts swirling around in her head, Layla kept kissing Wyatt . . . but it felt far more like the end of a chapter than a new beginning.

108 days until graduation . . .

ZOE heard all of Layla's words, but she did not understand them.

"What do you mean you're *done*?" she asked sharply.

"Okay, 'done' is maybe the wrong word," Layla backtracked. She pushed some of the lettuce from her half-eaten salad back and forth with her plastic fork as the girls sat around their lunch table. It was a Friday, the last day of school before spring break, and tensions seemed to be running high. "I just . . . ," Layla tried again. "I guess maybe I'm just trying to say that I don't think it's going to happen."

"Well, I didn't either at first." Zoe smiled. "I'm sure you'll figure it out."

But Zoe's certainty withered as she saw a gloss wash over Layla's eyes . . .

"I don't know," Layla said. "It doesn't feel like it's gonna work without Logan."

"Is it too soon to say it didn't exactly work *with* Logan

either?" Alex said, which made Emma and Zoe giggle—while Layla, noticeably, did not.

Zoe got the sinking feeling that it really *was* too soon. Or maybe too late. Or both.

"Sorry, Lay," Alex added quickly when she saw that Layla was actually upset.

"It's okay . . . ," Layla said meekly.

"Of course it's okay," Zoe insisted. "You've still got four more names on the kiss list. And it's not like that bullet point disappeared or anything. It's still there. There's still a due date and everything. All of the things. It's all still happening . . ."

Zoe was expecting a "right" out of Layla, even if only a tepid one . . .

. . . but instead she just got a short, clipped exhale.

And Zoe did not like the sound of it one bit.

It was off-putting and out of character and it made the little red, frizzy hairs on the back of Zoe's neck stand up straight. "Unless . . . ," Zoe started again slowly, " . . . 'done' simply means you're *done* . . . and then that's it."

"Well that's not *exactly* what I'm saying . . . ," Layla attempted to explain, but Zoe had heard enough. Now she really felt like an idiot. An absolute mess of a human. All of a sudden Zoe remembered the feeling she got the first time Layla had smiled at her about the pact as they sat at their table at The Bigg Chill. Right now, in this moment, she felt exactly the opposite. She could also feel a dark pit growing inside her stomach as if she already knew what Layla was going to say next. Zoe was *furious*.

She went from zero to livid in no time flat.

"That sucks," Zoe spit out with more bite in her voice than she'd anticipated.

Zoe realized that it might've sound off-putting to Emma and Alex, as if her fervor had come out of nowhere, but Zoe could feel Layla abandoning the pact and The Crew and maybe even her, too, even though she hadn't quite said that yet . . . and she hated all of it.

"I'm just trying to be honest," Layla said, which pissed Zoe off even more.

"Thank you, Layla, I *really* super appreciate your honesty . . ."

"Wait, what's happening?" Emma asked as her eyes darted back and forth between Zoe and Layla.

"Yeah. I think I missed something," Alex added. Her eyes were darting too.

Layla and Zoe were still stuck in a silent stalemate.

Zoe didn't want to have to be the one to say it out loud, but she couldn't stand it anymore. "Layla is quitting the pact."

"No, she's not . . . ," Alex said.

"She is. She just said she doesn't want to do it," Zoe exclaimed.

"It's not that I don't *want* to — " Layla tried to speak up.

"Right, sorry, *Logan* doesn't want to, so Layla couldn't possibly — "

"Hey, Zoe . . . ," Emma spoke up, trying to lower the temperature.

"Sorry, but this is bullshit," Zoe said to Emma before

turning back to Layla. "I'm sorry you and Logan broke up, but that doesn't mean you just have to give up on us, too . . ."

"I am not *giving up*—on anything—but can we be real clear for a minute? Logan dumped *me*. If it was up to me, we'd still be together."

"Yeah, but you probably *still* wouldn't've had sex with him anyway . . ."

"That's a low blow, Zoe," Layla said, raising her voice for the first time.

"I'm sorry, but I thought this was about us, all of us together. Or *together* together. Or whatever it was supposed to be . . . now I'm realizing that maybe this was just about Logan the whole time. Did you ever even care about the pact?"

"Of course I did! Zoe, you're being ridiculous!"

"Being 'done' is ridiculous!"

"I don't want to do this if I can't do it right."

"What does that even mean? *Right?*" Zoe asked, reaching a fever pitch.

"I don't know! I don't know what it means—but I know it's a problem! So I'm trying to tell you how I feel—or that I don't know how I feel—and apparently none of that is allowed . . ."

"Just do whatever you want, Layla," Zoe fumed. "Clearly, I can't make you do anything you don't want to do."

"Did I make *you* do something you didn't want to do?"

"No—"

"'Cause if you didn't want to sleep with Austin—"

"I never said that!"

"—you shouldn't have slept with Austin—"

"I'm not talking about Austin! I'm talking about you, Layla. You're giving up . . ."

"I tried, Zoe! I tried with Logan, I just tried with Wyatt . . ."

"Oh, okay . . ."

"Do you think I didn't? What else am I supposed to do?"

"Try again! Try harder! Eat pizza. Whatever! Just don't be a hypocrite."

"How about if you try not to be an asshole?"

"Fuck you, Layla," Zoe snapped.

"Should I just *pretend* I'm still in? Will that make you feel better?"

"Don't do me any favors."

"I feel like that's exactly what you're asking for—"

"It's not, I swear—"

"Good, because this isn't just a favor. This is a big, huge deal."

"I know *exactly* what it is, Layla. I'm the one that's actually had sex." It wasn't just what Zoe said, but also the way she said it, the harsh tone in her voice—and all the honesty behind it—that seemed to hurt Layla so much.

And Zoe felt how mean her words were before they even came all the way out of her mouth, but it was too late for her to take them back.

And Layla didn't say anything else.

She couldn't.

Instead, she just got up and walked away.

would've texted the girls all about it, but she felt like there was too much else she had to say first. She wanted to apologize to Layla for some of her words at the lunch table, but she was still mad that Layla wanted to give up on the pact, and she didn't know where to start, so it all just amounted to more silence.

LAYLA hated the sound of silence so *so* much.

Luckily, she'd had a bit of a distraction, as her family had rented a house in Santa Barbara for a week. They'd caught waves at the beach and played board games, and Layla had even managed to get a tan (and no tan lines), but it all felt like a bit of a consolation prize. The conversation had simply spiraled too far with Zoe, and Layla wished she could take back some of what she'd said, but she didn't know where to start either. Now that Layla was home, she couldn't help but miss Logan, and she missed the girls, too, and there was still another week until they'd all be back at school again.

Layla decided she needed a break from her spring break, and all the racing thoughts in her head, so she drove over to Alex's house after dinner Monday night.

ALEX had spent all day every day of the first week of spring break on the track.

Meanwhile, Oliver had spent all night every night texting her—or more accurately *begging* her—for a naked picture, so she was doing her best to avoid her phone altogether.

But of course she was happy to hear from Layla, and glad to see her too, and the girls ended up on the lounge chairs in Alex's backyard, swapping stories about Layla's trip and Alex's track practices and how the closer she got to breaking the record, the farther away it actually felt.

Then, their thoughts and the conversation drifted to Zoe and the fight . . .

"Are you really done?" Alex asked, treading carefully.

Layla thought for a moment.

Alex wanted her to say no as much as she knew Zoe did, but she could see the hesitation all over Layla's face.

"I don't know." Layla finally exhaled after a bit of time had passed. "It was my stupid idea in the first place."

"Oh no. It is *not* a stupid idea. In fact, it might be the most brilliant idea you've ever had," Alex teased, quoting Layla back to herself.

"Thanks," Layla said softly.

"Hey. Don't do it if you don't want to, but don't *not* do it because of Logan."

"It's not *because* of Logan. I mean, I want to say that he has absolutely nothing to do with how I'm feeling . . ." But they both knew that wasn't true.

"Zoe *does* have a point," Alex said after another moment. "It was *supposed* to be together."

"Yeah, well, it was *supposed* to be a lot of things," Layla added.

"Maybe that's the problem," Alex said, thinking back to that night with Cameron at sleepaway camp. "Maybe it's the way we think things are supposed to be that messes

us up most of all. If you *really* don't want to do the pact anymore, that's your call. But don't bow out now just because you're scared about what it might feel like if you don't end up crossing the sex pact off your to-do list," Alex said, sounding all Zen and wise even though she felt like a bit of an imposter. She wasn't sure if she'd be able to take her own advice to heart when it came to thinking about her upcoming track meets and breaking the record and her faith being greater than her fear and all of that, but at least she believed it wholeheartedly for Layla.

"Thanks," Layla said.

Alex could tell that she needed that, which made her feel good. And then it got quiet for a while as the girls sat together, thinking.

"What's on your mind?" Layla asked, after who knows how much time had passed.

"Honestly?"

Alex's mind had returned to Oliver's dick pic.

She still hadn't told anyone about it, but Oliver had been texting, over and over, asking for a pic of her. Maybe she should've just blocked his number or told an adult or done something (*anything*) that could be classified as responsible . . . but she didn't.

Instead, she'd done something stupid.

Alex put her knees inside a red, lacy bra, the sexiest one she had, and took a picture that made it look like they were her boobs. It was something she'd seen on the Internet, but the online version looked way better than her own. Alex thought her picture looked ob-vi-ous-ly fake, since there

was way more cleavage involved than she had in real life, but, objectively speaking, it *did* sort of maybe kind of look like actual cleavage. Still, she was more or less certain that Oliver would know it wasn't real.

She was wrong.

Less than ten minutes later, Oliver sent her back a *very* real video of himself really jacking off to her fake boob picture.

That's what Alex was thinking about.

But.

Instead of getting all into all of it with Layla, she simply said, "Oliver."

"Boys are stupid," Layla said.

"So stupid."

"Girls too, though," Alex said, laughing.

And Layla laughed too.

The truth was funny like that, Alex thought.

92 days until graduation...

EMMA decided it was time to break the ice in The Chat.

She knew Layla and Zoe were both equally stubborn, but the silence had lasted for far too long, more than two weeks, *sixteen* days to be exact, and now she had to do something about it.

Emma had spent the last few days of spring break in Minneapolis visiting her cousins and had taken a pretty stellar selfie while she was on the SpongeBob rollercoaster at the Mall of America. Then yesterday, once she got back to Los Angeles, she texted it to The Chat and hashtagged it as a sexie. If anything was going to get everyone talking again, Emma thought, it might be that pic.

But she was wrong.

Alex and Zoe didn't respond at all. Layla texted Emma back separately, directly, to say that the pic and especially the hashtag had made her laugh out loud, but that was it.

Even before the fight, the girls had decided to take

a break from froyo Sunday while they were on spring break, since everyone was going to be traveling at different times. But now, Sunday March 22nd, they were all back in town, and *still* no one was texting.

That afternoon, Zoe texted her just to say hi, and they decided to meet for coffee right across the street from The Bigg Chill. It felt weird to be near that intersection and not have any rainbow sprinkles on the table, Emma thought. But then, when Zoe asked her what she was thinking about, she said Savannah instead.

Emma still hadn't really talked to the girls about her, but this just finally felt like the right time to say something. "We've been texting over break," Emma explained.

And then she told Zoe how they kissed at her birthday party.

"Like. *Kiss* kissed?"

"Yep. Tongue. Butterflies. Goose bumps . . ."

"Wow."

"Yeah. And I liked it," Emma added before Zoe even had to ask. That last part, the part about *liking* the kiss, as opposed to just doing it, seemed like the more substantial details. Sometimes, girls would randomly get drunk and make out with other girls at parties just because. Because it was trendy. Or because it got them attention. Or whatever.

But this wasn't like that.

Emma knew this was so much more than a "just because."

"So then, you like Savannah?" Zoe asked.

Emma knew she meant *like* like without even having to ask for clarification.

And she knew that she did, too.

"All right, then," Zoe smiled. "That's cool . . ."

"What?" Emma asked, sensing that there was more to Zoe's thought.

"Are you going to, like . . . come out?"

"Oh . . ."

"I know how much you love labels . . ."

"It's not even about the label of it all," Emma said, trying to wrap her thoughts around her feelings. "It just feels like too much attention . . . and so definitive . . . and what if I change my mind?"

"I think that's allowed," Zoe said sincerely.

ZOE didn't want to make *too* big a deal about this moment . . .

. . . but she didn't want to make it too small, either.

This was important for Emma.

She could feel that it was.

And she knew that was part of the whole best friend thing: You could *feel* each other.

It was part of what had made her and Layla yell across the lunch table at school a couple weeks ago. Caring for a friend's emotions as if they were your own could be muddled—and difficult and confusing. Sometimes, even the togetherness could be overwhelming. *Especially* since there were four friends involved in The Crew dynamic. All the emotions felt exponential.

"I'm excited to hang with her," Zoe said about Savannah. It was her way of letting Emma know, without saying too much, that it mattered to her too.

"You will." Emma smiled. "You all will."

"Yeah . . . if Layla ever talks to me again."

"Or if you talk to her."

Of course Zoe was going to talk to her. That wasn't the problem. "I'm just not even sure who owes who an apology at this point . . . ," she explained.

"Maybe it's not an 'I'm sorry' kind of thing anymore. Maybe you should just start with more of a hi," Emma suggested.

"A hi?"

"Yeah. Like a little peace offering."

Zoe was just about to tell Emma how wise she was when an incoming text message buzzed into The Chat.

Hi.

It was from Layla.

"Whoa," Zoe said, overwhelmed by the serendipity of the moment. "Did you give her the same advice?"

"Nope."

"She must've felt it."

"Definitely."

And ten minutes later the girls found themselves sharing a side of rainbow sprinkles at their usual table at The Bigg Chill.

LAYLA was definitely still in.

"I was just having a moment . . . ," she explained once

everyone had settled into their chairs, and their phones had been stacked, and rainbow sprinkles had been distributed, and everything.

"I know," Zoe said, "but if it's more than that . . . you don't just have to say it for me."

"I'm not," Layla insisted. She didn't want to make any promises she couldn't keep, but she wanted to be a part of the pact. It mattered to her. "So. Tell the universe: it's all still happening."

"Totally happening," Zoe agreed.

ZOE finally felt like herself again.

It had only been two weeks, but she'd missed her girls. She filled them in on the latest Austin progress report. They'd now had sex four times. And each time was better than the one before, even if there were still no damn fireworks to be found.

EMMA told Layla and Alex about Savannah.

"Wait, wait, wait," Layla said with one of those giant smiles on her face. "You know what this means, right?"

"Do I?" Emma asked cautiously.

"You're gonna get to lose your *girl* V-card too," Alex said, totally hopping on Layla's train of thought.

"Ohmigod *yes* . . ." Zoe smiled.

Emma hadn't really thought about it like that, but the girls were right.

"Can't wait for *that* progress report," Layla said, laughing.

✻ ✻ ✻

ALEX still didn't have much to report in the progress department . . .

. . . but she finally told the girls about Oliver's dick pic.

"Can I see it?" Zoe asked, surprising everyone at the table and prompting another round of giggles.

"I deleted it," Alex said.

"Too bad." Zoe laughed. "Let me know if he sends you another one . . ."

Alex had already deleted his jacking off video too, but she didn't tell the girls about that. She still wasn't entirely sure how she felt about it, but she knew she didn't want to talk about it.

"Maybe you and Oliver should just do it already," Layla suggested.

"Oh *God*, you should talk," Alex teased back.

And everybody laughed.

And it felt like everything had fallen right back into place.

Unfortunately, that feeling didn't last very long . . .

91 days until graduation...

EMMA saw it first.

Nick forwarded her the email at 11:45 p.m.

You still up??? He texted her at the same time.

At first Emma thought it was just a horny text message, a sext-me-maybe kind of text, but something about all the question marks tipped her off and made her think that it wasn't.

Yeah...? she texted back.

Check your email, he texted. *Sorry, but I thought you should see.*

OH, she texted back as soon as she opened it.

It's totally obviously fake. I can tell, Nick texted.

Emma could tell too.

It was Photoshopped.

The skin tones were all wrong.

The body was two shades lighter than Alex's *actual* skin color, and it didn't match her neck or her face—at all.

But maybe the mismatching was something you'd only notice if you looked closely.

Emma had a feeling that everyone who looked at this picture was going to be looking closely . . . but she didn't think anyone would be looking closely at *that*.

90 days until graduation . . .

ALEX woke up on Tuesday morning in a panic.

Her mind was racing and her palms were sweaty.

It was as if her body knew what had happened, even before she saw a hundred missed text messages on her phone and dozens of copies of the same email forwarded to her in-box.

She scrolled to the bottom of her in-box, searching for the original email. It was sent at 11:37 p.m. last night, less than five minutes after she'd turned off her phone and gone to sleep.

The subject of the email was "superstar."

All lowercase letters.

There were no words in the email.

Only a picture.

Alex got up out of bed. She couldn't lie or sit or even just stay still anymore. Instead, she started pacing around her bedroom and her bathroom.

She finally stopped long enough to open the photograph . . .

As soon as she saw it—really, clearly saw exactly what it was—she turned around and threw up all over the tiles on her bathroom floor.

It was the most awful thing she'd ever seen. And most of it was her. Well, *some* of it was her. The head, at least. It was still entirely awful.

ZOE could feel every pair of eyes staring at her and Layla and Emma.

"This is insane," Zoe whispered as they walked down the hallway.

It felt like the sort of dream where she accidentally showed up to school naked. But it wasn't a dream. It was a wide-awake nightmare.

And it was really happening.

And the girls weren't really naked, but everyone was staring.

And Alex wasn't really naked either, but her picture made it look like she was.

And everyone was talking about it as if it were real.

And Alex's real head had really been Photoshopped onto a naked body.

And it wasn't her real body, but it looked real enough.

And everyone in the hallway had *definitely* already looked at it.

At all of it.

It was only the second day back from spring break, and Alex had stayed home from school. She had texted The Chat, something about plans and God and a sick sense of humor and how she simply couldn't face anybody. Not yet anyway.

The Crew met Alex's parents at the door to the principal's office. They had just been in a meeting with Mrs. Bowers, the principal, demanding swift repercussions, but the head of the IT department informed them that—long (and nerdy) story short—they didn't know who sent the email, and they couldn't trace the IP address associated with the account.

"Do you know who might've had a reason to send this?" Mrs. Bowers asked as if there were going to be a simple answer to that question.

As if Alex didn't have a reputation.

As if people didn't make up stupid stories about her all the time.

The girls were thinking all of that, but they didn't say any of it.

They promised to alert the principal and Alex's parents right away if they heard anything that might be helpful.

Afterward, they huddled up in the hallway.

"It had to be Oliver, right?" Layla asked.

All the girls wanted to say yes. They wanted to be able to prove that it was definitely Oliver. And of course that made sense. And it was probably more likely than not that it really was him . . . but they couldn't prove it.

And the hard part was, as Emma articulated, "it could've been anyone."

"At least it's not *real*," Zoe said. "I mean not *really* real."

She was trying to find the bright side, but it didn't seem particularly bright.

85 days until graduation . . .

ALEX hadn't really responded to anything or anyone all week.

She couldn't.

The Crew had unsuccessfully tried to come over after school on Friday. And then on Saturday, too. And now it was Sunday. It was a quarter to four. It was almost time for froyo.

But Alex just still couldn't get out of bed.

So the girls got the froyo for Alex instead and brought it over. They bought medium sized servings of every flavor on the flavor board at The Bigg Chill (ten flavors altogether) and brought all of them to Alex's house along with a dozen possible topping options.

"Bigg Chill Aaron says he's sorry and he hopes you feel better," Layla said as she passed out the plastic spoons.

"Oh my God . . . ," Alex said. "Bigg Chill Aaron saw the picture?!"

"Well. At first I was thinking, he just thought you were sick," Layla explained, "but then he also said to tell you to keep your head up, so I think it's probably safe to say he did."

Yep, Alex thought. Bigg Chill Aaron had definitely seen it.

Everyone with an Internet connection had seen it.

Ugh.

It . . .

Alex still couldn't bring herself to say "me," mostly because the picture mostly wasn't *actually* her, but also because the whole episode felt like such a mistake, such an awful, horrible joke that she still wasn't entirely sure it was real.

"At least the body is hot," Alex said, attempting some levity.

Ugh.

The body . . .

It's not that Alex *wanted* it to be her body, she act‌ually very much did *not* want that, but at least if it w‌as hers, she could claim some sort of ownership of it. could've said, *Why yes, that is me, take it or leave i* but it wasn't. It was a sick, Photoshopped fantasy, ‍ felt like a violation on top of a violation.

Everyone thought she *wasn't* a virgin. *She wa*‍

Everyone thought she *was* naked. *She wasn't*

Alex's reality was overshadowed by everyone's thoughts and feelings.

And, really, no one knew exactly where the picture came from.

"There's no proof," the girls had all said, resigned to the uncertainty.

Alex wasn't *entirely* sure where it came from either, but she had one pretty strong guess.

84 days until graduation . . .

ALEX needed to get back on track—literally and figuratively.

Her parents had given her permission to stay home from school again, but there were only so many track meets on the calendar, and the record certainly wasn't going to break itself. Luckily, her body seemed to agree. She found herself awake and dressed for school and leaning against Oliver's car a whole twenty minutes early. Her shoes were already on, and the laces were tied, and all her possessions were packed inside of her backpack.

None of that had ever happened before, let alone all of that at the same time.

She stood outside in the driveway, waiting. Watching. Noticing everything. Like the thin morning breeze. And the paint scratches on Oliver's car. The way her toes felt inside of her sneakers. And then Oliver walked outside. It felt like maybe he somehow knew Alex would be early for the first time all year. He raised his hands up as he walked toward her as if to say he came in peace, or that he wasn't guilty, or maybe a little bit of both.

"Alex," Oliver said in a tone of voice she'd never heard before.

This wasn't Oliver the Flirt talking, or Oliver the Basketball Star, or even Oliver the Asshole. This was just Oliver, the boy next door. "I'm sorry," he said. It wasn't like the way he apologized for kissing Caroline on the bus. This was an actual, real life "I'm sorry" for something seriously worth being sorry about.

"I didn't do it," he added.

Alex didn't know how to respond. She just stared at him for a moment. *Through* him, really. And into his piercing blue eyes. She didn't *want* to believe him, but there was something about the way he looked, his quiet face, his strong jawline, the way he held his body as it got closer to hers . . . something about the way he said he didn't do it— his tone, his sincerity, the measured speed of his words as they slipped out of his mouth—something about it forced a big lump in Alex's throat . . .

She hadn't cried since it happened.

Not once.

She had puked more times than she could count, and she wasn't really sleeping or eating or combing her hair, but she hadn't cried . . . until now.

The lump in her throat turned into a fire in her eyes. And the tears—the hot, sticky, uncontrollable tears—came spilling out. It wasn't just *a* tear. It was *all* of the tears . . .

tears for all of the bad jokes and the rumors. For the catcalls and the cattiness. The two minutes and thirty-five seconds that Max held his breath. The months—*years*—she'd lied to her friends about that night at sleepaway camp. All the Mona Lisa smiles and the city lights near Mulholland. The star charm on her sneakers. The superstar email with all lowercase letters.

The way it never happens the way you want it to.

All of it.

Oliver respected Alex's space, staying near, but not too close, until her sobs finally reached a crescendo, and he had no choice but to step forward. He moved toward her slowly, but purposefully, until he stretched out his arms and wrapped them around Alex's back, pulling her into his chest, holding her.

Even after that Alex cried for a very long time.

Oliver held her until she didn't need to be held anymore.

They were both late to school, but they both knew it didn't matter.

82 days until graduation ...

EMMA got her very first college acceptance on April Fool's Day.

Of course she did.

She'd spent the past few months, basically all of senior year, feeling like the universe was playing a giant practical joke on her, so, *of course* she'd get into college on a day where everything was supposed to be some sort of joke.

"Yeah," Savannah said, "you should probably check your spam folder." Emma hadn't considered that. But just before she started to panic some more, Savannah continued, "I'm kidding. Deep breaths. You're good. And I'm proud of you."

Then she put her hand on top of Emma's and squeezed it reassuringly. She held on for a moment longer. Soon Emma could feel a layer of sweat coating her palm. She pulled her hand away as slickly as she could (which wasn't very) and wiped it on her corduroys. Savannah didn't seem *thrilled*, but public hand-holding really wasn't her style. Emma tried to carry on the conversation, rambling about how her parents wanted to celebrate and have a whole big dinner. Her mom wanted to use the nice china plates. Her dad wanted to make a speech.

"So, dinner . . . ," Savannah said tentatively. "Do I make the cut on that?"

Honestly, Emma hadn't even considered it.

Her parents had insisted that she invite "the girls" but that just meant Zoe and Alex and Layla of course. "Or, just, forget I asked," Savannah said before Emma had figured out how to respond. It wasn't that Emma didn't *want* Savannah to be there, but it just felt like a lot all at once. "We wouldn't want to make any sudden movements or anything," Savannah added rather pointedly.

"Hey," Emma said, pushing back.

"I'm not . . . it's not about *dinner*," Savannah replied.

Emma could hear the frustration in her voice, and she couldn't exactly fault Savannah for that. They'd been hanging out at school a lot—and things were decidedly "good" between them—but their kiss count was still stuck at one. It wasn't that Emma was *avoiding* kiss number two, but she hadn't exactly put herself in a position to let it happen either.

"It just feels like . . . what's that expression? 'If a tree falls in the woods when no one's around, can anyone hear it?'"

"Oh, you mean: *Does it make a sound*?" Emma offered. "'Cause obviously if no one's around then no one can hear it, but the point is about sound. Like, did it really happen at all?"

"Right." Savannah nodded.

"Ha. Yeah," Emma said, still trying to understand what she was getting at.

"So it's sort of like: 'If you fall for a cute girl, but she's too embarrassed to tell anyone about it, are you really falling?'"

There it was.

That's what Savannah was actually mad about.

"No?" Savannah asked, forcing the issue. "Does that one not work?"

Savannah got up and walked out of the classroom.

Emma followed right after her. "Hey. Stop. I'm not embarrassed."

"You sure about that?"

"Yes! Jeez. Come to dinner if it's that big a deal—"

"I already said it's not about *dinner*—"

"Then why are you making such a big deal about it?"

"You make a big deal about everything!"

"And you don't! That's why this is so weird!"

"Emma, I know you don't want me to have, like, expectations or whatever, but I don't think that's realistic anymore . . . And I know you're confused, but the thing is: I'm not. I know who I am. And I know how I feel. And I'm not trying to push you . . . but if you weren't so scared, I'd kiss you right here in the hallway."

"I'm not scared," Emma said as forcefully as she could, but it still came out sounding shaky.

Savannah stepped even closer to Emma.

Now their noses were practically touching.

Emma could feel Savannah's breath on her lips.

She was basically daring Emma to kiss her.

Right here.

Right now.

In public.

Emma wanted to . . .

. . . but she didn't.

And before she could do much of anything else, Savannah spun around and took off down the hallway. Emma wanted to yell out *Wait*. She wanted to stop her.

But she couldn't.

So she didn't.

And Savannah didn't come to dinner.

ALEX felt like she was late for car pool even though it was seven thirty at night.

She'd stayed for an extra while after track practice and lost track of time, and now she was running late to dinner at Emma's house. Alex hustled toward Emma's front door.

Zoe's forest green Ford Explorer was parked right out front.

The engine was still running.

"Hi, Zoe," Alex said as she approached the driver's side window.

"Well it *rhymes* with Zoe," Joey corrected.

Alex's heart skipped a beat.

Actually, it felt like her heart stopped for an entire

moment as she laid her eyes on Joey Reed sitting in the front seat. "Spring break," he explained as he fiddled with the radio.

"Nice to see you."

"Nice to see you, too," Joey said. Something about the way he said it made Alex wonder if he'd seen the picture. Her stupid, fake, but also stupidly real picture. "I'm sorry," he added—and she didn't have to wonder anymore.

He'd seen it.

"Yeah . . ." was all she could think to say.

"Did you hear about that time I got pantsed in the middle of the track?" Joey asked, seemingly out of nowhere.

No. Alex hadn't heard about that.

And so Joey launched into a whole story about his sophomore year, and how his asshole friends had pulled his pants down around his ankles. In front of *everybody*. And how he was absolutely mortified. And betrayed. And never thought he could show his face again. But he could. And he did. And somehow Joey was able to explain the whole thing in a way that explained all the feelings Alex had *felt* but simply hadn't been able to articulate.

Joey just got it.

And truth was, his story was way worse than Alex's, because everyone really saw his penis. His actual, real penis. Luckily no one took a picture of it or anything. But still . . .

Joey explained that the infamous pantsing episode was the final straw that helped him lose all the "baby fat" he'd been holding on to for so long.

"This is way more of a conversation than I was expecting

to have right now...," Joey admitted once he'd reached the end of it.

"Thank you," she said.

"You're welcome." He ran his fingers through his hair.

It felt like they were both trying to figure out what to say next when Zoe burst outside. She'd forgotten her cell phone in the car. Joey unplugged it from his charger and handed it over.

"Nice work, goober," he said. "You're lucky I didn't drive off yet."

"We were just catching up," Alex offered. She felt lame for thinking the situation needed any sort of explanation at all.

"Cool, cool," Zoe said, mocking the way Joey would sometimes. "But, like, get your own friends? Thanks, bro."

Zoe seemed mostly oblivious to the sexual tension simmering between Joey and Alex. She slipped her arm through Alex's and pulled her toward Emma's front door.

Alex glanced back over her shoulder one more time before they went inside.

Obviously, he'd been waiting for her to look back.

He winked at her.

Oh wow.

That wink, Alex thought.

She could feel it in her entire body.

Later that night, as she stood in her bathroom, getting ready for bed, she could still feel the wink as if it had just happened. She'd thought about it all through dinner too. And then after dinner when Emma's dad made a speech.

And also after all of that when the girls snuck away and climbed out Emma's bedroom window and onto her roof to smoke a celebratory joint.

"Wyatt's dad has a medical card," Layla had explained as she pulled the tightly rolled joint out of her pocket. The Crew didn't get high together very often, but everyone decided they could use a break from the inside of their heads and all their rambling thoughts and feelings for a minute or two. They passed the joint around for a while and then they sat on Emma's roof, laughing about how big the universe was and how small they all were—and they officially decided they needed more quality time together.

"Time and *quality* time are two totally different things," Emma said, all high and introspective.

Zoe had suggested that they have a sleepover. Her parents were going to be out of town Friday night. She said Joey might be home, but he could probably score them some alcohol. All the girls were down, but Alex was especially glad she didn't have to come up with an excuse to see Joey again.

That wink.

Alex was still feeling it.

Now she was also feeling a new sense of contentment pouring over her as she washed her face and brushed her teeth. She wasn't sure exactly where this new-ish feeling was coming from, but she knew that she liked it. Maybe it was because she was still high. Or maybe it was because this was one of the best nights she'd had with her girls in a really long time. Or maybe it was because of the story Joey had told her outside of Emma's house. . .

Whatever it was, she couldn't stop thinking about that wink.

It was totally possible that she was reading too far into Joey's wink, the same way her friends at camp had read too far into her Mona Lisa smile. Maybe she was exaggerating their connection. Maybe it wasn't really as strong and seemingly instantaneous as she thought it was. Maybe she was overanalyzing the situation. Maybe she was just simply crazy.

Then she glanced down at her phone.

There was a waiting text message.

It was from Joey: *Heard you're sleeping over Friday night . . . glad I don't have to make up an excuse to see you again.*

And there it was.

He felt the same way too.

Maybe, actually, she wasn't so crazy after all.

80 days until graduation . . .

ALEX couldn't remember the last time they'd had an actual sleepover.

The girls crashed at each other's houses all the time, after parties or late nights or for no real reason at all. But the last time the main plan of the evening was a sleepover? Alex had no clue.

"Wanna watch a movie?" Zoe asked, turning on the movie projector in her parents' guest house. She was expecting to see the Netflix homepage, but instead . . .

"Oh shit." Layla laughed.

"Are those . . . ?" Zoe asked, turning her familiar shade of red. She wondered why her cheeks didn't just stay that way permanently.

"Yup. Those are two girls kissing," Alex said, smiling.

There were, in fact, two naked girls making out on the screen.

Cherry

"It's Joey's . . . ," she explained. His laptop was still hooked up to the screen.

"Well, it's hot," Alex said. She wasn't sure if she meant the video itself or the thought of Joey watching it. Probably a little bit of both.

"I'm down," Emma chimed in.

"Me too," Layla said.

"Ohmigod." Zoe squirmed, clearly outnumbered. "It's fine. I'll just be over here trying not to think about my brother getting turned on by this . . ."

Now that was all Alex could think about.

"Can we at least pick a different video?"

Alex's phone buzzed. It was a text from Joey: *Upstairs.*

Alex couldn't help but notice the period at the end of his text.

It wasn't a question.

It was a statement.

And she liked it.

"Pick something hot," Alex said, and then added a stupid excuse about wanting to go grab a Diet Coke real quick. It was the only thing she could think of that they hadn't already brought out to the guesthouse. She would have to go back into the kitchen to get it. "Anybody want anything else?" she asked, trying to appear casual. Inside, her heart was already racing.

She walked into the Reeds' living room, right past the kitchen and upstairs toward Joey's room. Her bare feet were cold against the hardwood floor. She could feel the

295

word "magnetic" swirling around in her head, as if that explained everything: She was being drawn toward Joey.

"Hi," she said as she walked into Joey's room.

"Hi," he replied, standing up to greet her.

Before she knew it, they were only a few inches apart.

That magnetism.

A spark from Joey's deep brown eyes slid down his face and parted his smile, and in one fluid movement he pulled Alex toward him, pressing his lips—firmly, sweetly, *perfectly*—against hers. The kiss was so natural and so obvious and so necessary, that it was actually the pulling apart afterward that felt strange. All she wanted to do was kiss him again.

But before she could, her phone buzzed. It was the girls, getting anxious.

"They're waiting for me—to watch your porn collection," Alex explained.

Joey smirked and then pulled her in for another soul melding, mind crushing, body bursting kind of kiss.

Alex's phone buzzed again.

"Ugh. Okay." She smiled. "To be continued . . ."

"Please stay?" Joey said as if the words had escaped through his lips without permission.

"I can't," she said. She wanted to, but she couldn't. Not right now. "Chicks before dicks," Alex added with a little laugh, knowing it would drive him crazy.

It did. And she liked that.

"All right, fine . . . ," he said with an adorable shake of his head. He ran his fingers through his hair. "Me and my 'dick' are gonna go take a cold shower."

79 days until graduation...

EMMA woke up the next morning with a hangover.

It felt like a happy hangover, but still, her head was throbbing.

The girls had an incredible time last night. They drank and ate and giggled and watched porn. They spent some time in the Reeds' Jacuzzi, laughing about the warm jets and how if they positioned themselves just right on top of them, it might set off a fireworks display. It had been perfect—except for the fact that the hours they spent together might as well have just been a few minutes. Their time felt like it was flying, dripping away, and there was nothing any of them could do to hold it or stop it.

Emma's stomach was growling and her heart felt strange. All she wanted to do was be with Savannah. And talk to her. And maybe dance with her. Or maybe even kiss her again . . .

. . . but Savannah had stopped responding to her text

messages ever since Emma had been stupid enough to forget to invite her to dinner.

Clearly, Emma should've handled the whole situation better, but she hadn't. She'd messed up.

Emma went home and took a nap and woke up to a flurry of new texts in The Chat. Layla had sent a whole string of new inspirational quotes, as Layla so often did, and the last one was particularly pertinent for Emma's current state of mind. It was a picture of a bike along with the words: *to keep your balance you have to keep moving.*

Emma felt that.

For months, basically all year, she felt like she had been out of balance, entirely unsteady. But now she realized that maybe she was going about it all backward. Maybe her unsteadiness came from the fact that she was effectively attempting to stay in the same place. Everyone around her was moving forward. Because that's what people did. They moved. They evolved. Despite her fears Emma wanted all that too. But first she needed to find her balance.

All Emma wanted to do was jump on and pedal to Savannah's house.

So she did.

In her car, this hill leading up to Savannah's house just seemed like a little incline. Now, on her bike, it might as well have been a mountain. When Emma finally did make it to the top, she was covered in sweat. This certainly wasn't how she envisioned this moment with Savannah, but she didn't work so hard just to chicken out now.

She took a few deep breaths, attempting to steady

herself, but she knew the only way she was going to find steadiness or balance or whatever she wanted to call it was to actually move forward.

So that is exactly what she did.

She walked up the steps and knocked on Savannah's front door.

"What are you doing here?" Savannah asked, stepping outside to talk to Emma and closing the door behind her.

"You said I didn't need to make up excuses to hang out with you. . . ." Emma smiled, which made Savannah smile back too. And then Emma could feel why she was there. *This*, she thought as she looked into Savannah's eyes. This is what it was supposed to feel like. The hormones. The racing. This moment felt like everything she'd heard Layla and Alex and Zoe talk about. This was good. And it wasn't like Emma *hadn't* felt good before, because she definitely had. And it wasn't like she hadn't been aroused before . . . she had. But all of that? All of that *before*? It simply wasn't *this*.

She could feel that much for sure.

Emma could also feel her blood and her boobs and the butterflies and all of the sweat, still dripping down her back and neck and knees. She could see it all from the outside and feel it all from the inside, and she knew she owed Savannah an apology and more honesty and a grand gesture, too, and so she stepped forward, onto Savannah's welcome mat, and kissed her perfectly pink lips.

This kiss was long and hard and on purpose.

This! Emma thought.

This was balance and movement all at the same time.

"Look at Emma O'Malley, kissing in public and everything . . . ," Savannah said after Emma pulled away.

Emma laughed. "Does it count as being 'public' if there's no one around to see it?"

"I don't know. What if a tree falls in the woods and there's no one around to hear it?" Savannah asked, joining in on Emma's laughter.

This, Emma thought again as she caught Savannah's eyes.

"So. We can agree this is good, right?" Emma asked, repeating Savannah's words from the water polo match.

"Emma. If you're trying to *expectation* me right now . . ."

"I'm not *expectationing* anything," Emma said, smiling with her entire face.

After a few more kisses on the front step, Emma found herself pedaling home even harder and faster than she had on the way there.

I kissed a girl and I liked it, she texted The Chat as soon as she got home.

OHMIGOD YES, Zoe texted back almost immediately.

I love it so much, Layla texted.

Lucky Savannah, Alex added.

Lucky me, Emma thought.

ALEX's thoughts had been entirely consumed by Joey Reed.

The last time she saw him was about twelve hours

earlier as she'd snuck up into Zoe and Joey's Jack and Jill bathroom to say good-bye before she went home after the sleepover. She'd said hi—and then he'd said hi—and they'd been stuck staring at each for a moment until Joey said he had to see her again before he went back to school. And then he kissed her, and it rattled her soul, and it took every single ounce of self-control in Alex's body not to melt into a puddle on the floor right then and there. And then somehow she'd manage to survive the rest of the day and most of the night. As soon as her parents went to sleep, she'd texted Joey to come over. He'd snuck out of his house and now here he was, tiptoeing into the Campbells' kitchen through the back door as quietly as he could.

At first sight Alex wanted to kiss him everywhere and all at once, and the urge was so strong and overwhelming it had the exact opposite effect: It stopped her in her tracks. Alex felt like once she started to kiss him, she might never be able to stop, and the thought was absolutely terrifying and amazing all at once.

"I know . . . ," Joey said, as if he could read her thoughts.

"You know?"

"You're bad news, Campbell," Joey said, grinning.

Alex led him up the stairs and into her bedroom, slowly closing the door behind her. "Hi," she whispered, not wanting to wake up her parents or Max.

"Hi," Joey whispered back. Then he laughed.

"What's funny?"

"I feel like I've been with you all day because I haven't been able to stop thinking about you. And now that I'm

here, literally looking at you, I already miss you . . ." Joey
laughed at himself. "So much for playing it cool, huh?"

"Cool is overrated," Alex said with another smile.

"Thanks . . ." Joey laughed.

"You know what I mean," Alex said. Besides, she felt
the same way.

Alex and Joey spent the entire night kissing.

Basically *just* kissing.

There was some touching, too, but mostly they were
just running from first base to second base and back again,
in the most enjoyable circles. They'd stop every once in a
while to laugh or hold each other or share a secret or tell a
story, and then they'd inevitably start kissing again.

And again and *again* . . .

And again and again it felt like things might escalate
physically, and they *could've*, certainly, but Joey and Alex
just didn't seem to be in that kind of a rush. For Alex, the
girl who had been known to get bored with a boy before
the end of their first make-out session, the girl who felt like
she was always rushing, the girl who was always trying to
move faster—*to literally break speed records*—this was an
incredibly important moment of stillness. Of slowness. Of
general *now*-ness. Most of the time Alex felt like she was
being pushed and pulled and prodded to be something she
wasn't . . . Right now with Joey, the only thing she had to
be was herself.

78 days until graduation . . .

ALEX and Joey managed to kiss until the sun came up . . .
. . . but it still didn't feel like nearly enough time.

"I'm gonna miss you," Joey whispered. He smiled with a little pink in his cheeks, as if he were surprised that the words had come out of his mouth.

"I'm gonna miss you, too," she said, thinking it was strange, considering how little time they'd actually spent together, but knowing it wasn't strange at all considering all the feelings she was feeling through her whole body.

"I miss you already," Joey said, laughing at his own corniness.

"Same," Alex replied, all full of sincerity and a little bit of sadness.

She'd known Joey for about twelve years, ever since she and Zoe had been friends, and even though they'd formed their own friendship through the track team, they'd never really spent any time alone together.

Until now.

And it felt like the most natural thing in the entire world.

Being together, with their lips and everything touching or their fingers and legs intertwined, felt right. But Joey had to leave. He had to sneak out of Alex's house and back into his before Zoe or his parents had a chance to notice he was gone.

So he kissed Alex good-bye one more time. Softly and slowly.

He said he'd text her as soon as he got back to his dorm room at Berkeley. And he did.

Hi, he said simply.

Hi, she texted back.

I miss you, he added. And then, also: *Ugh*.

Alex felt exactly the same way . . . all the way down to the *Ugh*.

I miss you too, she texted back.

She really did miss him. It was actually almost physically painful. Alex wasn't sure how to explain her feelings for Joey because they came on so fast and strong, but if she knew anything, anything at all, it was that they were the most real feelings she'd ever felt. For eighteen years, she'd had this space inside her, below her heart and above her stomach—maybe it was the place where the butterflies and the fireworks live—but it hadn't really registered before now. Like, if she'd walked through an X-ray machine, even just yesterday, there would've only been blank space inside her. But now . . . *ugh*, she thought, which was both the best and worst feeling all at the same time . . . *now* Joey Reed—and his spiked hair and those teal glasses and that wink—were all sitting inside of her, filling a space that she didn't even know existed.

Now she didn't want to even consider feeling any other way.

74 days until graduation . . .

ZOE was starting to worry that something was seriously wrong with her.

She and Austin were still dating. And they were still sleeping together semiregularly. And it was mostly fun, and she liked it, but she still hadn't had an orgasm. "Maybe I'm, like, physically incapable of having one," she'd proposed at froyo last week, but none of the other girls were willing to humor her.

It's totally gonna happen, they all assured her.

"Trust the process," Emma had said, giggling.

Zoe did trust the process—sort of.

But she decided she also wanted some professional reassurance that everything was working down there the way it should, so she'd made an appointment with her gynecologist. Also, she figured it was probably a good move to go on the pill. She and Austin had been using condoms, but still.

Zoe stood by the oak tree next to the senior parking lot,

waiting for her mom to pick her up, when she saw Dylan heading toward her. Well, really he was heading toward the pool with a pack of water polo boys, but it was the closest they'd come to being in the same place at the same time in a long time.

She wasn't even expecting him to wave, let alone walk over and say hi, but he did. Zoe didn't realize how much she'd missed him until he was standing right there in front of her, but she didn't realize the words were just going to tumble out of her mouth . . .

"I've missed you, too," he said before her cheeks even had time to redden.

"I got into Michigan," Zoe blurted out, realizing she hadn't told him yet.

"Oh hell, yeah," Dylan said. He'd already gotten early admission into Colorado. His older brother went there, and it was the only school he wanted to go to. And he got in. It was pretty undramatic as far as the college process went.

Zoe's college applications had been that way too. She wanted to go to a big school where people rooted for things and wore face paint and went to frat parties, but she also wanted a theater department. Zoe thought Michigan would be the perfect fit. Luckily, Michigan thought so too.

Then, Zoe's mom pulled up and waved. It was time to go. But before Zoe walked away, Dylan asked if she wanted to phonefall later that night.

Zoe had never said yes faster.

72 days until graduation . . .

ALEX and Joey had been texting constantly.

Ever since they'd spent the whole night kissing, they'd been continuously texting about anything and everything. Embarrassing stories. Childhood memories. Stupid jokes. They'd text back and forth about their hopes and dreams. About all their thoughts on God. About drugs and alcohol and rainbow sprinkles. About Alex's running shoes and how they occasionally didn't match. They texted about their daydreams and nightmares . . . Alex admitted that lately *he'd* been keeping her up at night, mostly just in the best possible way. She even texted him in the middle of the day just to say that she couldn't stop thinking about him, which wasn't the kind of thing she normally wanted to admit to a boy, or anyone really, but it felt like Joey already knew. He texted her back and said he felt exactly the same way. She already knew that too.

Alex couldn't imagine having all of these text message

conversations with anyone else. She'd never really cared what *any* boy thought about these topics, let alone what one particular boy thought about *all* of them. But with Joey, she wanted to know everything.

The only strange thing about all of their texting was that it accounted for a hundred percent of their communication. Alex liked texting much better than talking on the phone. She appreciated having the time and space to respond in exactly the right way.

But.

Considering the fact that none of these words *had* actually come out of her mouth and that she hadn't actually heard any of them come of Joey's mouth either, the whole thing was starting to seem like a strange dream. And to make matters worse, she still hadn't told the rest of The Crew about Joey. She certainly didn't want to lie to Zoe, not after all the Cameron stuff, but she knew how weird Zoe could get about things, especially things that involved her brother. She didn't want to get all into it with her if things with Joey weren't going to last anyway. Maybe that was lying by omission, but Alex wanted to figure out what was actually going on between them before she opened it up to The Crew.

Alex climbed into bed for the night and grabbed her phone.

Can I ask you a question? she texted Joey, innocently enough.

If it's "what am I wearing?" it's gonna be awkward, he texted back.

Alex smirked. That *wasn't* what she was going to ask, but now she wanted to know.

(The answer is nothing), he added almost immediately.

She and Joey had texted for an incredibly long time without crossing into any sort of sext message territory, and Alex had recently started to wonder if Joey was ever going to make that sort of a move.

What about you? he texted after a moment had gone by. The truth?

Alex was wearing flannel pajama bottoms and an over-sized track T-shirt, but she was pretty sure that wasn't the kind of answer Joey was hoping for. She lied, well, fibbed, and texted that she was wearing *black panties.* She hated the word "panties," but "underwear" just didn't sound sexy enough.

UGH, he responded in all capital letters. *I want to take them off.*

Yes, please, she texted back quickly.

And then, just like that, it was on . . .

. . . and they began turning *each other* on as a flurry of sext messages replaced their usual text message conversation. Joey told her where he wanted to touch her—*her thighs, her neck, her breasts*—and how he wanted to touch her—*mostly with his tongue*—and before Alex knew it, she really was touching herself and texting Joey about it. And Joey was touching himself, too, and texting her back . . . and pretty soon there were fireworks on both ends of the phone.

Or so Alex had to assume.

It was still hard to know what was actually happening.

She liked texting Joey, and she liked sexting him too, but all of that was only taking place on the glow of her phone screen.

Alex was starting to worry that it wasn't real.

Part of the problem was that it simply felt too good to be true.

70 days until graduation . . .

LAYLA was still spending far too much time thinking about Logan.

It wasn't that she was still mad at him anymore or hurt by him or anything like that, but she simply couldn't get him out of her head for any extended period of time, and it was driving her crazy.

And now.

Logan and Vanessa were *officially* a couple, and they were almost always making out all over campus. And Layla was pretending not to notice or care, both of which were horrible lies. She was focusing on schoolwork mostly, still trying to get her grade up to an A in AP Lit, doing some extra credit assignments. She was also trying as hard as she could not to focus on the calendar or her to-do list and its due date. And so, for the first time all year, Layla had actually succeeded in losing track of time, which was very un-Layla-like.

But then.

Last night, as she was lying in bed, searching for new quotes online and feeling uninspired, she suddenly felt compelled to count the days on the calendar. And so she did. She counted down, all the way down from today, Monday, April 13, to graduation day on June 22 . . . and she just simply had to laugh. She certainly believed that the universe had a mind of its own, but she didn't think it was *perverted*. But maybe it was. She counted the days on the calendar again, a second time, and then, just to be safe, a *third* time too, and realized that as of tomorrow, Tuesday, there would be exactly sixty-nine days until graduation.

Sixty-nine.

Of course she would reignite her interest in the calendar and the counting and all of that right before the most overtly sexual day of the whole countdown.

If Layla had ever gotten a sign from the universe, this might be it.

She texted Wyatt right away and made a plan to see him after school. They'd hooked up a couple times since that first make-out session at the skate park before spring break. He was still fun and still uncomplicated—but Layla still knew that she didn't want to sleep with him. Even so, she decided she'd still like to make some sex pact related progress with him.

"You're gonna sixty-nine him?" Alex asked as she unwrapped a protein bar.

"I think we have to say that I'm gonna sixty-nine *with*

him," Layla said so seriously that it caused everyone else to laugh.

"Okay, grammar police . . ."

"No, it's just . . . it's not something I can just do to him. He has to do it to me, too, which is kind of the whole point . . . ," Layla said, trailing off.

69 days until graduation ...

LAYLA drove over to Wyatt's house right after school.

They quickly found themselves alone in his room.

On his bed.

With the door closed.

Wyatt's parents weren't home from work yet, but Layla got the vibe that they wouldn't care about an open door policy even if they were. Wyatt was pointing out all the constellations on his ceiling: the Big Dipper, Orion's belt, and all the rest. He'd painted them with glow-in-the-dark paint. He was very proud.

"Wyatt?" Layla said, interrupting his tour of the galaxy.

"Yeah?" he asked with a big smile on his face. A big smile crept over Layla's face too. "Whatever you're thinking, I can already tell that I like it."

"I've never ...," she started, and then stopped to make

sure she was choosing her words carefully. "I graduate from high school in sixty-nine days."

"Whoa, crazy . . . ," Wyatt said.

Layla could tell that he didn't entirely understand what she was trying to say. "And. Also. I'm realizing that's something I've never done before."

"Graduate from high school?" Wyatt asked, clearly teasing.

"The other part. But the reason I've never done it is because no one's ever . . ."

" . . . gone down on you?" Wyatt asked, completing her sentence. "Is it because you didn't want them to?"

"I'm not really sure what I wanted," Layla said truthfully.

"But now you do," Wyatt said, his grin still finding ways to grow.

"I, um, well . . . ," Layla said, trying to qualify her statement or maybe just even lessen it in some way, so as not to seem too brash or demanding, but Wyatt didn't seem to need any of that.

"I got you," Wyatt said before sliding down to the bottom of the bed, taking Layla's jeans and underwear down with him.

The universe might have a sick sense of humor, Layla thought as she looked back up at the constellations on Wyatt's ceiling, but in the grand scheme of things, it definitely seemed to know what it was doing. After Wyatt spent some time between Layla's legs, he stopped what *he* was doing and asked if she wanted to sixty-nine, since it was numerically appropriate and all.

The answer to Wyatt's question was unequivocally yes.

Yes, she wanted to do that.

And yes, it was the right day and all that, but that wasn't *why* she wanted to do it.

To be totally honest: She just did.

It was the same but opposite way she knew she *didn't* want to have sex with Logan.

She just didn't.

And that was okay.

And this was okay too.

Once they finally (awkwardly) got situated in a sixty-nine position (on their sides facing each other), it all became so much more than okay.

So. Much. More. And then . . .

. . . after a while of tongues and lips and pressure and pleasure . . .

. . . it all exploded into *synchronized* fireworks.

Yes, Layla thought afterward.

So. Much. Yes.

68 days until graduation . . .

ALEX had been successfully avoiding Layla's progress reports for a few weeks.

After Oliver and the picture and all that, the girls had given Alex some space in the boy department. But now they were starting to ask questions again.

"You sure there's nothing you want to tell us?" Layla asked.

"Oh, I'm sure." Alex grinned, trying to play coy.

She *wanted* to tell the girls about Joey, she really did, especially after how mad Zoe got about Cameron and camp and everything. But the problem was that she didn't know what to say. She wanted to at least know *what* was happening before she told the girls that it *was* happening, but in order to get any clarity about the situation she was going to have to ask Joey. Her fear was that asking him about what it was (exactly) would ruin whatever it was (actually).

Whatever it was it all just seemed so strange and dreamlike.

No one (except for her and Joey) knew what had happened. Alex had never even said the words—*I kissed Joey Reed*—out loud. She had no one to say them to.

To Alex's surprise Joey was the first one to bring up the issue of telling Zoe. *You can tell her if you want*, he texted late one night when they were both already in bed.

I don't want to tell her if it's just gonna be a fling, Alex texted back.

After an oversized pause, Joey replied: *Yah.*

Alex noticed that Joey had added a period to the end of his *Yah* and she suddenly hated it so much. That period. It was so small, but also so stupid and so frustratingly definitive. What she wanted him say was *Of course it's not a fling*. Or *The truth is, I'm really into you*. Or *I want to be with you*. Or *I might even love you—let's make out forever and ever.*

Any of that—or all of that—would've been perfect.

Alex waited for what felt like another forever for him to type something else, something more, something *anything . . .*

But he didn't.

Unfortunately, for now, that one small, stupid word was all Alex was going to get out of him. So she texted it back exactly the same way: *Yah.*

She hoped he'd notice the period at the end.

She hoped he'd hate it as much as she did.

She hoped he'd be hoping for more too . . .

. . . and maybe he was, but he didn't text anything else.

And so neither did Alex.

She turned off her phone just to be sure.

64 days until graduation . . .

EMMA and Savannah held hands in the movie theater.

It was their first real date night. And Emma figured that hand-holding was the sort of thing you were supposed to do on a real date night. All in all the holding only lasted about five minutes, but that was approximately four minutes and thirty five seconds longer than Emma had ever held anybody else's hand. She could tell that it meant a lot to Savannah. And that was the whole point anyway.

After the movie the girls ended up back at Savannah's house. Emma's parents texted her to say they were running late to pick her up. Emma certainly wasn't complaining about the lateness. *Especially* when she and Savannah found themselves alone in Savannah's bedroom. Sitting on Savannah's bed. And Emma realized it was the first time they'd ever been alone somewhere that wasn't the yearbook room.

Savannah pulled Emma in for a kiss . . . which then

quickly turned into a whole *string* of kisses . . . and soon Savannah's hands were everywhere, and then Emma's hands were also everywhere, and things were decidedly different (and better) for Emma than ever before, because part of that "everywhere" included Savannah's boobs. Emma had touched her own boobs, of course, and that always turned her on, but touching Savannah's boobs was a whole new ball game. And then—*then*—when Savannah touched *Emma's* boobs . . . Emma didn't really have words to describe the sensation, except that it felt like there was a direct connection between her nipples and her vagina and it felt like all the hormones in her entire body were swirling between her legs and Emma started to feel like she might firework from that feeling alone . . .

. . . but then Savannah pushed forward and unzipped Emma's pants and slid her hand into Emma's underwear . . . and all the feelings and all the swirling just went into absolute overdrive and it felt like Savannah's fingertips were somehow all over Emma's entire body all at once.

And it was the fastest orgasm she'd ever had in her whole life.

"Shit," **ALEX** said in an uncharacteristic whisper as Emma finished recounting the whole date night/hookup story at the froyo table.

"You should've taken a sexie." Zoe smiled.

"Yeah, but Savannah didn't firework and then my parents showed up like two seconds later, and I had to go home, so . . ."

"Oh. Is that how it works?" Zoe asked sincerely. "Is it only . . . I mean . . . like . . . ?"

"Zoe . . ." Alex laughed.

"I'm trying to ask how exactly you would define having sex with another girl, but that might just be a stupid question."

"Definitely *not* stupid. I think I still have that same question," Emma said, laughing.

"*Basically* you're saying it was good, but you're not sure it was totally sex?" Layla said, trying to clarify the situation.

"I guess we have to define what 'it' actually is," Emma said as her thoughts drifted back to the day after she'd first had sex with Nick. She remembered they'd had to define some words then too. With a boy the "it" was easy: penis in vagina. Ironically, the "good" was more elusive. With Savannah, it was exactly the opposite. The "good" was incredibly obvious while the "it" that was proving more difficult to wrap their heads around. "I think Savannah and I would both have to firework in order for it to really count as sex . . ."

"Since when do you care about counting?" Alex asked. "I thought it was all about the process . . ."

"Well, the process is totally fun"—Emma laughed again—"but I want to make Savannah feel that way too."

"Oh, you will . . . ," Layla said reassuringly.

"Oh. Cool," Zoe said, newly frustrated. "According to that definition, if I was a lesbian, I'd still be a virgin."

"Or maybe then you would've orgasmed?" Emma

asked, trying to make a joke, but she realized it came out sounding rather insensitive. "Sorry, Zo," she added.

"It's okay," Zoe said, returning to her froyo.

"Savannah said her ex-girlfriend considered 'sex' any hookup that involved an orgasm for either girl," Emma added. "If we're looking at it like that then maybe technically you could say we did have sex, but I think it should be all systems go before I'll feel like it's official."

The other girls realized that was the first time the G-word had come out of Emma's mouth. G-word meaning "girlfriend," not "graduation." Still it was a big deal. But none of the girls pointed that out to Emma. They didn't want to freak her out. And, to be fair, she hadn't described Savannah as being *her* girlfriend . . . she was talking about Savannah having an *ex*-girlfriend who used to do the kind of things with Savannah that Emma was now doing, but still . . .

Suffice it to say the word did not go unnoticed.

Then, the stack of phones in the middle of the table started to buzz.

Zoe thought it might be Austin. She had told him that he could come over later. She told Emma that she could check. Emma reached for the phone stack. She checked Zoe's phone, but the new text wasn't for Zoe.

It was for Alex.

ALEX had a sinking feeling about the situation.

"Who is J?" Emma asked slowly.

"Um. Why?" Alex asked, trying to sound as nonchalant as possible.

"Well. He just asked what you're wearing, so . . ."

The girls all laughed as Alex breathed a little sigh of relief. Considering some of the other sext messages Joey had sent her recently, she knew his question could've been *a lot* worse. Also, she was *so* incredibly grateful that she'd put him in her phone as J and not Joey. She had no clue how she would've explained *that* to Zoe right here and now.

Luckily, she didn't have to.

"It's Jordan, isn't it? From the basketball team?" Layla asked, in detective mode.

And Alex smiled that Mona Lisa smile. The one that kept getting her into trouble. This time, she thought, it might actually be her saving grace. She still didn't want to tell the girls about Joey. Not yet. Not until she knew if it was real or not. So she just let her smile say yes.

"I knew it!" Layla laughed, thinking she'd solved the case.

"Should we text him back?" Emma asked.

"Oh no . . ." Alex shook her head.

But then Alex's phone buzzed again.

And it was still sitting in the middle of the table, and the girls saw the text before Alex could hide the screen.

PLEASE tell me it's the panties again

Now Zoe, Emma, and Layla all lost it, exploding into a new burst of giggles, and that made the heads of all the Bigg Chill customers turn toward them and their corner table. "Again?" Layla squealed.

"Who says 'panties'?" Zoe laughed.

"At least he didn't call them *moist*—that is *literally* the worst word."

"Shhhhh," Alex said as her light brown cheeks turned a distinct shade of red. She slid the phone toward her, trying to hide the screen, but it was too late.

"You have to text him back," Layla insisted.

"Yes," Zoe agreed.

Alex knew Zoe would die, *absolutely die*, if she knew who J really was, but she wasn't sure how to get out of it now, especially as another string of texts poured in:

Or just say ur wearing nothing
In my head I've already taken them off
With my teeth.

"Oh. My. God," Layla said.

"Okay, see, now you have to say something," Emma pushed.

Alex didn't seem to have much of a choice.

Mmmhmmm, she texted back.

"And what does that mean exactly?" Layla asked, taking mental notes.

TURNED ON, Joey texted back in all capital letters.

"Oh, okay, got it," Layla said, laughing.

"And now what?" Emma asked after a few minutes. "Why isn't he saying anything else?"

"He's probably jacking off . . . ," Alex said matter-of-factly.

"Ohmigod," Zoe said, shaking her head. She turned her attention back to her vanilla froyo as Emma and Layla brainstormed some sexy things for Alex to text next. Alex couldn't help feeling bad about how Zoe would feel if she knew who was on the other end of this phone, but she was already feeling bad about Austin, and Alex didn't want to do anything that might make the girls suspicious. She knew there was nothing left to do but go with it. And so they did.

Laughing and squealing and sexting . . .

"Can everyone just please remember that we are in public?" Zoe asked when it all got particularly loud at one point.

"Sorry," Alex said.

Really, she was apologizing for the entire situation and not *just* for the volume of their conversation . . . Luckily Zoe was blissfully oblivious.

Alex decided that was definitely for the best.

61 days until graduation . . .

ALEX sat in the front of Oliver's car, texting Joey on the way to school.

Lately, Alex and Oliver's car pool rides had been quiet and friendly, mostly just filled with the sound of the radio. They'd nod to say hello. And then they'd wave good-bye on the way out of the car. But that was it. They really didn't have much to say to each other. Not since the crying and everything. It was just too much. And now that Oliver was *dating* Caroline—not just hooking up—there was even less to talk about. This morning Alex found herself laughing out loud at one of Joey's text messages. She wasn't trying to rub it in Oliver's face, but it just sort of happened like that. She could tell that Oliver wanted to ask her about who she was texting with and what the text message said and all that, but he didn't or he wouldn't or whatever, and Alex wasn't going to offer up the information, so the silence continued.

Then, Joey texted that he had something serious to tell her.

The word "serious" jumped off her phone screen. *Ugh.* He's breaking up with me, Alex thought. But then she felt stupid, because they weren't even officially together. What exactly was there to break?

But then Alex realized that the seriousness wasn't about them at all . . . it was about her.

Her picture.

Joey was still friendly with some of the younger guys on the track team, and he'd been in a big group text, along with a bunch of athletes, for a while now. But just last night Oliver admitted to doing it. *Doing what*, Alex started to type before she realized she didn't have to. Joey was trying to tell her that Oliver had, in fact, Photoshopped the naked picture of her and sent it to everyone on the Internet. Joey explained that Oliver had been bragging about it pretty extensively. At first Alex wanted to argue with Joey. She wanted to say that Oliver couldn't *possibly* have done it — he'd told her he hadn't . . . but, then again, she knew that his word didn't really mean much of anything at all.

Joey texted Alex a screenshot from the group chat, and there was absolutely no use in arguing any more. There it was, in black-and-white, right on her phone screen.

You're welcome, Oliver had texted all the guys as he took credit for his photo editing skills, like the cocky asshole he was.

"Stop the car," Alex said.

"Excuse me?"

"Stop. The. Car." Alex's words were calm and measured, but they were also unwavering. "I'm getting out."

"We're, like, two miles from school."

"I'm not asking you."

Oliver pulled up to a red light and was forced to stop, which gave Alex just enough time to hop out of the car. "What are you doing?" Oliver yelled at her through the open window.

All Alex knew for sure was that she couldn't sit next to him anymore. She hadn't really thought about anything else. Alex took off, running toward school. Fortunately it was a flat, easy jog along Ventura Boulevard. Once the stoplight turned green, Oliver had no choice but to drive off without Alex. He couldn't stop traffic, and Alex refused to get back into the car.

About fifteen minutes later, by the time Alex got to school, a bit sweaty from the run, Oliver was standing at the entrance, waiting for her. "What is your problem?"

Alex didn't have a problem.

Not anymore.

She bent down and untied her shoelace, all slowly and deliberately.

"What are you doing?" Oliver asked, getting more and more agitated and flustered with each passing moment, which made Alex want to move even slower. She knew she was driving Oliver absolutely crazy. It was an empowering feeling. She slid the star charm off her shoelace and held it up for Oliver to see before dropping it in a nearby trash can.

"You're actually crazy," Oliver said when Alex still hadn't spoken to him.

"And you're *actually* an asshole," she finally replied. "You're welcome," she added, echoing the text message he'd sent the boys. "For the Photoshop skills."

Oliver's face turned instantly pale. He was so cocky and stupid; he thought he was actually going to get away with the whole thing. Not just the picture. Not just the embarrassment and all the ache he'd caused Alex. But the bragging, too. He thought he could get away with that. And that was the worst part, Alex decided. Oliver asked her if she was going to tell on him. He sounded like a small, sad, sniffling child.

"No," Alex said, making the decision as the word came out of her mouth. "What's that going to do? Make your life miserable? Maybe, but I don't need that. You know what you did. And I know who you are. So. As far as I'm concerned I've already won. Forever, I get to be me—and you have to be you—and I feel incredibly good about both of those things." Before Oliver could respond, she added, "And I'm glad you had so much fun jacking off to my knees . . ."

Alex turned triumphantly and walked away with her head held high.

59 days until graduation . . .

EMMA drove to Savannah's house without wearing any underwear.

She wasn't expecting to make that sort of bold move at 11:00 p.m. on a Friday night, but she wasn't expecting a lot of the things that had happened to her over the past few months. Recently, her older sister Heather told her that the secret to being an adult and knowing what you were doing just meant Googling the answer without asking anyone else first. So, mostly as a joke, she Googled: *What should I do with my life?* And it led her to a website about taking a gap year. Emma had never considered that option before. The only option that seemed to be on the table for the following year was her freshman year of college, but now, she realized that simply wasn't true. Emma spent some more time Googling—and exploring the real possibility of a gap year. It was an exciting prospect. But not nearly as exciting as spending more alone time with Savannah.

Can I come over? Emma had texted.

PLEASE, Savannah texted back almost immediately.

Emma was already wearing her pajamas, so she got up and got re-dressed.

Or undressed.

Or both.

Either way, she decided she needed to be only minimally dressed for what was going to happen next. She put on a pleated jean skirt. And her favorite purple zip-up hoodie. And a pair of flip-flops. And that was it. No underwear whatsoever . . .

Emma's parents were already sleeping, so she slipped out the front door as quietly as she could. And she snuck into Savannah's house too, making sure not to wake up her parents. And then, as soon as Emma stepped into Savannah's bedroom, the girls picked up right where they'd left off after their date night . . . all kissing and touching and fingertips . . . and Savannah reached for the zipper on Emma's hoodie . . . and the moment she realized Emma wasn't wearing a bra was absolutely priceless. It felt like an instant, immediate memory. The kind of thing you can remember in real time, long before before the actual moment even ends.

Savannah's face and eyes and *everything* . . . it all just lit up.

"Oh, if you think that's fun . . ." Emma smirked.

And Savannah seemed to know exactly what she was getting at, because she wasted absolutely no time slipping her hands under Emma's skirt . . . and confirmed her happy suspicion that Emma didn't have any underwear on down there, either.

"You. Are. The coolest . . . ," Savannah said as the kisses continued.

They pulled off the rest of their clothes, and moved over to Savannah's bed and soon Emma found herself on top of Savannah . . . Savannah started to slide her fingers between Emma's legs, but Emma grabbed her hand, stopping her . . .

"This first," Emma said, pinning Savannah's hands up above her head.

Emma kissed her way down from Savannah's lips, past her neck and her boobs and her stomach, until she found herself between Savannah's legs . . . and the truth was she didn't know what she was supposed to do—*at all*—but she knew what *she* liked . . . and she remembered the last time she was in the darkroom with Nick and how worried she'd been about where his face had to be, and now that her face was there, she realized she had wasted way too much time worrying about that. Even though she certainly enjoyed the, um, *process* with Nick she knew now that she could've been and should've been just enjoying it so much more . . .

Savannah didn't seem to have any of those same fears— or if she did, Emma couldn't tell. . . . Especially since Savannah was too busy telling Emma how much she liked what she was doing with her tongue and her lips and her fingers. . . and then, just as Emma felt like she was really getting started . . .

Savannah finished.

Fireworks.

Everywhere.

This, Emma thought.

And then Savannah flipped over, on top of Emma, and it only took a few more minutes of Savannah's lips and fingertips before Emma set off her very own display . . .

Afterward, Savannah curled into Emma's arms.

"So. This is good," Emma managed to say with a bit of a laugh.

"Yeah, it is . . ." Savannah laughed back. "Ineffable," she added as if she'd been waiting for the right moment to say that.

"Ineffable?"

"That's the word for when something's too great to be described in words."

Exactly, Emma thought.

Ineffable.

That's exactly what this was.

58 days until graduation . . .

ZOE knew what she had to do as soon as she saw Emma's new sexie.

Emma and Savannah had "officially" had sex last night, and Zoe could see the glow on Emma's face and feel the "rightness" of it all even just by looking at the picture on the phone screen, and it helped confirm what she'd known was true for a few weeks now . . .

Zoe didn't want to be Austin's girlfriend anymore.

And not *just* because she didn't want to have sex with him anymore, even though, truthfully, she didn't, but mostly because he didn't make her feel the way Emma looked in her sexie. She didn't have any *bad* feelings toward Austin, but there just weren't enough good feelings left to force it anymore.

Zoe knew it was time to break up with Austin.

But it was still easier said than done.

Finally, after stressing about it all day, she worked up

the courage to call him just before dinnertime. She kept the conversation short and mostly sweet. She explained that she simply didn't like him like that anymore. And that she wanted to break up. He didn't argue with her. Maybe he felt like it had been building to this, too. Regardless, it was done.

Zoe realized she probably should've driven over to his house and told him in person, but she couldn't. At least she didn't text it to him.

Even though Zoe caused the breakup, she was still upset about it. She'd never had a boyfriend before Austin. He'd always be her first. And now he was her first *ex*-boyfriend too.

She texted The Chat.

And everyone texted back quickly. They all loved her very much. And they were all there for her. But of course she knew all that already. And the girls made her feel like the luckiest, as always, but then she also felt like crying too.

And so she did.

And she felt worse for a while but then also better, too.

Alex was right.

Tears were *so* underrated.

50 days until graduation . . .

ZOE could not bring herself to order vanilla frozen yogurt again.

Layla ordered "The Layla."

Emma ordered cake batter.

Alex ordered Graham Cracker Caramel.

But, for Zoe, today was the time for something different.

She ordered strawberry.

"You reached maximum vanilla capacity?" Layla teased as the girls settled around their table.

"Yeah something like that. Maximum vanilla capacity. Maximum *Austin* capacity . . . I just had to get all of this out of my room." Zoe gestured to the shoe box she'd brought with her. It was full of little memories she'd collected over the past couple of months. Each item on its own felt small, but it all reminded her of Austin and all piled together they were more than Zoe needed.

The dried carnation from Valentine's Day sat on the top.

"Is it lame that I want to keep this? Not 'cause of Austin, but just . . . it dried so perfectly."

"Well. It's not from Austin," Layla said, treading carefully.

"What?"

"Dylan bought it for you."

Zoe laughed until she realized that Layla was serious, then suddenly she got serious too. "Why didn't you tell me? Why didn't *he* tell me?"

"He said all he wanted was for you to be happy. That was his 'mission accomplished.'"

Zoe had been *so* happy that she hadn't even thought to press Austin about the flower. She just assumed it was from him because that's what she'd wanted at the time. Now, looking backward, she would've been even happier to know that it was from Dylan . . .

But that's not how life worked.

Life had to be lived forward. And it all had to happen exactly the way that it did or she may not have found herself here, in this moment, with her best friends and a brand-new frozen yogurt flavor. After the girls finished, Zoe threw the Austin shoe box in the trash can in the parking lot of The Bigg Chill, but she made sure to hold on to the red carnation. She put it on the passenger seat next to her and drove toward Dylan's house. She blasted his mix CD as loud as she could and turned what might've been a twenty minute ride across the city of Los Angeles and into the valley into a two hour drive. There was still so much that Zoe didn't know, but right now she knew she needed this time and this space and most of all she needed this music.

She pulled up in front of Dylan's house and turned off the car's engine, but she left the key in the ignition so she could listen to the end of the last song on the mix: Jimmy Eat World's "Sweetness." It was Dylan's all-time favorite song, and one of Zoe's, too. Even after the song ended, the last lyric—"with a little sweet and simple numbing me"—still continued to ring in her head as she sat in the front seat, trying to build up the courage to get out and go talk to Dylan . . .

And then . . .

After two minutes of sitting in silence.

After two full minutes of getting lost in her thoughts and her feelings and holding out hope that Dylan might just telepathically realize she was sitting outside and come open the front door.

. . . another song started to play.

Zoe had been listening to Dylan's mix CD on repeat for weeks. She had heard every song on it *at least* a hundred times. But, up until this moment, she'd always started the CD over again immediately once it ended. She'd never thought to wait for something more—why would she? There was no way she could've known there was a secret song, *but* then again, maybe she didn't need to know about this song until this very moment. It was a "God Bless the Broken Road" cover by Rascal Flatts. Zoe had heard the song so many times before but never quite like this.

Now it all made sense.

And now, as the song ended, Zoe knew that the timing was finally right.

She'd had feelings for Dylan since that first day they got paired up in Chem class. But those original emotions—that first crush or attraction or whatever it was—couldn't even begin to compete with the layered and complex love she felt for him now. Her feelings were real . . . but she needed the whole entire broken road to get here.

Now all Zoe had to do was get out of the car. And ring Dylan's doorbell.

So she did.

And he answered and invited her inside. He wasn't expecting her, but he wasn't all that surprised to see her either. They made their way down the hallway into his room. It was all dark blue and plaid. Lots of trophies and sports memorabilia on the walls. She looked at Dylan's bed and tried to count how many times she might've heard his voice from it.

"Why didn't you tell me about the carnation?" Zoe asked.

"Why did you pick up the phone that night?" Dylan smirked.

"Ohmigod . . ." Zoe rolled her eyes. "'God bless the broken road,' I guess," she added with a bit of a laugh, which felt like it answered both of their questions at the same time.

"You found it."

"Took me long enough."

"I wanted to tell you, but then that ruins the secret."

"It's not really a secret anymore," Zoe said, talking about so much more than the song.

And then finally—*finally*—after all their phonefalls, after all the thousands or maybe even millions of words they'd exchanged . . . there were only four more that Zoe wanted to say:

"I love you, too."

Dylan pulled Zoe in close for the kind of first kiss she'd (literally) been dreaming about for oh-so-long. Then they moved to Dylan's bed and kept kissing and kissing and *kissing* until Dylan finally found the courage to move his hands from Zoe's back . . . and onto her boobs.

Zoe laughed.

It wasn't a nervous giggle.

It was a big, rich, full body kind of laugh that made her boobs jiggle in Dylan's hands.

"Ohmigod," he said through kisses, the way Zoe always did. "I've wanted to do that for-*ever*."

"Okay, but I've only had them for like four months," she teased.

"What. Ever. Feels like forever," he teased back.

For the first time, their "for real" in person conversation felt like it did when they spoke on the phone. Zoe kissed Dylan again. And again and again. And even though they'd only been doing that for about four *minutes* it felt like forever, too, but in the best possible way. They spent the next couple of hours rolling around on his bed, laughing and teasing and talking and kissing some more. . . until Zoe had to leave so she wouldn't be late for curfew.

She sang along to "Sweetness," on repeat, all the way home.

She got ready for bed as quickly as she could and then called Dylan like he made her promise she would before she left his house. And he picked up on the first ring. And they talked for another hour or two—or tonight it might've even been *three*—until they both managed to fall asleep . . . together.

47 days until graduation ...

EMMA had taken more pictures in her lifetime than she could count.

She couldn't even count how many she'd taken in the last five months, which was proving to be a bit of a problem, as she'd gotten the idea in her head that it was time to develop all of them. She needed them. But right now, staring at the filmstrips in the darkroom, it seemed like an overwhelming task.

Thankfully, there was a knock on the door.

"Em?" Nick asked. "You in there?"

Emma's lips curled into a smile as she was transported back to the memory of the last time she had heard Nick knock on the door of the darkroom . . . and all the fireworks that followed. She opened the door, still smiling. She knew she didn't have to explain why. She could tell by the look on his face that he remembered too.

"Thank you for agreeing to help me . . ."

"You. Are. Welcome." Nick laughed. "Last time you asked me for help, I offered you my penis, so I figured it couldn't be any more awkward than that."

"Hopefully this won't be awkward at all," Emma said as Nick walked across the small room and slid up next to her. "But I have the strongest sense of déjà vu."

"My mom says that having a feeling of déjà vu means you're exactly where you're supposed to be," Nick explained.

"I love that," Emma said, feeling the truth in Nick's words. They were so simple and also so profound. Emma's thoughts drifted back to the very first time she met Savannah in the yearbook room, and she remembered the sense of déjà vu that had washed over her then. Of course, at the time, things were just starting to fall into place, but they were clearly already aligning themselves in the right direction. Now Emma was more clearly rooted in this time and place—but all of it just felt right. Weirdly right. Emma was so present and so in the moment. Thankfully the "right now" was all she could think about . . . but she did her best not to *over*think it for once.

She was just in it.

Emma had learned that moments like this one were fleeting. But she'd also learned that every once in a while, if you trusted the process and let things develop, everything would fall into place.

It wouldn't *stay* in place—not for very long anyway— but at least it would balance for a moment. And then the next moment of balance required more movement.

And so on.

And so forth.

Emma and Nick spent the rest of the afternoon in the darkroom, developing pictures. For the first time in the longest time, Emma felt like she was really truly getting somewhere—and it was exactly where she wanted to be.

43 days until graduation . . .

ALEX was still in the same place she'd been many times before . . .

In a galaxy far, far away, watching *The Empire Strikes Back* with Max.

Her phone buzzed. It was a text from Joey, unsurprisingly.

What are you doing?

Alex was relieved he didn't ask what she was wearing this time. Being with her girls was one thing, but she would not have humored him like that while she was sitting on the couch with her brother watching her favorite Star Wars movie.

Joey said *The Empire Strikes Back* was his favorite Star Wars movie too.

I love it, he texted.

The word "love" jumped out at her.

There had been *endless* text messages sent between

them, but no one had dropped an actual "love" bomb yet. Normally, Alex would've waited and played some sort of game to make sure that Joey was the one who said— or typed—it first. But Alex was tired of playing. This— whatever this was exactly with Joey—felt so much more real than that.

I love YOU, she typed.

She watched as the message was delivered.

She knew he had seen it.

She waited for a response.

And waited.

And waited . . .

. . . until she felt so incredibly stupid that she decided she might never send Joey Reed a text message ever again. Honestly, she might never send *anyone* a text message ever again in her entire life. *In fact,* just as she was about to decide to give up her cell phone altogether and become a monk and live by herself on the top of a mountain, out of the middle of nowhere, Joey texted back . . .

I know.

Five letters. Two words. One period.

THAT'S HIS RESPONSE?! she thought. I say *I love you* and he says *I know?* Alex was about to lose it and throw her phone across the room . . . when, as if on cue, Max pointed to the TV screen and said, "I know."

"What?" Alex asked as she looked up from her phone.

Max's words had sounded like an echo of the thoughts in her head, but they weren't about her at all. Max's eyes were glued to the screen. To the movie. To his favorite scene.

"I love this part," he said. And Alex watched along with Max as Princess Leia turned to Han Solo to tell him that she loved him, and then—then!—Han Solo responded with his perfectly infuriating, incredibly classic line: "*I know.*"

Alex's heart burst inside her chest, filling her entire body with an incredible amount of warmth. It was as if she could feel Joey winking at her through the phone.

Thank you, Han Solo, she texted back as quickly as she could.

Ugh! Joey responded, including that well placed exclamation point.

You're perfect, he added, this time without any punctuation.

And then he added: *I love you too.*

Alex noted the period at the end of that last text.

Joey Reed and his stupid periods, she thought.

Right now, she even loved those, too.

ZOE picked up the phone on the first ring. "What's wrong?" she asked.

"Well hello," Joey laughed.

"Are you okay?"

"Why wouldn't I be okay?"

"'Cause you never *just* call me. Only if something's wrong or you're trying to find me in a crowd."

"Okay, well, I'm not *just* calling, but . . . don't be mad."

"Uh-oh . . ."

"No, no. It's fine. It's *good* actually—"

"Joey. You are killing me right now—"

Cherry

"I kissed Alex when I was home for spring break."

"Excuse me?" Zoe asked, her voice squeaking.

"I kissed her in my bedroom the night of your sleepover, and then I kissed her all night, the next night, in her bed-room."

"I don't even understand what you're saying right now," Zoe said.

Joey explained that there had been a lot of kissing between them. And now, ever since then, there'd also been a lot of texting. And Alex wanted to tell Zoe what had happened right away so as to avoid lying or anything, but they had both decided it was better to wait and not say anything official until they were sure that the whole thing was worth talking about.

"We wanted to make sure it was real."

"Okay . . . ," Zoe said, still trying to put all the pieces together. "So. Is this your way of telling me that it's real?"

"Very real," Joey said after a bit of a pause.

"Oh my God, wow," Zoe said. But not in her usual freak-out kind of way. The words were slow and deliberate. "You're in love with my best friend."

"I am . . . ," he said with a happy exhale. "She's in love with me too." Zoe could hear the smile in Joey's voice, but then her mind started to wander—back through the last few weeks, replaying all of her moments with Alex in her head—and all of a sudden her thoughts found their way to The Bigg Chill and the group sext message conversation three weeks ago and all she could say was . . .

"Wow."

349

"Uh oh. You sound like you're about three seconds away from freaking out on me . . ."

"No. I'm . . . *ohmigod* . . ." Zoe started to laugh.

"I knew it . . . ," Joey said, mistaking Zoe's laughter for a meltdown.

Really, it was just the realization that her brother—*OHMIGOD* HER BROTHER—was the J they had all been texting with on Alex's phone that afternoon.

Despite the awkwardness Zoe had a feeling they would all laugh about this together one day, but she said she'd let Alex fill him in on the details.

38 days until graduation . . .

ALEX was actually, technically, and completely about to run out of chances.

This was it.

Today, Friday, May 15, was the last official qualifying track meet of her high school career. It was time to "go big or go home." Well, realistically, Alex was going to have to go home either way, but hopefully it wouldn't be empty-handed.

Either way she knew it would be a relief. For so long she'd felt as if she had been carrying the weight of the world on her shoulders. Since the first day of her life, she'd been carrying part of Max and all of the things her parents had hoped for him. As she grew up, she held on to the way people looked at her. With all her speed, she'd convinced herself that she was capable of outrunning her baggage and leaving it behind her in the dust. But that wasn't what she had been doing at all. She wasn't actually leaving anything behind. Instead she was still forcing herself to carry it all with her. Now she could see the difference between what she had and what she actually needed. It would've been too simple and trite to say that it was because of Joey—or because of the way she felt about him—or even the way he felt about her. That would've given him far too much credit and power. She knew he never would've accepted a compliment like that anyway, but she also knew that something real had happened between them. It felt so right, and they just fit together so well, that she didn't have to carry any of it. It was just there all on its own. And it was exactly what she needed.

Every track meet of her high school career Alex would stand on the same spot on the track and take a minute to visualize the race before it began. For the past few months she'd been standing in that spot trying to convince herself that she could break the record. Today, she knew that whether she broke it or not, she was going to run the race in a way it had never been run before. She was going to do her best no matter what the outcome.

As Yoda liked to say: "Do or do not. There is no try."

Today, Alex knew she wasn't trying. She was doing. She wasn't worrying. She was being. She was alive and completely in the moment . . . but she couldn't help but think that the moment would be even better and sweeter and more complete if Joey had been there too.

And then . . . there he was.

Standing on the track in front of her as if he'd just appeared out of nowhere. But he hadn't, of course. He'd bought a plane ticket and flown from Oakland to Burbank.

And Zoe had picked him up at the airport in his Ford Explorer and driven him to the track.

"You're a dream," she said as soon as he finished the explanation.

"And you're the most real," he said with a seemingly endless smile.

It might've been the best compliment Alex had ever received in her entire life. And this might've been one of the best moments of her entire life. She loved Joey, and he loved her, and at the very same time they both just said, "I know."

"Okay, cool." Alex smiled. "Now I'm gonna go do this thing."

"You got this."

And Alex knew that she did.

But.

She didn't break the record.

She won the track meet as she had so many times before.

And she was the fastest runner on the entire track.

But, it still wasn't enough.

Alex felt like a giant failure. And there was nothing she hated more than that feeling. It stung. And it sucked. *So much.* But the world kept spinning, and Alex didn't fall apart. Coach K insisted that all of the seniors take a victory lap around the track. Alex led the pack. A few months ago Alex might've said this last lap was just a consolation prize, but she knew now that the journey to get here—all the hours of practice and beads of sweat—was the real victory.

It wasn't until a couple hours later, sometime between

dinner with her family and ending up watching a movie on the couch in Zoe and Joey's guesthouse that Alex realized what her buddy Yoda really meant when he said "Do or do not. There is no try." He wasn't saying that it was impossible to try, or that it wasn't worth trying . . . he was saying that trying *is* doing. Of course, you had to do whatever the "it" was in the right way. You had to try with every ounce of yourself, but if you did that—if you whole-heartedly tried—then that was doing, too.

Alex could not have trained harder.

At least for now, for this moment, this really was the absolute best she could do.

And the truth was, she loved herself more in the midst of this supposed failure than she ever had before. Alex's thoughts drifted to her sex dream and Cameron and summer camp and then high school and the pact . . . at first she thought she'd been waiting to have sex until she felt the right way about another boy . . . and then she felt like she was supposed to do it together with friends . . . and both of those things could still possibly be true, but now Alex knew that what she had *really* been waiting for was the opportunity to feel that way about *herself*.

Joey made her feel like herself without even trying.

There was that "try" word again.

Even though she understood what Yoda meant, she also knew that trying to have sex wasn't the same as actually having sex. Not technically, not completely, not at all. And even though there was a time when *she* thought and wished that Cameron had been her first, clearly God or the universe or whatever was in charge had other plans.

And those plans led her to this moment.

To this couch.

With Joey and Zoe.

After a little while, Zoe's phone buzzed. It was a text from Dylan. "I'm gonna go talk to my *boyfriend*," she said. "Have fun with yours . . ."

It was only after Zoe left that Alex realized that she and Joey hadn't been alone together since their all-night make-out session almost six weeks ago.

They wasted absolutely no time and picked up exactly where they left off . . . but then this time all their kisses turned into so much more than that.

This time would be Alex's first time.

Technically.

Actually.

Completely.

Joey was on top, and Alex's shoes were on the floor next to the couch, and he knew to put a towel down underneath them, and she had a smile on her face the entire time—even when it got awkward and she wasn't sure where to put her hips and he wasn't sure where to put his hands—and she couldn't stop staring into his eyes, and he looked right back at her the very same way, and it was all sort of sexy and fun and—most of all—magnetic.

"Yes," Joey said afterward. He was lying on his back, looking up at the ceiling. Alex was curled on her side next to him. He turned his head to look at her. "You . . . ," he started sweetly, but something about the sound of the word made Alex roll her eyes. "Oh, stop with that eye roll . . . you don't even know what the end of my sentence is going to sound like yet."

"Something about the way I look right now? The beauty of it all?"

"The beauty of it all has absolutely nothing to do with the way you look," Joey insisted. "You're gorgeous, Alex. Deal with it. But that's not . . . I think your looks pale in comparison to the way your soul feels when I look at you."

She felt Joey's words all over her body . . . and deep inside, too.

No one had ever talked about Alex's soul before, but she appreciated it more than any other compliment she'd ever received.

Afterward, Alex went into the bathroom to pee and wash up . . . and then she took a moment to look at herself in the mirror. She couldn't help but think that it may have been the first time she'd ever really seen herself in her entire life. Or maybe it was the first time she'd seen herself the way she'd always wanted to. Either way she snapped a sexie. And sent it to The Chat.

ZOE had been expecting the picture, but it still made her groan into her phone.

"What?" Dylan asked.

Brotherfucker, Zoe texted back to Alex and The Chat.

She added a smiley face to make sure the girls knew she was joking.

Well.

She wasn't *joking*, that was a totally accurate description of the situation, but she wanted to make sure the girls knew she wasn't mad about it.

"Are you texting?" Dylan asked.

"Yes. Sorry. The girls . . ." Zoe realized that in order to explain Alex's sexie, she would have to tell Dylan about the pact. So she did. She explained everything. "So that might explain the time you called and I was . . ." She knew he knew exactly what she was talking about. The now infamous phone call.

"Yeah . . . So. Would you now?" Dylan asked quietly.

"Would I now *what*?" Zoe was pretty sure she knew what he meant, but if Dylan wanted it to happen she was going to make him say it out loud.

"Would you . . . I mean . . . Do you want to touch yourself?"

"Only if you tell me where," Zoe said rather boldly. She could feel her entire face and all of its redness. And her entire body and all of its *everything* as their conversation got sexy and intimate in a way it never had before . . .

The girls had all told Zoe (and she'd also read it in Layla's Sex Doc) that the key to having an orgasm was foreplay and she realized as their conversation turned sexual, that she and Dylan had effectively been *foreplaying* on the phone for almost four years. They'd had so many conversations and had spent so much time talking and laughing and flirting (even when they were supposedly just friends) that now, as they talked about how *hard* or *fast* or *slow* to touch themselves and exactly where and how they wanted to touch *each other*, it wasn't much of a surprise that all of it finally—*FINALLY*—erupted into Zoe's first orgasm.

It was more than worth the wait.

And it really did feel an awful lot like fireworks.

"Then, why are you crying?" Alex asked, feeling the tears welling up in her eyes too.

"Because now this really feels like the end," Layla said.

"No! We still have three weeks!" Zoe said. "And summer! And grad night! And prom!"

"Right . . . ," Layla said. She always had lots of grand visions about prom, but they all circled back to Logan.

"We're going together, right?" Alex asked.

"Of course," Layla said.

"No, I mean we're going *together* together. 'Cause I literally can't think of anyone I'd rather pose for pictures with . . ."

As soon as Alex said the word "picture," a single tear ran down Emma's cheek. She'd been the last noncrying holdout. "Not you, too, with the tears . . . ," Layla said through more tears of her own.

"I can't help it," Emma said. She sincerely couldn't.

None of them could.

They were all crying now.

And the tears were mostly happy.

Or at least more happy than sad, but they were still a little bit sad, too.

The girls knew that no matter what happened from here on out, it would never be exactly the same between them. After graduation, they would simply never all be in high school together again. And soon even the memories would fade. All the late nights and the all-nighters and the rainbow sprinkles. All the crushes and the soul crushing kisses, and all the texting and the touching and sexies and sex . . . one day all of it would blur together.

"Kind of like an orgasm . . ." Emma laughed.

"Yeah," Layla agreed. "At some point, all the feelings and sensations just kind of blur together. I think that's how our memories will be too: blurred into us, into our souls."

"A soul of fireworks," Alex said, clearly liking the sound of that.

"Fireworks really are the perfect metaphor," Zoe agreed. "They're so bright and bold and fill up the entire sky, but then they also fade away just as quickly."

"Oh, now you get it." Alex laughed.

"I do, actually. I *finally* do."

"Zoe. Reed," Layla said, putting the pieces together. "Tell me everything . . ."

"Phone sex, late last night."

Everyone erupted into a familiarly epic fit of laughter.

"Finally!" Alex squealed. "I love that so much."

"Me too," Zoe agreed.

"Me three," Emma added.

"This is perfect," Layla concluded.

"The only thing that would make it even more perfect is if we had . . ."

" . . . frozen yogurt," Emma and Zoe chimed in, along with Alex.

"It's already in my fridge," Layla said.

"You got frozen yogurt? For all of us? Even though we were assholes and didn't show up?" Zoe asked as both a question and an apology.

"Have you met me?" Layla laughed. "Of course I did."

Layla didn't know for sure that they'd all end up on her trampoline like this, but she had certainly hoped that they might. It was a dream. And, in Layla's head, hopes and dreams and plans were all still sort of the same thing.

The girls went inside, into the kitchen, and ate all of the frozen yogurt and toppings.

Now Layla couldn't help but think that it was wrong when she had said that this felt like the end. It wasn't. Not yet anyway.

But it was, perhaps, the end of the beginning.

28 days until graduation . . .

EMMA invited Savannah to come over and have dinner with her parents.

"First prom, now dinner with your parents?" Savannah teased. "What happened to the expectation-less Emma I know and love?"

Good question, Emma thought.

But the question was also the answer.

Savannah *did* love her.

And Emma loved her back.

And there were very few things in the universe that Emma was sure about, but at least for right now, and the foreseeable future, she was entirely and without-a-doubt sure about Savannah—and she wanted to make sure her parents were too.

The O'Malleys seemed to be in a good mood before dinner even began, but they were absolutely thrilled to have a teenager at the dinner table who was glad to answer all of their questions. Savannah talked to them about school and her classes and her plans for the future. She still had another year left in high school, but still, unlike Emma, she didn't cry every time anyone mentioned the word "college."

Then, the conversation wound its way around to prom.

"We're actually . . . we're going to prom together," Emma said.

"Oh yeah?" Her mom smiled. Emma could tell that her mom wasn't entirely registering what that meant. "Layla and Alex are going together too, right?"

"Yeah. They are"—Emma nodded—"but they're just going as friends."

That statement seemed to get her parents' attention.

"Savannah is my girlfriend," Emma said simply.

She didn't say it to shock them or try to rile them up.

She said it because it was true, and because it mattered to her.

And she wanted her parents to know.

Emma's parents looked at each other and then glanced back at Emma and then across the table toward Savannah . . . and then her dad said, "Sounds good" and her mom asked if Emma knew what she wanted to wear to prom—and that was it. The conversation marched on. Emma said she had no clue what she wanted to wear, but Savannah chimed in and said she was thinking about buying a new suit. Savannah felt like one of them should wear a suit—'cause it would look better for the pictures or something—and Savannah said she wanted to be the one to do it. Emma's mother agreed that it would look nice. Especially if Savannah's suit or tie was color coordinated with Emma's dress. Turned out, that's *exactly* what Savannah was thinking too.

And the rest of the dinner conversation continued like that, back and forth across the table.

This, Emma thought as she listened to the pleasant chatter.

Just simply: *this*.

23 days until graduation . . .

LAYLA could not have been happier to cross it off her to-do list.

It had been 146 days since she first wrote it down. Now she finally had blond highlights in her hair. It was even more important for her to cross this bullet point off her list, especially since it was looking less and less likely that she was going to cross off anything else . . .

But it was prom night, and Layla was determined to have the best time of her life.

Layla and Alex, Emma and Savannah, and Zoe and Dylan all lined up on the staircase—and took a million and one pictures. The girls were glowing—and honestly, Dylan was too. And Layla's highlights looked absolutely perfect.

The Crew (and company) took a limo to prom, which was at a fancy hotel in Santa Monica and the six of them basically spent the entire night on the dance floor. At one point, when the DJ switched songs and everybody screamed, Layla looked across the crowded dance floor and saw Logan and Vanessa, dancing. And also kissing. Really, it would've been more accurate to say that she was just sucking on his tongue. But Layla didn't care. Well. It wasn't that she didn't *care*, but it certainly wasn't enough to ruin her night . . . absolutely nothing could do that. At some point, as things started to wind down, Layla and Alex realized that Emma and Savannah had disappeared and so had Zoe and Dylan . . . but Layla and Alex were still there, still dancing—and having the time of their lives.

It might as well have been just the two of them on the dance floor.

ZOE and Dylan headed upstairs to their very own hotel room.

As they were getting undressed, a new thought occurred to Zoe, something she hadn't considered until this very moment. Dylan had dated a whole string of girlfriends throughout high school, but he hadn't slept with any of them. Thinking back through all of their phonefalls, she couldn't remember him even ever mentioning it as a possibility.

"What were you waiting for?" she asked.

"You," Dylan said.

"Oh, yeah, I'm sure. . ."

"I was waiting for you to get boobs," Dylan teased. "Obviously, I can't say I was *actually* waiting for you," Dylan added more seriously, "because that wouldn't be entirely true. But looking back on it now, it kinda feels like that."

That's how it worked, Zoe thought.

You couldn't fully understand things until you looked backward.

The hard part, of course, was that you still had to live it all forward.

But Zoe knew that it could not have happened any other way.

At the beginning of the semester she couldn't even *say* the word "orgasm," let alone try and have one. And now . . . here they were. Dylan put on some music—a perfectly curated prom night playlist—and Dylan and Zoe got lost in each other for a while . . . in their nakedness and paleness . . . in their laughter . . . and in oh-so-many kisses.

"I love that I can feel you smiling while we're kissing you. And blushing, too."

"No, D, come on . . ."

"You come on . . ."

"You cannot *feel* my blushing. You just know that I am because I *always* am . . . it's an unfair advantage."

"Oh, Z, don't tell me what I can and cannot feel." Dylan laughed.

And that made Zoe laugh too.

And they continued kissing. . .

It was incredible how natural it all felt. After so many years of friendship and phone calls and inside jokes . . . this just felt *right*.

Afterward, and after some more cuddling and more kissing, Dylan went to take a shower and Zoe found herself lying alone in bed. It seemed rather fitting, considering how many nights she'd spent alone in bed, talking to Dylan on the phone. And then she remembered her own phone, and The Chat, and the fact that The Crew was all waiting for a prom sexie. Zoe never liked the way she looked in pictures, but she wanted to take one now. She stayed in the bed with the sheets wrapped around her. She held her phone straight out in front of her, her arms fully extended, and snapped the picture. Just one. She looked at it, expecting to need to take another one. Or two or three more even. But she didn't.

This was it.

Her face was as red as her hair.

Her hair was as frizzy as it had ever been.

And she'd never felt prettier.

4 days until graduation...

LAYLA got an A plus on her final AP English paper of the year.

Officially, that lifted her overall class grade from an A minus up to an A, which meant that she'd crossed every single bullet point off her high school to-do list . . .

. . . except for the one about having sex.

As glad as Layla was to cross off this second-to-last point, it was also one last glaring reminder of the one she wouldn't finish. It looked so lonely all by itself.

Luckily, Layla didn't have to stare at it very long, as Alex was already outside, honking. "Usually I'm the one getting honked at," Alex said as Layla climbed into the backseat of her car along with Emma. Zoe rode shotgun and DJ'd as The Crew drove out to Malibu for a party at Trevor Morgan's beach house. The party was fun, in that everyone-was-wasted sort of way, but after a while it just felt like too much fun, and Layla needed a breather. She walked down to the waves, pulled off her sandals, and stuck her toes in the Pacific Ocean. The water was freezing, but she liked the cold. And she liked the way the moon reflected off the waves. And just as her eyes and thoughts drifted up to the stars—or at least whatever stars she could see through the California haze—she heard a familiar voice behind her.

"There she is . . ."

It was Logan.

He said it as if he'd been looking for her, which, apparently, he had.

"What are you doing out here?" he asked. "Hiding?" She wasn't, but all of a sudden she wanted to. "You know I love you to the moon and back, right?" he asked as if they hadn't broken up back in February. As if he hadn't chosen Vanessa instead. As if he still really loved her. He had *tried* to ask as if he weren't actually drunk, but clearly he was. He was wasted. And all his words just slurred together.

Layla didn't know quite what to say, so she didn't say anything at all.

"A penny for your thoughts?" he asked.

It was the kind of question Layla would've found so charming back when they were dating. Now he just reeked of alcohol and a bit of desperation.

Layla held out her hand as if to ask for an actual penny. Logan didn't have one to give her and probably mistook her gesture anyway, so he grabbed her hand and held on, squeezing it tight, which felt familiar but also foreign all at the same time . . .

After a brief moment Layla pulled her hand away.

"We broke up." Layla knew that Logan was talking about Vanessa, but it was also what she wanted to say to him.

"I heard," she said instead. She'd been trying not to pay *too* much attention to Logan and Vanessa's relationship, but apparently something dramatic had happened between them on prom night, and Vanessa ended up going home with someone else.

"Shoulda listened to you . . ." Logan laughed. "But then you should've listened to me, too."

"O-kay . . ." Layla didn't quite know what Logan meant, but she was more than ready for this conversation to be over.

Clearly Logan was not: "There were gonna be rose petals."

"What?"

"On the beach. That was going to be the last clue on Valentine's Day. I was gonna decorate the sand in front of my aunt and uncle's with a whole entire, like, *bed* made out of red rose petals. And we were gonna have sex on top the petals, on top of the sand, under the stars, and the moon and back—"

"Logan, I really don't . . ." The missing word at the end of Layla's sentence was "care," but she decided she didn't want to say it out loud. Or she couldn't. Either way, she decided it was time to go back inside the party. Layla started walking back to the house.

Logan followed closely after her. "Okay, I'm sorry—"

"I don't need you to be sorry—"

Logan reached out and grabbed Layla's hand again.

And she pulled hers away again, just as fast as she could.

"Why are you mad at me?" he asked.

"What kind of a question is that?"

"You don't seem to want to talk to me . . ."

"Logan, I'm not gonna make *small talk* or whatever—"

"We can make big talk if you want." Logan laughed.

"You're drunk, Logan. Go home."

"Would love to," Logan said with a crassness in his voice. "But first can we agree that we should've lost it to each other?"

"No."

"No?"

"I didn't lose it," Layla said, feeling strangely liberated.

Logan certainly wasn't expecting her to say that. "What about your to-do list?"

"What about it?" Layla smiled.

"O-kay," Logan said, sounding even more drunk than he had just a moment before. "What happened to the Layla Baxter I dated for two years? That girl would've made sure to finish her to-do list."

"Yeah, well, maybe that girl isn't me anymore . . . ," Layla said. And she meant it too. She didn't have to pretend. Not with her face. Not with her voice. Not with any of it. It was a glorious feeling. "And that's okay," she added.

"It *is* okay," Logan said, smirking, "but it could be better . . ."

Before Layla could ask him what he meant, Logan pulled her in for a kiss.

It was big and hard and fast and slow all at the same time.

And all of a sudden all the old feelings came rushing back.

The attraction, the hormones, the love . . . all of it.

And Layla kissed him back just as hard and fast and slow as he kissed her. And even though she knew it really would be okay—*way more than okay*—if she didn't complete her to-do list, she also couldn't help but think, at least for a fleeting moment, that maybe she and Logan should just . . . do it. They could have sex on the beach—right here and now—and Layla could cross it off her to-do list, and that would be it.

But then, forever, that would be it.

And it simply wasn't what Layla wanted . . .

. . . at least not right now.

And since right now was all there really was Layla pulled away from Logan, stopping his kisses.

"Aw, come on, Lay. Let me help you finish the to-do list. You'll be happy. I'll be happy . . ." He leaned in for another kiss, but Layla held up her finger, touching it to his lips. "What's wrong?" he asked.

"Nothing." Layla smiled. "But we're not doing this."

"Oh, come on," Logan said, sounding all drunk and harsh and mean. "You're gonna miss your deadline."

"Due date," Layla corrected him with a laugh. She couldn't help herself. She couldn't be something she wasn't either. And she certainly wasn't going to do something she didn't want to.

Layla walked away—back to the party and away from Logan—and she knew, without a shadow of a doubt, that *not* doing her very last bullet point was actually the most important thing she'd done all year.

1 day until graduation . . .

LAYLA laid out her outfit for graduation on her bed.

It was hard to believe that it was all really happening in the morning.

HAPPENING, she texted The Chat as the doorbell rang.

"Lay-la!" her mom called from downstairs a few moments later. "Guess who's here?" Layla had teased her mom for thinking that someone might show up to her front door without texting first, but that's exactly what Logan had done.

"I figured you might tell me not to come over," Logan explained as Layla closed the front door behind them and joined him outside. They sat down on the front steps. Logan had asked if she wanted to hang out on the trampoline one last time, but Layla had said no. This felt better. "I just wanted to say sorry . . . "

"Doesn't love mean never having to say you're sorry?"

"Yeah, well, my mom thinks that's the stupidest thing she's ever heard, so . . ." Logan smiled, popping that signature dimple into his cheek. Now that he wasn't dripping with alcohol, he looked and sounded like his old charming self again. They hadn't been alone like this, really alone and just themselves together, since the day they broke up. Layla had missed him so much, but looking at him now, and smiling with him, she could feel that he wasn't the same person from before.

And neither was she.

And Layla couldn't help but think that was a good thing.

"I still love you to the moon and back," Logan said as the beginning of his good-bye.

"I love you, too," Layla said.

And she meant it.

But it was a different kind of love than she'd had for him before.

She knew that no matter how many times she'd fall in love in the future, there'd always be a small, quiet place in her heart that belonged only to Logan.

And that was okay.

More than okay.

In a way, Layla loved Logan more now than she ever had before. The good news, though—maybe the *best* news—was that she loved herself more.

Graduation Day . . .

. . . was as bittersweet as it gets.

Layla, Zoe, Alex, and Emma posed for pictures on the athletic field in their caps and gowns. At some point, as the cameras were flashing from every direction, Emma thought to whisper to the girls that the real reason she liked photographs so much was that they never changed, even when the people in them did. Everyone wanted to say that wasn't true, that they wouldn't change, or at least, if they *did*, they would still manage to grow and change in the same direction and fit this neatly together forever.

But they all knew that they couldn't say that.

They knew it wasn't the sort of thing you could promise.

Later, The Crew spent their graduation night at Disneyland. Twelve glorious, uninterrupted hours spent running around the happiest place on earth. No boys or other girls. No sex. No distractions. Just four best friends. And a hundred rides.

The last ride of the night (slash morning) turned out to be Splash Mountain. It was Zoe's favorite, even though the big drop at the end scared her beyond words. It had actually been their first ride of the night too, but Zoe asked to ride it one more time. Layla loved the symmetry of that, and Alex and Emma were game, and so the girls ran back through the park for one last splash. As they crept up the conveyor belt in their fake plastic log, edging toward the largest drop, Layla, Alex, Zoe, and Emma all managed to have the very same thought at the very same time: The best part about this ride was that they were on it together. Honestly, that was the only thing that really mattered.

Just before the sun came up, the girls stood all together watching an *actual* fireworks display in the sky above the magic castle. Of course they couldn't help but think about their own personal fireworks, the ones they'd set off by themselves or with the lucky people they'd let step inside. And the thoughts and feelings were enough to make them want to cry . . . but it all turned into laughter instead, because sometimes emotions are so close together it's impossible not to feel them all at once.

Sometimes emotions know what you need even when you don't.

This was it: the final, fleeting moment of high school.

All of it was bright and exploding, and then just as quickly fading away and finally disappearing into the sky. The girls felt each blast as if it were happening just for the four of them alone and no one else in the world. And the whole thing was already a memory—a forever-and-always kind of memory—before the fireworks display even ended. Maybe, honestly, before it had even really begun.

It was just that special.

This moment.

This magic.

This friendship.

This glorious time of their lives.

And they knew it couldn't last forever, not really anyway, but they already felt like it was all a part of them, like it had burrowed into their hearts and melted into their minds and blurred—irrevocably blurred—into the depths of their souls.

This was it—and this was everything.

The end of the beginning.

The story started in a froyo shop, and that's effectively where it ended, too.

Even though it didn't officially—*actually*—happen for Layla until the very end of the summer, it was all set in motion right in the beginning on the first day after graduation. After the girls came home from Disneyland, and napped, The Crew decided the only thing they wanted was froyo. This meant breaking tradition and showing up at The Bigg Chill on a Tuesday, which would've been fine, totally, absolutely fine, *except* for the first time all year— maybe even possibly for the first time *ever*—there was no peanut butter flavor option on the Bigg Chill menu.

There was *always* peanut butter.

And Layla always ordered it.

But now this time would have to be different.

Layla tried very hard to act like it wasn't a big deal, but Bigg Chill Aaron could tell that it was a VERY big deal.

He decided to be bold and recommend his favorite flavor instead: Honey Greek Yogurt. "It's not for everyone," he cautioned, "but I'm a big fan." Layla tried it. She liked it. And ordered it without too much of a fuss.

Then, the girls sat at their usual table, in their usual corner, and laughed and ate too many rainbow sprinkles and were just happy to be together.

And that was it.

Alex had a week until she had to leave for Stanford and summer track practices. Emma's one-way ticket to Southeast Asia was scheduled to leave two weeks after that. She'd officially decided to defer her freshman year of college and take a gap year. Emma was going to travel around the world, volunteering and working and taking pictures as she went. Zoe had to move into her dorm at the University of Michigan the second week of August. And Layla would start her freshman year at USC a week or so after that.

It was all happening.

That first day after graduation Layla had left The Bigg Chill feeling strangely alive. She felt invigorated, like the world was an open door, a book with only blank pages. Layla climbed into her car, stuck the key in the ignition . . .

. . . and simply got stuck.

She couldn't drive. She could barely even move. She was petrified. She desperately wanted to be the kind of person who could speed off into the sunset and not look back, but that wasn't Layla's style. Yes, plans could change and she would survive. There was no peanut butter froyo, and she had lived to tell it. But she liked her lists and her systems and all of her due dates. Layla was unapologetically *Layla*, and she wasn't going to stop being that now . . . but apparently and unfortunately, it felt like she wasn't going to be able to go anywhere either.

And then.

Just when she thought she might actually get stuck sitting in the parking lot of The Bigg Chill forever, her phone buzzed.

It was a phone number she didn't recognize, with a 267 area code.

Too soon to make a plan?

Layla looked up from her phone and saw Bigg Chill Aaron smiling at her through the wall of glass windows. Layla had given him her number just a few minutes earlier. She said she would love to hear from him sometime. And she meant it. The fact that he texted her almost immediately *and* used the word "plan" in his very first text message was an absolute dream.

Almost instantly Layla and Bigg Chill Aaron fell hard and fast, as text messages and timid smiles turned into full-fledged butterflies and endless make-out sessions. He insisted he wasn't normally like this, all head over heels and all in and everything, but their connection was infectious and palpable, and there was no reason to fight it. Bigg Chill Aaron's name was soon shortened to "Aaron," because there was far too much discussion about him in The Chat to keep typing all three words over and over again. A few weeks later Aaron officially asked to be Layla's boyfriend. A few weeks after that, they said "I love you." And then, about two months after that very first text . . .

. . . it happened.

It wasn't even an official date night. It was just an end of summer Sunday, a few days before Layla was scheduled to move into her USC dorm. Aaron texted Layla when he got off work at The Bigg Chill earlier than usual. They decided, last minute, to grab a quick dinner and see a movie. They shared fries. They held hands. They laughed at the big screen. And then, what began as just another seemingly endless make-out session, turned into the first time Layla never realized she always wanted.

It was passionate.

It was spontaneous.

It was sexy.

And loving.

And a little bit silly, too.

And, it all went down *exactly* sixty-nine days after high school graduation. The sexy numerological wink from the universe seemed almost too good to be true. But it wasn't. It was very real. And absolutely right.

LAYLA Baxter lost her virginity in the backseat of her car.

To be honest, the sex pact wasn't always part of the plan.

Even Layla could not have planned it better if she tried.

It was perfect.

All of it.

Mostly, because the girls did it all together.

Together together.

And that really was, without a doubt, the very best part.

Acknowledgments

You never forget your first time.

Trust me, I know.

And I'm already certain that I will never forget *this* first time either. The process of writing my first novel—spanning from the first blush of an idea, to this final, finished product—has been exhilarating, terrifying, humbling, and immensely rewarding. I am sincerely grateful—for all of it. And I know it would not have happened without the unwavering support of my family and friends who have held my hand—both literally and figuratively—every step of the way.

Thank you to everyone at Simon Pulse for championing the story of these four friends and their fireworks. Thank you, Mara Anastas, Liesa Abrams, Mary Marotta, Lucille Rettino, Carolyn Swerdloff, Tara Greico, Jennifer Romanello, Jodie Hockensmith, Christina Pecorale, Mandy Veloso, and Regina Flath. An extra-special thank-you to my editors, Jennifer Ung and Sarah McCabe, whose enthusiasm knows no bounds. Thank you for your fearlessness and your patience. Thank you for helping me find the rhythm and pace of the book. You are the best.

Thank you to my wonderful literary agent, Jess Regel, for helping me navigate this process and for being excited about *Cherry* from day one. Thank you you to my manager, Josh Turner McGuire, for helping me keep my head on straight. I don't know what I'd do without you. And thank you to the rest of my team: Melissa Orton, Bryan Diperstein, and Tara Kole.

Thank you to my crew of early readers, fellow writers, "technical" consultants, and very best friends: Elyssa Caplan, Caroline Rothstein, Emma Sugerman, Aaron Karo, Jordan Ross, Harper Dill, Marissa Freeman, Melanie Mason, Sasha Salinger, Samantha Billett Rosenblum, Sara Sargent, Jessie Rosen, Emma Goidel, Ilana Caplan, Lindsay Katona, Jamie Epstein, John Krause, and Molly McCook. Thank you all for your notes and wisdom and insight. Thank you for your pep talks and the "you got this" text messages. Thank you for humoring me. And loving me. And reminding me to laugh and sleep and breathe. *Cherry* wouldn't be what it is without you—and neither would I. An additional and endless thank-you to Elyssa, Caroline, and Emma—my *girls* and founding members of my tribe and executive committee—who went above and beyond the call of friendship and read every single draft of *Cherry* along the way. We really are the luckiest.

Thank you to my friends from high school. The ones

whose pictures were taped to the walls of my bedroom. The ones I made mix CDs for. The ones I hung out with in Rugby Theater, or in my parents' backyard, or the back seat of my car. And *especially* the ones I've eaten frozen yogurt with at The Bigg Chill. Thanks for being a formative part of the story of my life.

Thank you to my extended Rosin and Passman families—my relatives by blood and the ones we've adopted by choice. The regular days and the holidays and all the moments in between wouldn't mean nearly as much if I couldn't share them with all of you. I want to especially thank my 99-year-old grandmother, Helen Rosin, who I've had the privilege of updating about the *Cherry* writing process every step of the way. The first time I told her about the plot of the book I chose my words rather carefully, saying that it was a story about four friends during their senior year of high school. Then I added that it was "a little bit sexy." Without missing a beat she replied, "That's okay, people like that." I'm so very glad she said that. Hopefully, she was right.

Thank you to my Andy Grammer and "Ain't It Fun" Pandora stations and all the songs that played on repeat. Thank you to all the baristas at my favorite Coffee Bean and Tea Leaf (10897 Pico Blvd.) for making the best vanilla lattes around. Thank you, Santiago Huckleberry scented Voluspa Candles. Thank you to Converse sneakers. And thank you, Pilot G2 pens (size 1mm), which I used as I wrote the entire first draft of *Cherry* by hand.

Thank you to my dog, Dodger, who sat by my side or at

my feet or on the purple shag carpet on my office floor as I wrote almost every word of this book.

Thank you, Mom, Dad, Maxine, and Avery—for everything. I'm not sure what life would be like without the "lovies" group chat, but I wouldn't want to live it any other way. I love you all to the moon and back—and so far beyond that too.

Thank you to my husband, Josh. I love you forever. Long story short: there were two ducks.

And finally, thank YOU for reading.

About the Author

Lindsey Rosin is a screenwriter, playwright, producer, and director. A fourth-generation Los Angeles native, Lindsey lives in West LA—in close proximity to her favorite froyo spot, The Bigg Chill—along with her husband, Josh, and their adorable poodle-mix named Dodger. For more about Lindsey, please visit lindseyrosin.com and follow her on Twitter @lindseyrosin. *Cherry* is her debut novel.